Trail to Treason

Patricia Clough

Text copyright © 2024 by Patricia Clough

Cover Illustration © Nat Mack
Distributed by Simon & Schuster

ISBN: 978-1-998076-98-7
Ebook: 978-1-998076-99-4

FIC014040   FICTION / Historical / 20th Century / World War I
FIC098050   FICTION / World Literature / England 20TH Century
FIC014080   FICTION / Historical / 20TH Century General

#TrailtoTreason

Follow Rising Action on our socials!
Twitter: @RAPubCollective
Instagram: @risingactionpublishingco
TikTok: @risingactionpublishingco

Trail to Treason

Part One

The Fall from Grace

Chapter 1

PILLOWELL, A COAL-MINING VILLAGE IN GLOUCESTERSHIRE, JANUARY 1901

Florence Ada Harris's contribution to twentieth century history had its origin, one might say, in a violent shove between the shoulder blades which hurled her out of the front door of the manse and flat onto her face on the flagstones outside.

Her husband was ranting. Through the ringing in her ears she heard, "Whore! Harlot! Shame on me, on my mission, on your family, your sons!" And, loud and clear, "You will burn in hell!"

He was standing above her now, and she flinched, fearing more blows.

"Get out of this place!" he hissed. "I give you one hour to pack your things and go—and take your bastard son with you! Godfrey will stay with me. Do you hear me? Go—I never ever want to see you again!"

She heard him turn, there was a slight scuffle, then he stepped past her, dragging another man—obviously her lover, Rob—and throwing him down the steps to the road, shouting, "Foul adulterer ... everlasting damnation! How dare you! Don't ever show your face in the chapel again!" Her husband followed the culprit down the steps. She heard him cross the road and walk up the path to the large stone chapel on the other side. There was a clatter of the key in the lock, then the door slammed and was locked again from the inside.

She lay on the ground a few moments, aching and trembling. Her head hurt, as she had hit her forehead on the stone. Her ribs were bruised, and her right arm was badly grazed and bleeding. Heavy steps were approaching, and voices—miners coming off the night shift at the colliery, probably. Dawn was breaking. Painfully, she picked herself up, brushed the grit off her face and hands, gathered her nightdress around her, and turned to go back into the house. Just inside were her two boys in their nightshirts, shivering and white in the face.

"What are you doing here?" she cried, shooing them in. "You will catch your death of cold! Get back into bed quickly, it's not time to get up yet."

"But Mama, what happened? Why did Papa do that?"

"What was Rob doing here?"

"It was nothing, my darlings," she tried to reassure them. "Your father was just a bit upset about something; he doesn't really mean it. Don't worry. Just go back to bed."

"But … but …"

"No, go now."

Silently, they obeyed.

Florence, or Flo as everyone had called her since childhood, went into the kitchen and sat down on a stool at the old wooden table, shaking, too stunned to cry. For several minutes she sat immobile, in a state of shock, her mind blank. Then, like a deluge, the whole horror crashed down on her. What had she done? How could she have been so wicked? How could she betray her devout, clergyman husband—and with a member of his flock! What had possessed her? And in any case, why had it not occurred to her that Josiah would come back on the early train that brought many of the miners to the first shift of the day?

She had never seen her husband in such a fury. But he was right, she knew. She had committed a terrible sin. She had betrayed him, her upbringing, everything she had been taught since earliest childhood. She could expect no forgiveness either from Josiah or his congregation. This was the end of her.

Shivering, she rose, threw a shawl round her shoulders, and automatically stoked up the embers in the old, blackened range and filled the kettle. A black terror enveloped her. What should she do? She had no money, no means of support, and now no home. She felt naked, like a tortoise without a shell. How could she survive without a husband and a home? Where could she go? Certainly not back home to her widowed father. She shivered at the thought. Yet she must leave, as quickly as possible. Those miners might have seen what happened just now. The news could already be flying around the village. Oh, the shame of it!

Her arm was hurting. Wincing, she bathed it in the sink and bandaged it. She went to the old, dim mirror and dabbed at the bruise on her forehead. It was turning blue and swelling. She looked disheveled. Her oval face, surrounded by rich red hair, was still pretty but it was pale and fine lines were beginning to show. She was thirty-one now. Ten years of pious poverty, hard work, and two children lay between her and the effervescent young girl she used to be. Where were the sparkling eyes, the enchanting dimples, and the endearing smile which those around her, particularly men, had found irresistible?

A cup of hot tea lifted her spirits slightly. "There must be someone who can help," she said to herself. And all at once it dawned on her where she could go.

"Cyril!" she called. "Get dressed, put your sailor suit on. We are going to visit Aunt Emily!"

"Aunt Emily!" The boys came thumping downstairs, their feet still bare. They adored Flo's oldest sister who in their early years had been like a second mother to them.

"I'm coming too!" cried Godfrey, the younger one. Flo felt as though she had been punched sharply in the stomach. She was being doubly punished—she was not only being cast out into a frightening world alone with the older boy, but she was forced to part with the younger one, her darling, her secret favourite—who knew, maybe forever! She could not bear the thought. She would refuse to go! No mother should ever be told to do such a thing. She paced up and down in front of the stove. No. Never!

But moments later she saw the hopelessness of her position. She knew Josiah and their puritan world only too well. The Primitives, as they called themselves, were very democratic, as the laity had even more say in decisions than the clergy, but she knew that their congregation would support Josiah to a man. Disgraced and dishonoured, she could hardly appeal to them—indeed to fight and call attention to herself would only make things infinitely worse.

She went over and hugged Godfrey, pressing the child tightly against her. *What can I say to him?* she agonised silently. *I can't tell him the truth. I'm going to have to pretend.* Fighting back her tears, she swallowed hard and took Godfrey's face in her hands. "Not this time, my darling. You must stay with Papa, or he will be lonely. We won't be gone long and if you are very good, Papa

might take you to stay with Aunt Martha and the boys. And," she added, improvising wildly, "next time you can come with me, and Cyril will go to Aunt Martha. How about that?"
Godfrey was not convinced and began to cry. "But why? It's not fair, Mama! I want to go with you!" He wailed and ran upstairs, weeping bitterly.

With tears running down her face, Flo went into the bedroom and put on her "good" dress, a severe, high-necked gown of navy serge, such as befitted the wife of a Primitive Methodist minister. She had made it herself. It was old and regrettably ratty, but her other one was even shabbier. Automatically she scraped her long, red hair back into the prim bun she had worn since she married. What should she take? She had so little. She took down the photograph of her late mother from the mantelpiece and looked at it sadly. "Oh, forgive me, Mama, forgive me! If only you were here to help me now!" she murmured and held it for a moment against her breast before putting it carefully into her battered hold-all. After it went her other dress, underwear, stays, nightdresses, spare boots, Cyril's few belongings, her Bible, and their prayer books. She looked in her purse and saw that the remains of the week's housekeeping money would probably not even cover their train fare. After some hesitation, she went into her husband's study and took out the contents of a tin box in his desk drawer, leaving in its place a scribbled note saying, "I will pay this back as soon as I can." She looked around the house to make sure she had not forgotten anything important, then put on her cape, gloves, and hat, gingerly positioning the latter at an angle and tugging at the short veil to hide the bruise on her forehead. *Looks a bit saucy, but it will have to do,* she thought.

As they reached the door, she stopped and clung tightly to the doorpost. She ached to run upstairs and carry Godfrey off with her. If only! Instead, she called, "Goodbye, my darling, be good! We'll be back soon!"

Taking a deep breath, she grasped Cyril's hand, and with her large hold-all in the other, set off, chin in the air and a fixed smile on her face.

It was a cold, windy January day. The half-mile walk through the village to the station seemed endless. They were passing little houses where she, the minister's popular wife, had visited or tended the sick, passing members of the congregation with whom she had so often prayed and sung hymns and children she had taught Bible stories. She greeted them all with forced gaiety as she went by. "We're off to visit my sister! Back soon," she called, again and again.

They seemed to know nothing yet, but who knew what dreadful rumours and stories would circulate when they found out that she was never coming back?

Chapter 2

On the Great Western Railway, 1901

She huddled, comatose, in the window seat of the compartment, her bruised head and rib cage throbbing to the rhythmic *da-da-da-da* of the wheels. Ten-year-old Cyril, opposite her, seemed to have forgotten the events of the morning in his excitement at being on a real train, with a genuine, big black engine which belched black smoke and let off piercing whistles. He was watching, fascinated, as fields, woods and houses, signals, and the odd other train sped past. He wanted to pull the thick leather strap to let down the window, but she feebly raised her hand to stop him.

"No, dear, you will be covered in smoke and get cinders in your eyes."

After a while, she realised she should pull herself together and try to take stock of her situation. She opened her handbag and counted the money. The contents of Josiah's tin box, his parishioners' contributions to the chapel repair fund of which he was the treasurer, was more money than she had seen for a long time. She felt deeply guilty and promised herself she would pay it back as soon as ever she could.

How she would achieve this she had no idea, but she hoped fervently that Emily would help her sort her life out. Her older sister had always been a tower of strength, especially after their beloved mother had died. She and her Scottish husband, John, were practical, sensible people; they would know what she could do. Except, she reminded herself, she could not tell even Emily what had really happened that morning. No one must ever know. She would have to prepare a good story.

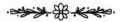

At the next station, the door between them opened and a youngish, distinguished-looking man in tweed plus-fours climbed into their compartment with a polite "good morning" in Flo's direction. Flo quickly sat up straight and surreptitiously adjusted her hat and her dress.

The man lifted his leather suitcase onto the overhead rack and settled down to read a newspaper. He had a dark red, squiggle-like birth mark down the left side of his face. Cyril clearly noticed it too, and she silently signalled to him not to stare.

After a while, Cyril suddenly piped up, "Mama, what's a bastard?"

Flo stiffened and looked quickly at the man. "It's a bad word that people sometimes say when they are very angry," she replied in a hushed voice. "You must never use it."

"But why did Papa call me one?"

Flustered, Flo glanced at the man again, but he seemed engrossed in his newspaper. She grasped at a straw.

"Perhaps because you let Mrs. Evans' chickens out."

"But Godfrey was there too, and Papa didn't call him that."

To Flo's relief, the thought of his beloved younger brother distracted Cyril. He began to cry. "Why couldn't Godfrey come with us? Why did he have to stay at home?" He sobbed.

Struggling not to cry herself, Flo fished for a handkerchief and tried to comfort him. As she did so, the answer to the boy's question slowly sank in. Josiah had known that Cyril was not his son. Unbelievable. He had never said a word when the baby arrived "prematurely." Never a word, even when the midwife thoughtlessly let it drop that he was remarkably big and bonny for a "seven-month" baby. In his distant way, Josiah had always seemed as fond of Cyril as he was of Godfrey. When and how did he learn that Cyril was not his? And why had he never spoken of it until this morning? She could not know, as they had never, ever, discussed intimate matters. He was totally engrossed in his mission: bringing the Gospel to the poor and downtrodden, the miners, the factory workers, and the farm labourers who, the Primitives felt, had been abandoned by the Church of England, and even by the official Methodist church as it became more "respectable" and middle-class. Indeed, they called themselves "Primitives" because they had felt they were returning to the original, purer, more fundamentalist teachings of the early days of Methodism with their open-air sermons and prayer meetings and their focus on the poor. Pale, slight, and with mousy hair and a moustache which joined up with his sideburns, Josiah was almost fanatical in his beliefs and a surprisingly passionate, fiery preacher in front of a congregation. But at home he was a quiet, almost ghostly presence, his mind always on his sermons and, when he had time, his Hebrew and Greek studies.

Flo had told no one her secret, not even her sisters: that she'd "had" to get married. It had put an abrupt end to a happy, innocent girlhood as the youngest and prettiest of three sisters living in a Buckinghamshire farming community. Their father, Zachary Summers, was a farm bailiff, the manager of several farms belonging to a big estate, and a pillar of the local Primitive Methodist congregation. Zachary was a domineering figure, irascible and severe, who imposed an austere, puritan lifestyle on his family in accordance with his stern beliefs. He wanted his three daughters to grow up to be pious, God-fearing girls who, after leaving school at fourteen, would devote themselves to learning to cook and keep house, feed their rabbits and chickens, and engage in good works in the neighbourhood until such time as suitable young men, preferably non-conformists like himself, would come along and marry them. And the older two, Emily and Lizzie, had obliged, becoming virtuous and obedient young women who gave no trouble, but Flo—Flo was a handful. Her bubbly, fun-loving, impulsive nature was constantly landing her in scrapes. She tried to be good, Zachary would admit in his mellower moments, but she was never able to repress her high spirits for long.

"I don't know why the good Lord has sent us this little hussy," he would growl to his sweet, docile wife, Betty, shaking his head sadly. As children, Emily and Lizzie would tease Flo that the fairies had stolen their real sister and put Flo in the cradle in her place. When she became a teenager and dazzlingly pretty, she was courted by a bevy of boys and young men and delighted in evading her parents' strict supervision, if only for a few moments, to flirt, tease, and kiss. Kittenish and vivacious, she was adored and petted by her friends and family—all except for Zachary who became ever more censorious and heavy-handed and would frequently resort to angry canings. Far from beating her into demure submissiveness, though, his severity prompted Flo to defend herself by inventing what she would think of merely as "stories," but later had to admit that they were—she was ashamed to admit—lies.

Zachary was desperate to marry her off before she went seriously astray and had been pressuring Flo to marry Josiah Harris, the quiet, intense, young trainee preacher attached to their chapel. He knew it would very likely mean that she would be much poorer—for although he imposed a simple, frugal lifestyle on his family, he was able to keep them in more comfort than would a young preacher. But Josiah, he felt, would be just the man to turn her into a devout, God-fearing housewife and mother. Flo, joyous as a struggling butterfly free its chrysalis, was not interested. She was in no hurry to settle down.

I have to admit, Papa was right, she thought ruefully, trying to find a position in which her ribs hurt less. She had been foolish, she now realised. Foolish and innocent. Furtive kisses had become furtive trysts in the woods while she was supposed to be visiting the sick. With only the haziest idea of what people called "the facts of life," she thought these simply romantic escapades, but one day things happened which she was not prepared for and did not know how to stop. And soon she discovered to her horror that she was pregnant. To make it worse, her lover, a handsome, young, farmer's son, had gone to join relatives in Canada. She was alone, facing what her father had always warned her was a "fate worse than death." Panicked, she immediately agreed to marry Josiah and, fearing she might change her mind, Zachary arranged a speedy wedding. In a conveniently short time, she was safe—and sealed up in her chrysalis again. She was twenty-one.

Funny how history repeats itself, she thought, reflecting on the last years of her marriage. She had tried so hard to be a good, pious, preacher's wife. She had enchanted his successive congregations, performed innumerable works of charity, and raised the boys as best she could on their tiny income. But with time their extreme poverty began to grind her down. She struggled to find enough food to put on the table and all too often it was just stale bread and potatoes with, in summer, such fruit and vegetables as members of the congregation could pass on—although most of them were desperately poor too. Often, she went hungry so the boys could have enough to eat, but too often there were times when they had to go to bed hungry too. She had to rely on hand-me-downs from relatives or neighbours to clothe them, and she was constantly mending them and re-knitting the wool from outgrown jerseys. In winter, she often had to beg miners to smuggle out lumps of coal, so they did not freeze to death.

She became desperate for human warmth and intimacy, but Josiah, his mind always on his work, was awkward and scarcely responsive and provided little solace. She sometimes wondered whether he subconsciously felt that even marital sex was sinful. Increasingly she felt unloved, lonely and resentful.

Sometimes she dreamed of a better life, a life with money, comfort, pleasure, happiness. But it never occurred to her to leave Josiah. Women like her could never do that: marriage, for better or for worse, was for life. This would be her fate as long as she lived.

A brief flirtation with a passing tradesman reignited a spark in her crushed spirit. Then came another, and another, each less innocent than the one before, but each a thrilling escape from the misery of her daily life. Then came Rob—and disaster.

"Are you going to London?"

She was jolted out of her reverie. The gentleman in the plus-fours was talking to Cyril. Cyril seemed unsure what to say, so Flo came to the rescue. "We have to change trains in London. We are going to visit my sister in Warley, near Brentwood."

"That's only a short train ride from London. But you will have to change stations," said the man. "You will have to take a cab to Liverpool Street. Why don't you ask the cabbie to show you some of the sights while you are at it? You could see Buckingham Palace, Westminster Abbey, Trafalgar Square, Piccadilly, and St Paul's without going too far out of your way."

"Oh, Mama, can we do that?" exclaimed Cyril.

"Why not?" Flo said. "It sounds a lovely idea."

They chatted for half an hour or so until the man looked at his fob watch, stood up, and pulled down his suitcase from the rack. "I have to get out at the next stop. Goodbye, it was nice meeting you, ma'am." And, to Cyril, "Look after your beautiful mother, young man. Make sure she comes to no harm." And with what looked suspiciously like a wink, he was gone.

Flo was taken aback. What a compliment! But did he mean it? Did the wink mean he was joking? She stood up and looked in the mirror above the row of seats opposite. Well, a bit better than this morning, she thought. Maybe she was not so bad looking, after all. A small trickle of self-confidence began to seep back into her battered spirit.

"Cab, lady?"

"Cab, lady, cab!" A bewildering assortment of cabs was waiting as Flo and Cyril emerged from the station. The cabbie on the nearest leapt down from his dickey seat and opened the door and said with a thick London accent, "There y'are, lady, Where y'going?"

"To Liverpool Street station," replied Flo. "But could you take us past Buckingham Palace, Trafalgar Square, and all those wonderful places on the way? I want my son to see the sights." They set off merrily, looking over the back of a lively chestnut horse, the reins from its harness going up and over their heads to the driver on his high seat above.

Flo and Cyril were enthralled by the guards in their red jackets and busbies outside Buckingham Palace, the famous buildings they had heard so much about, the fountains, the elegant folks in their carriages, the horse-drawn buses, even—to Cyril's delight—some motor cars. Forgetting the time, they disembarked to see inside Westminster Abbey, to buy roast chestnuts, and to look in the windows of Fortnum and Mason's. At the sight of their delicacies, Cyril started to complain he was hungry, and Flo asked the cabbie to leave them at Lyons Corner House. But the man, who was hungry for his own packed meal, agreed to wait for them outside at no extra charge.

When they set off again, the sun was sinking in a rosy haze, dusk was falling, and the lamplighters with their long poles were out and about, lighting the streetlamps one by one. It was late by the time they reached Liverpool Street. Flo paid the cabbie and left Cyril with their bag while she went to buy the tickets. She returned distraught.

"Would you believe it, Cyril! We have missed the last train! And by only a few minutes! There is none now till tomorrow morning. Oh, if only we had spent less time in that wretched cab!" She had dispatched a telegram to Emily from the post office before their departure, announcing that they would be arriving that evening. Now what should they do? She stood there, perplexed, her mind blank. Finally, Cyril spotted a sign: Waiting Room.

"Thank heavens," exclaimed Flo. "We will just have to go there and make ourselves comfortable till morning." The waiting room was empty; they settled down on one of the wide wooden benches and soon Cyril was fast asleep, stretched out with his head on his mother's lap. Flo, exhausted by the turmoil of the day, was nodding off herself when a policeman came in accompanied by a woman from the Salvation Army.

"You can't sleep here, ma'am, it's not allowed," said the policeman.

"But officer," protested Flo, "we have missed the last train to Brentwood. We have no choice but to wait till the morning. Where else can we wait but in the waiting room?"

"No sleeping allowed in the waiting room at night," the policeman replied. "Or we would have all the tramps in London dossing down here."

"Well, I am certainly no tramp ..." began Flo indignantly, but the Salvation Army woman stepped in. "Of course you aren't, ma'am, but why don't you go to the Station Hotel? It's just here and it's open all night. It's not at all expensive and you can sleep in proper beds."

"I never thought of that," Flo said.

"Well, come with me, I'll show you the way," the woman said.

Before long, exhausted by the day's events, they were sleeping soundly in the Station Hotel—so soundly that neither stirred until ten a.m. the next morning. It was almost lunchtime by the time they reached the Norton's house in Warley.

Chapter 3

WARLEY, NEAR BRENTWOOD, 1901

"**S**o there you are! Thank God!" exclaimed Emily as she opened the door. "We were really worried. We were expecting you last night like you said in your telegram!" Flo's sister, her hair a lighter red than Flo's and her figure fuller, was a kindly, motherly woman. Clinging shyly to her skirts was her five-year-old daughter, Madeleine. Emily hugged Flo and Cyril delightedly. "Don't tell me you decided to go on the razzle in London instead!"

"Well, not quite," Flo said. "We let the cabbie take us on a detour to see the sights of London as we changed stations, and we just missed the last train. We had to spend the night at the station hotel."

"Featherbrained as ever," a deep, rasping voice came from behind Emily. "Josiah should not have let you out of the house." There was a tap and a shuffle and a short, wiry man with a bald head and white sideburns, a wooden leg, and a knobby stick came into view.

Flo's heart dropped to the floor. Her father. She had to summon all her willpower to step forward and embrace him, exclaiming with forced delight, "Papa! What a lovely surprise! What are you doing here?"

"Staying with your sister, of course," was the terse reply. "I shall be attending a reunion with some fellow Germans over in Epping. You two should be coming too, and taking some interest in your heritage." This was a reproof. Their father, who was born in a village near Braunschweig, in northern Germany, had tried to teach them German and had even engaged a shy Fraulein for a time to teach them German folk songs and fairy tales. Quite why he had gone to live in Dorset in his early twenties, changing his name from Zacharias Sommer to Zachary Summers, and why he had never gone back to Germany, not even for a visit, no-one ever knew. He never cared to explain. But there were quiet mutterings among farming folk in the local pubs that he had come to England all those years ago to escape some kind of "trouble."

"And what brings you here?" Zachary demanded.

"Josiah is away at a Primitive Methodist conference, and so I decided to come and visit Emily. It is a long time since we have seen each other," she replied.

"And Godfrey?"

"Staying with Aunt Martha and her family, Father."

"You should have brought him too." He always had something to quibble about. "And what's that bruise on your forehead?"

That her heavy, iron, jam-making pan had fallen on her as she tried to pull it down from a high shelf, was the answer.

Her father's presence cast a chill over her arrival, and the sisters could not relax and talk freely until he left the next day to meet his Germans.

"Let's make lunch," Emily said after he had gone.

As she prepared the lamb chops and Flo peeled the potatoes, Emily remarked, "I am so happy to see you, but why did you decide to come all of a sudden?"

Flo had her story ready. Emily must never know the truth. No one must. The explanation she had devised was entirely credible, she thought. It was true too. It just left out the crucial part. "Emily," she said in a low voice so that Cyril could not hear, "I cannot bear it any longer. I cannot begin to tell you what my life is like. You knew we were desperately poor, but now I can tell you that often we don't even have enough to eat. Can you imagine what it is to put your children to bed hungry? Josiah gets paid less than a farm labourer, and sometimes he doesn't get paid at all because the circuit authorities have no money. And you know what it is like in his kind of congregation—no 'vain and worldly amusements' as they like to say, not even beer. It's all chapel, Sunday School, sermons, and parish visiting.

"We haven't had any quarrels, nothing like that. It would almost be better if we did. Josiah's mind is always on his congregation, or he is away preaching. He has no time for me. I often think he does not even care about us anymore. When I tell him we don't have enough to eat, he just says we must trust in God! He thinks I have just come here for a short stay, but he has another thing coming. All this time I have never complained to anyone else, but now I have had enough. I'm not going back."

"But Flo, you can't do that! You can't abandon your husband—and a minister at that. It's unheard of. There'll be such a scandal!" Emily was so overcome she had to sit down. "Josiah is such a good man. And you helped him so much with his work. Remember in Guernsey, when he was put in prison, and you campaigned so hard to have him freed that the Queen decided to pardon him!"

Flo smiled wryly. That had happened just after Cyril was born. It was Josiah's first congregation as a full minister. Still inexperienced, he had married a couple without knowing that they were blood relatives—uncle and niece. As soon as he discovered the truth, he reported the case to the authorities but was nevertheless thrown into jail. The congregation believed that powerful Anglicans hostile to successful non-conformist churches were at work behind the scenes. Flo had joined in the protests and encouraged petitions by the islanders to have him freed and eventually the Queen, made aware of the injustice, pardoned him.

"Well, he said he was grateful to everyone, of course, but in fact, he was convinced it was the Almighty who did it, not us," remarked Flo, wryly. It did not improve their marriage, she might have added.

"And what do you think you will live on?" Emily went on. "You know, of course, that you would never be able to marry again. Even if he could ever possibly afford it, Josiah would never dream of getting a divorce; it would be completely against everything he has ever taught. How could you possibly manage on your own? You have the boys to think of!"

"I don't know, but we could not possibly be poorer than we are now. If only I could work ... that's what I want to discuss with you and John. You two know more about the world than I do, and I'm sure you can give me good advice."

"We can talk about it when John comes home tonight. But you know, Lizzie and I could never understand why you married Josiah in the first place. No matter what our father said, you were not cut out to be the wife of a minister, especially not a poor, travelling preacher like Josiah. Of course, we sometimes wondered if you had another reason for getting married so quickly," she went on, with a sly glance and smile at Flo, "you gave in so suddenly."

Flo laughed but said nothing.

As it grew dark, Emily's husband returned from his rounds. John Norton was the local representative of a well-established London drapery firm which provided him with a generous salary and a horse and carriage to reach towns and villages over a wide area to display its wares and take orders. A little later Dolly Norton, John's sister, appeared, who was engaged to be married. Dolly Norton could not be called pretty, with her long, pale face and prominent nose framed by thin, mousy hair. She spoke little, but what she said revealed her as sensible and intelligent. She was currently working as an assistant to a local dentist and living with John and Emily until she and her fiancé had saved up enough to get married.

After supper, the children were put to bed and the four of them sat in the parlour, contemplating Flo's future over cups of hot cocoa.

At first, John was adamant that Flo should go back to Josiah. "You must learn to accept the path you have chosen. Life may be hard there, my dear, but I don't think you realise how very much harder life is for a woman without a husband and an income. What would you live on? How would you bring up the boys? And have you thought about the scandal it would cause, how people will gossip about you behind your back and cast doubt on your morals? I fear you are jumping from the frying pan into the fire."

"I will say I am a widow," Flo protested. "There's nothing immoral about being a widow."

"Until you get found out," John said, frowning. But Flo was not to be persuaded.

"Look, it can't be *so* bad, John," Emily said after a while. "If Flo is really determined to leave, there are perfectly respectable things she could do. She could be a governess, like Miss Milford up at the hall. I don't suppose she is paid too much but she is living in a nice house and shares meals with the family, and even goes travelling with them."

"That would be lovely," mused Flo, "but I couldn't teach, either as a governess or in a school. It's true I taught Bible stories in Sunday School, and I tried to teach miners' children how to read and write, but I left school myself at fourteen and have hardly read a book since. I don't know what I would teach them!"

"You could be a housekeeper, then," suggested Emily.

"Oh no," wailed Flo. "And be someone's servant? I hope I never will be reduced to that!"

"But that's what we married women are anyway," interjected Emily, wryly. "You wouldn't need any special knowledge and you would get paid for it." But the look of horror on Flo's face put an end to that option.

Dolly had been silent during the discussion but then she began, slowly, "It seems to me the best solution would be to become a nurse. I'm not saying you should necessarily work in a hospital, as that's very hard and you would probably need special training. But there is always a need for what they call monthly nurses, to care for children or sick, old or dying people—well-off families are only too happy to pay someone to live in and look after them. Or to look after women during their confinement and after their babies are born. You just have to do what the doctor tells you to do, that's all."

"Now that's a good idea," Emily said. "You are actually very good at nursing, Flo. You were marvellous with our mother when she was dying."

Flo's face had lit up. "That's a wonderful idea, Dolly!" she exclaimed. "You know I learned some first aid after I left school, and I not only nursed our mother, but also several people in Josiah's congregation when they were ill. I could do that!"

"But what about the boys?" John repeated. "You wouldn't be able to take them with you."

Flo had not told them yet that she'd had to leave Godfrey behind, as it was too painful even to speak of.

The group fell quiet for a while, thinking. There seemed to be no obvious solution.

"Well, why doesn't Cyril stay here for the moment?" Emily offered generously. "It would be fun for Maddy to have another child in the house, and he could go to the local school. We'll look after him until you can work out a better solution. I would imagine Martha would be willing to keep Godfrey for the time being too."

"That is *so* kind of you, Emily," Flo said, much relieved. "I'm sure we'll think of something more permanent before long. Though I don't imagine I would ever be able to afford anything like boarding school," she added sadly.

"Then why don't you go and see Dr. Willoughby?" suggested Dolly. "Tell him of your plan and ask if he has any patients who need home nursing. He is bound to have some. And you should get yourself a nurse's uniform, so you would look more professional."

"Now that's a good idea. Where would I get that?"

"There is an outfitter's I know in London that specialises in such uniforms," John said. "I have to go to London on business at the beginning of next week, so if you like, you could come along and get what you need. But I warn you, it would mean leaving at the crack of dawn, and we would have to go by train."

"Marvellous!" Flo exclaimed, clasping her hands in joy. "I'd love to go to London again!"

The next day she called on Dr. Willoughby. She told him she had been recently widowed and needed to support herself. She had plenty of experience in nursing, she claimed. The good doctor was interested. He often had patients who needed live-in nursing help, he said, and since he knew her sister and brother-in-law well, he would not hesitate to recommend her. As it happened, he did not know of any vacancy at the moment, but she should come back in a few days.

Back at the house, a letter had arrived from Josiah. He had guessed she would be at her sister's.

"You are doubtless aware that you have committed an unforgiveable sin which condemns you for eternity in the eyes of God and my own," he wrote. "But to avoid scandal which would wreak great damage on the congregation, our family and of course my own ministry, I do not propose to reveal to anyone the true reason for our separation. I believe Godfrey, who has been quiet and withdrawn ever since that event, can be relied on not to say a word. I trust you can say the same of Cyril and yourself.

"For the same reason, I have not reported to the police your 'borrowing' of the monies in the chapel repair fund, outrageous though it is. I demand that you send them back immediately, as I have no way of making good this terrible and embarrassing loss.

"You cannot, of course, expect any financial support in future from me for yourself or your son. And divorce, I hardly need to add, is out of the question, being an abomination in the eyes of the Lord."

She could not have expected anything else, Flo thought, but it still hurt. Yes, she would send the money back as soon as she could. But what a relief that Josiah did not want the truth to be known either! That made her situation a little easier.

Emily was dying to know what was in the letter.

"He wants me to go back straight away," Flo lied and stuffed it in her pocket. "I'm going to have to write and tell him I'm not going to. I'm worried about Godfrey, though. He says he is quiet and withdrawn. That's not like him at all."

"I think I'll go and have a look around Brentwood to cheer myself up," said Flo that afternoon. "It's been ages since I saw any decent shops." What she did not say was that despite all her good intentions, the money she had borrowed was burning a hole in her purse. She went and came back a couple of hours later with a mysterious package which she took up to her room.

"What have you bought?" Emily asked.

"It's a secret," Flo said, laughing. "After supper I'll show you."

As they were sitting and chatting over their cups of cocoa as usual, Flo disappeared upstairs. Eventually there was a rustling on the stairs, and she appeared in the sitting room, her arms outstretched dramatically. "Tra-la!" she exclaimed.

She was transformed. She had backcombed her hair and piled it up in the bouffant style that fashionable ladies were currently wearing, with curls on top and wispy ringlets framing her face. She was wearing a beautiful apricot-coloured dress with a slim skirt that flared slightly from her knees to her feet and an elegant wide-brimmed hat to match. She radiated beauty. The family were staggered. "Flo!" exclaimed Emily, "you look fabulous! What a wonderful dress!"

"You look like a princess!" marvelled Dolly.

John sat speechless. He could not take his eyes off her.

"I wanted something smart to wear in London," Flo said. "All these years I have had to wear such plain, frumpy clothes. Josiah always said I must never look better than a miner's wife—and in fact, I could never afford to. I always so longed for something pretty." She pirouetted ecstatically around the room. "Oh, it is so wonderful to have a nice dress at last!"

As they were saying goodnight and preparing to go to bed, Emily murmured to Flo, "That outfit must have cost a fortune. It's none of my business but …"

Josiah's tin box flashed through Flo's mind. "It wasn't expensive. They had made it for a lady whose husband suddenly died, and she felt it was inappropriate. It fitted me perfectly, so they let me have it at a large discount. And I'll let you into a secret: for a long time, I squirrelled away a little of the housekeeping money." She was fibbing again. "Just a little at a time, so as to have something by me for the day when I couldn't bear it all any longer. I always knew that sooner or later I would need it. And don't worry, I have enough left over to buy a nurse's uniform."

When the day came, they had to leave early, as John had warned her. In the train, they chatted and joked. John had been one of Flo's admirers before he had married the steadier Emily, and Flo had to admit the two were far better matched. Nevertheless, she sensed that he was still much attracted to her, which pleased her.

He took her first to the outfitters, introduced her, and told the salesman to give her the best of attention before going on to his own appointments. The shop had everything she could have wanted. She chose two pale blue dresses with high, white, starched collars, four white aprons, and a couple of stiff, white caps. She was delighted to find that the pale blue and white of the uniform, its slightly puffed shoulders and neat waist, greatly flattered her and vowed to wear it as often as possible. Finally, she spent the last shilling from Josiah's box on a nurse's chatelaine, a leather pouch containing a thermometer, a syringe, scissors, tweezers, and other useful instruments.

She and John had agreed to meet under Nelson's column at one o'clock. They lunched at a café in the vicinity and were heading for St. James's Park for a stroll when they became aware that a small crowd was gathering on the street. John asked a man what was going on and was told, "The Kaiser is coming! The Kaiser is coming to visit the Queen!"

Policemen appeared, making sure the crowd did not spill into the carriageway. It was not a state visit, or even an official one. Kaiser Wilhelm II was on his way to Osborne, on the Isle of Wight, to be at the bedside of his grandmother, Queen Victoria, whom he knew—although her own subjects did not—was dying.

Before long, the Kaiser's carriage approached, drawn by four gleaming, black horses. Two or three people cheered and some waved at the upright figure with his outsized moustache waxed into upturned peaks at each side, but for the most part, the little group was silent and slightly hostile—Germany was building up its navy in an alarming manner and many feared it would soon threaten Britain's sea power. Nevertheless, people behind Flo were jostling to get a better view, and Flo found herself pushed off the pavement almost in front of the carriage. Giggling, she looked up and caught the eye of the Kaiser. He smiled and the next wave of the Imperial hand seemed intended directly for her.

"Did you see, John? Did you see? The Kaiser waved at me! He waved specially at me!"

"Well, it certainly looked like he did," said John.

"Papa would be so happy—do you know that he is German?"

"Yes, but I think he should keep quiet about it, and you too, the way the wind is blowing nowadays. If his Imperial Majesty does not watch out, before long we could end up at war with Germany."

They were making their way back toward the station when Flo's eye was caught by an establishment calling itself "American Bar."

"What's an American bar?" she asked.

"It's one of these fashionable new places where people go to drink cocktails."

"And what are cocktails?"

"They are drinks made from mixtures of various wines and spirits. They are all the rage in London at the moment," John said.

"Ooh," Flo exclaimed, "I'd love to try a cocktail! Do let's go in and have one!"

They went in and immediately Flo's eyes lit up. A pianist was playing jazz tunes, and the bartender smiled and called out "good evening" as they entered. John felt proud to see how many heads turned to look at the lovely lady in the apricot-coloured dress.

After much discussion, Flo ordered a Manhattan.

"Are you sure? It's very potent," warned John. "Have you ever drank alcohol before?"

Flo hadn't, but she did not want to admit it. "Don't you worry, I'll be fine," she assured him confidently.

She was in her seventh heaven. She was chatting vivaciously, tapping her foot to the music, and dimpling and smiling at the gentlemen who threw her admiring glances. *Think what I have been missing all these years!* she thought to herself. Eventually John looked at his watch and said they must be going. But Flo would not move. "No, no, I'm having such a lovely time, I could stay here all night! Please can I have another drink, please, please!" Against his better judgment, John gave in and ordered her a Gin Fizz and a second Old Fashioned for himself.

He soon regretted it. None too steady himself, he had to manhandle Flo, swaying and singing merrily, together with her parcels, first into a cab and then into a train where she promptly fell asleep with her head lolling on his shoulder. At Brentwood he had no option but to take another cab home.

Emily and Cyril were out when they arrived, attending a children's play at their chapel. Once through the front door, John ordered Flo sternly, "Upstairs, immediately!" He made a cup of tea, took it upstairs, and knocked on her door.

Flo was already in bed. "How sweet of you! You have been so very kind to me, John!" she exclaimed tipsily. "It has been such a wonderful day, thank you, thank you!" Spontaneously she flung her arms round his neck and covered his face with kisses. She was soft, warm, and perfumed. Laced with fumes of bourbon and vermouth, and without anyone intending it that way, the embrace became longer and closer …

"Mama's door is locked," Cyril called down to Emily, who had sent him up to bed.

"I can't imagine it would be. Maybe it's stuck, it does that sometimes," Emily suggested. "John!" she called. "Would you go up and have a look at it?" But John was nowhere to be seen. "Where's your Uncle John?" she asked Cyril. Cyril did not know. Emily went upstairs herself.

She stopped on the landing, poleaxed. Unmistakable noises were coming from Flo's room.

"I don't believe it!" she gasped. She tried the handle, but the door was indeed locked. She hammered on it wildly, shouting, "Stop it, you two! Stop it this instant! I'll kill you!"

The noises stopped. Emily was trying to break the door down when John, looking extremely sheepish, unlocked it from the inside. "Flo is not feeling well. I was bringing her a cup of tea," he stammered lamely. Emily landed him a stinging slap on the face, charged into the room, threw herself at her sister, and grabbed her by the throat. After a fierce struggle, John finally managed to pull her away and pushed her out of the room, following closely. Flo locked the door again behind them, opening it briefly a few minutes later to let Cyril in.

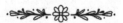

Her head spinning and her heart thumping, Flo lay in bed petrified, aghast at what had happened. How could she? What had possessed her? Her beloved sister's husband—was there anything more shameful than that? She felt filthy, wicked.

She could hear Emily shrieking at John downstairs and John, quieter, struggling to apologise and begging her to keep her voice down for fear the neighbours would hear. She could tell that Cyril was awake and listening too and wondered how on earth she would explain it all to him the next day.

At some point she must have slid into oblivion for when she became conscious again the house was quiet, and the first light was creeping through the gaps in the curtains. Her head was splitting, she felt sick, and memories of the events of the evening were crowding hideously back in. She wished she could die.

When she heard Emily moving around downstairs, she decided to send Cyril down for breakfast and see what happened. After a while, he returned bearing a piece of paper reading, *Get out of my house, now! And never come back. I shall never speak to you again!*

Flo was torn. Part of her would have been relieved to leave the house without looking her sister in the face ever again. But she knew that she must at least humbly apologise and seek forgiveness. Still in her nightdress, she went downstairs. There was no sign of John. She found Emily in the kitchen.

"Emily, I'm so, so sorry. Please forgive me! I must have been so drunk—you know I had never drunk alcohol before, I did not know what I was doing ..."

"Get out of this house, you slut! You whore!" Emily hissed through clenched teeth.

Flo, abject, fell on her knees, crying. "Please, please, Emily, I did not mean to ..."

"You are not my sister anymore! Now *get out*! I'll never ever speak to you again!" Emily stormed out of the kitchen and slammed the door.

Flo had no choice but to go upstairs and pack their things.

For the second time in a week Flo, hung-over, hungry, and by now penniless, was out on the street.

Chapter 4

WARLEY, 1901

"What do we do now, Mama?" Cyril asked miserably.

Flo was shaking and felt ill. But with a great effort, she took deep breath, grasped her hold-all firmly in one hand, and took Cyril's hand with the other.

"We will go to see Dr. Willoughby and ask if he has work for me yet," she said and set off with a determined stride. She was glad she had at least had the presence of mind to put on her nurse's uniform before leaving.

But Dr. Willoughby was very sorry, he still had no-one who might need her. He suggested she try the other doctor in Warley, Dr. Atkins, and perhaps even the chemist. Again, she drew a blank.

"Very well, we will walk into Brentwood and see if the seam-stresses will buy back my new dress," she told Cyril. But when they got there the seamstresses said they were very sorry, they could not take it back, especially since they spotted some dirt on the hem. Flo had had to admit she had worn it once.

By then it was lunchtime, they were extremely hungry, and Cyril was whining. They found a market where the stallholders were packing up to leave. She sent Cyril to ask if they had any produce to spare but all he could glean was a bag of damaged apples. They found a secluded bench in a small park and devoured them voraciously.

"Fortitude," said Flo, half to herself. "We must be strong, steadfast. Courageous. The Lord will help us."

Cyril said nothing.

That afternoon they trailed round doctors' surgeries and chemists' shops in Brentwood, but in vain. By the end of the afternoon, Flo was becoming desperate. They had nowhere to go, no money, nothing to eat. Apart from Emily and John, who were lost to them, probably forever, they knew no one. Who could possibly help them?

"Where are we going to sleep tonight?" whined Cyril. Where, indeed.

They were passing a large church and suddenly Flo stopped. Of course. Churches helped people in difficulties. At least sometimes. She and Josiah had always tried to. There was even a board outside on which was written "All Are Welcome."

"Here, Cyril. Let's see if someone can give us some advice." She banged the huge knocker on what appeared to be the vicarage door, but there was no reply.

"Let's just sit in the church for a while, somebody is bound to come sooner or later."

Across the road was a baker's shop which was just closing. She sent Cyril to ask if they had any bread left over. He came back with a bag of stale rolls, which made their supper. They settled down in a pew and waited. Flo racked her brains for stories to tell Cyril. It grew dark. Still, no one came.

Eventually, Cyril stretched out on the pew with his head on a hassock and went to sleep. Flo must have dozed off too, because she was jolted awake by the sound of a big key turning in the lock of the church door. It was some moments before she realised that the person was not coming in but going away. She ran towards the door and banged on it, shouting, "Help! Don't lock us in!" But whoever it was seemed not to hear, and the door remained firmly locked. They were shut in for the night.

It was pitch dark and icy cold. She had sharp hunger pains in her stomach. She kept bumping on pew-ends as she felt her way back to Cyril and her hold-all. Her shuffling steps echoed through the huge, empty church. Her feet and hands were numb with cold. *Josiah said I should burn in hell, but here I am freezing in hell,* she thought bitterly. As she sat in the dark, cavernous church, the events of the past few days crowded in on her. The scene at the manse, the scene at Emily's—why, oh why, had she been so wicked? Josiah, for all his faults, had not deserved that, neither had Emily, her dearest sister. Whatever had possessed her? That was not the way she had been brought up; she had always tried to be a "good" girl, even if she did not always succeed. She had betrayed her parents, her family, her religion. And now she was being punished. She had no home, no money, nothing—and it was all her own fault.

Seeking comfort, she fumbled around in her old hold-all until she could feel the cheap metal frame that held the photograph of her mother and pulled it out. When she was small, her mother's voluminous skirts had often been her refuge from the anger of her father. As she grew older, she would seek comfort in the large bosom and gentle embrace. Her mother would never contradict Zachary but try to persuade Flo in a soft voice that Papa was right, and she had to behave better. But she always felt that somehow her mother understood and forgave her.

"Mama," she said to the picture silently, straining to make out her mother's face in the dark. "I've been so wicked, but I didn't mean to, believe me, really, I didn't. I'm so terribly sorry. Poor Emily! I shall never, ever do anything like that again, I promise! Mama, please help me!"

Thank heavens her mother was not here to see her, she thought, alone with her poor son, and destitute.

What became of women like her? What would happen if she didn't find work? Once again, a black terror engulfed her. Would she and Cyril have to beg in the streets? How would they find enough to eat? Would she be forced to prostitute herself? Horrors! Or would they end up among those poor people in the workhouse, slaving away under the grim supervision of supposed benefactors, hungry, mistreated, and ashamed?

She threw herself on her knees. The words of a psalm came to her: "Out of the depths I cry to thee, oh Lord!" She could not remember the rest but begged, "Lord, I vow never, ever, to do anything like that again. I will be good, I promise. But please, you must help me—to survive."

Part Two

A Respectable Woman?

Chapter 5

BRENTWOOD, 1901

"Who are you? What are you doing here?"

Flo sat up abruptly. A thin figure in a grey suit and white dog-collar was standing at the end of the pew, blinking at them through steel-rimmed glasses. Morning sunshine was pouring through the stained-glass windows.

"Oh, Vicar, thank goodness you have come!" Flo exclaimed. "We wanted to ask for help; the church was open, but nobody came. And then someone shut us in. We didn't mean to sleep here."

"Well, you can't stay here," said the vicar. "The church is not for vagrants."

"I'm not a vagrant! I'm a respectable woman!" Flo burst into tears. The vicar looked appalled. He put his arms out awkwardly as if to console her, then dropped them, not knowing what to do.

"What's going on?" A plump, grey-haired woman bustled over, carrying a sheaf of flowers and a vase. She immediately looked at Flo's uniform.

"Are you a nurse?" she asked.

Flo blew her nose and nodded.

"So, what's the matter?"

Flo started crying again and blurted out a confused story about her husband dying, needing a job, no money, nowhere to go.

Cyril listened in silence.

"I hoped someone could tell me what to do," Flo stammered amid sobs and snuffles. "But no one came."

"And who is this young man?"

"Cyril," answered the boy, and, tugging on Flo's sleeve: "I'm hungry, Mama."

Flo threw him a reproving look.

The woman evidently decided she needed to take charge of the situation.

"I'm Vera Snodgrass. The vicar here is my husband. Let me just put these flowers in water and we will go round to the vicarage and have a talk. And we will give Cyril something to eat."

Visibly relieved at that the problem had been taken out of his hands, her husband went off to attend to other matters.

At the kitchen table in the vicarage, Flo regained her composure and, while she and Cyril tucked hungrily into bread and marmalade, she gave Mrs. Snodgrass a carefully edited version of her predicament.

Mrs. Snodgrass's heart went out to her.

"You poor dear," she said. "How terrible! It makes me wonder what would happen to me if my dear Arthur were to die. I really don't know what I would do. But let us see if we can find a solution to your problem. I am not aware of any our parishioners who need a live-in nurse at the moment, but I will certainly ask.

"But then, what will you do about this young man here?" she wondered. "I can't imagine any family would be willing to take a child too. It would be very unusual."

Flo had not thought about that. There was of course no longer any question of Cyril staying at Emily's. "I'm not sure. I could ask his aunt in Dorset"—meaning her other sister, Lizzie—"to look after him, but at present I cannot even afford a train ticket to take him there."

"Perhaps for the time being we could ask Mr. and Mrs. Cooper at the Waifs and Strays to take him in. I am on the committee and I'm sure he would not refuse me."

Cyril did not look happy.

"Don't worry, young man. The Coopers are very kind and will look after you well. And I'm sure it would only be for a very short time," Mrs. Snodgrass tried to assure him.

A few minutes later, Flo was certain that the Lord had answered her prayers. She, Mrs. Snodgrass, and Cyril were walking through town to the Cooper establishment when Flo heard her name called. It was Lucy Green, Dr. Willoughby's assistant.

"Mrs. Harris, Mrs. Harris!" Lucy came hurrying across the road. "There is a patient who needs you urgently! The nurse who was looking after her left all of a sudden this morning! Can you come and talk to the doctor?"

Flo was ecstatic.

"Listen, my dear, you run along to Dr. Willoughby," said the kindly Mrs. Snodgrass. "I'll take Cyril to see Mr. and Mrs. Cooper, and then we can meet up again late this afternoon at the Vicarage and you can pick up your bag."

Flo thanked her profusely and went.

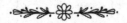

"I'm Nurse Harris. Dr. Willoughby sent me," Flo announced briskly as the door of the red-and-grey brick house on Warley Mount opened. The doctor had told her that her patient was a Mrs. Darnley, a pregnant woman who was suffering from consumption and was not at all well. It might not be an easy assignment, the doctor warned her diplomatically, but he would be very grateful if she was able to take it on at such short notice.

"Ah, thank heavens you've come, nurse. And so promptly too." Relief was written all over the round, slightly ruddy face of the woman, presumably the housekeeper, who let her in. The face, with small, dark, beady eyes, was topped by a stiff brown cap holding back grey curls. Below it, she wore a brown dress and a reddish apron tied round her plump waist. Flo had the irresistible feeling of being let in by a harassed robin.

"Come on in, nurse. Let me take your things."

As the front door closed behind her, a harsh voice like the cawing of a raven came from upstairs, "Who is it?"

Another bird? Flo giggled to herself.

"It's the new nurse, ma'am," called the robin. Then, in a low voice to Flo, "Be patient with her; she's having a very difficult time."

Flo nodded and followed the housekeeper up the stairs to her employer's room.

The room was dark, hot, and almost unbearably stuffy. Heavy, velvet, maroon curtains were swathed over the windows, with more festooned around the old-fashioned, four-poster bed. Dark, flowered wallpaper and equally dark, overstuffed furniture added to the gloom. A dim, coloured-glass gas lamp by the bedside gave the only light, revealing the pale, once-beautiful face of a younger woman, surrounded by a mass of dark hair, sunk into a pile of lacy pillows.

"And who are you?" rasped the figure in the bed who promptly succumbed to a fit of violent coughing.

"I'm Nurse Harris, Mrs. Darnley. Dr. Willoughby sent me. He will be coming himself any minute now," Flo bustled purposefully to the bedside with a reassuring smile, determined to look businesslike and competent, as if she had all the experience in the world.

"Let me sit you up a little straighter, so you can breathe better," she said, moving to lift her up.

"Leave me alone," snapped the woman. "It doesn't do the slightest bit of good. I know best. I'm sick and tired of you nurses telling me what I should do. I suppose you will leave after a couple of days like all the rest of them, stupid good-for-nothings. They have no idea what they are doing."

At that moment, to Flo's great relief, the doorbell clanged, and the robin went downstairs and returned shortly with Dr. Willoughby, a tall, avuncular man in his fifties, with a high collar, bushy moustache, and a reassuring manner.

"Doctor, will you please tell the nurse what she should do and what she should not do; she really seems to have no idea."

Flo was about to protest that she had only just arrived, but Dr. Willoughby made a motion to keep quiet and said, "First, I will examine you, Mrs. Darnley. How are you feeling today?" He opened his large black leather bag.

After examining the invalid, taking her temperature, and finding her no better than the day before, he said gently, "Well, we're going to have to let a little blood, Mrs. Darnley. I think it will do you some good." Misjudging the startled look on Flo's face, he added, "I do it myself, don't worry, nurse. I never let a barber near my patients. Nor do I use leeches. It is necessary to reduce the danger of infection in ladies in madam's condition. Fetch a small bowl, would you? There will just be a small quick cut, ma'am," he added in the direction of his patient, ignoring her protests.

Flo knelt, holding out a bowl in one hand and Mrs. Darnley's right hand in the other while the doctor cut a vein in Mrs. Darnley's left arm. Blood dripped into the bowl. Flo felt a little faint but steeled herself—the doctor must not know it was the first time she had seen a bloodletting. She had heard that the practice was now controversial, but Dr. Willoughby was obviously a doctor of the old school. In any case, she must do everything he said. *This is my work now, and I have got to learn to cope*, she thought.

When the arm had been neatly bandaged and the contents of the bowl removed, Dr. Willoughby took her aside and wrote out a prescription for some medicines. "The ones she has are nearly finished. I have written down the times and dosages here," he said, giving her another note. "Be very careful with the laudanum. No more than two drops in the morning and midday, and five in the evening to help her sleep. And it's important that she should eat as much as she feels able to," he added. "Give her plenty of stout to drink; it's good for ladies in her condition. And a little fresh air when you can, although," he added in a low voice, "I know she does not take kindly to the window being open."

They returned to the bedside. Mrs. Darnley lay immobile, her eyes closed. Flo could not tell whether she had passed out, was sleeping, or just ignoring them.

The doctor took her pulse. "She'll be all right, just let her rest for the moment," he said. And as Flo handed him over to the housekeeper outside the room, he turned to her and said very seriously, "The baby is due in a month, and she is not strong. It's not going to be easy."

Flo cautiously opened a window slightly to let a little air and light into the stuffy room and busied herself sorting and tidying the bottles of medicine which had been left in some disarray by her predecessor. The silence was suddenly broken by a screech from the bed.

"Close that wretched window! It's cold! Do you want me to get pneumonia on top of everything else?!"

Flo rushed to close the window.

Lunchtime was approaching and, despite Mrs. Snodgrass's bread and jam at the vicarage, Flo was hungry. Before long, the maid arrived bearing a tray with Mrs. Darnley's lunch.

"You should have asked me before bringing this!" the patient barked. "Take it back, I don't want it. Just bring me a small bowl of broth."

"But the doctor said …" Flo protested.

"Hold your tongue, I know what is best."

Flo's heart sank even further. She wondered how long she could put up with this shrew.

The housekeeper came to ask where Flo wanted her lunch. Flo paused. She knew that the status of nurses, while below that of the family, was above that of the servants and that they often ate alone in their own rooms. But she badly wanted to know more about the Darnley family and her impossible patient, and to get on good terms with the staff.

"May have it in the kitchen with you?" she asked.

"Yes, go and have your lunch and leave me in peace," said Mrs. Darnley, turning over.

In the kitchen, Flo was introduced to the maid, a slip of a girl with mousy hair by the name of Nellie, who, after a shy "pleased to meet you," said nothing. The robin turned out to be a Mrs. Betts and said she had been with the Darnleys since they came to live in Warley ten years earlier. Flo must have looked surprised, because Mrs. Betts hastened to add that "it wasn't always like this. They were young and very much in love. They are both very musical. Mrs. Darnley is Irish; her family live in Dublin, but she had come to London to study. She was very beautiful, and a very promising young singer, she had a lovely voice and could have had a wonderful future. Very much a prima donna, even then, I have to say. Mr. Darnley used to indulge her to no end; she could have or do anything she wanted.

"She gave up her career—or at least postponed it—when the children arrived. Then she fell so very ill. You can hear what it has done to her voice. Even if she gets better, the doctor says she may never be able to sing again. It has made her very bitter—and you see how she has become.

"There has been one nurse after another, they could not stand it for more than a few days. But I could not leave them. I love the children so much and Mr. Darnley is so very kind. And I feel sorry for her, because I know what she used to be like, and how she is suffering."

Flo was moved. "I'm glad you told me that," she said. She hoped it would help her deal with her difficult patient.

"And when will Mr. Darnley be here?" she asked.

"Probably not till the end of the week," Mrs. Betts replied. "He has to be away often for his work." Then, in a lower voice as if imparting information of great importance, "He's something in the government, you know."

It sounded impressive.

"You will have to arrange with him about your pay and so on," Mrs. Betts went on. "Providing, of course, that Mrs. Darnley wants you to stay." Flo realised that that meant she would have to put up with her patient at least for several days if she was going to get paid at all. But unpleasant though it was likely to be, at least for the time being, she had a roof over her head.

"The children will be back from school at four," Mrs. Betts said. "Then they will have their tea and go up to see their mother, if she feels strong enough. Then they will play and practise until they go to bed at six thirty."

"Practise?" Flo asked.

"Yes, Mr. Darnley is teaching the children to sing and play the piano. You will hear them; they sing like little angels. He plays the organ in church, and he even has a small organ here in his study."

Flo returned to the sickroom. Mrs. Darnley had thrown off all her bedclothes, the bed was drenched in sweat, and she was gasping for air. Flo sat her in a chair, wrapped in an eiderdown, while she changed the bed and then managed, with much difficulty, to persuade Mrs. Darnley to let her sponge her down, brush her long black hair, and put her back into bed.

As soon as her patient was asleep, Flo hurried into Brentwood to collect her hold-all from the vicarage and to thank Mrs. Snodgrass for her help, then went to the Waifs and Strays to take Cyril his belongings. Mr. Cooper greeted her effusively. She was a little surprised that he did not invite her in but merely assured her that Cyril was very happy and settling in well. Flo was content to take his word for it; she was relieved to have found a solution for Cyril, at least for the time being. She had heard that Waifs and Strays homes were supposed to be small and create a warm, family atmosphere which many of the children would be lacking in their lives, and Mrs. Snodgrass had recommended this one. Flo did not know that by no means all such homes lived up to these ideals and it did not occur to her to look more closely.

She returned quickly to Warley to find her patient awake again and demanding to know where she had been.

Around half past four, the Darnley children, a small girl and an older boy, arrived at the bedroom door, accompanied by Mrs. Betts.

Flo welcomed them with a cheerful smile. "Hello, you two, I'm Nurse Harris and I have come to look after your mama. And you are …?"

"Mary," said the girl, shyly.

"I'm Paul," said the boy. He looked about the same age as Cyril, Flo thought.

"Come in, dears, but be very quiet, your mama is very tired." They tiptoed in, kissed their mother, answered her whispered questions about their day, then returned them to the care of Mrs. Betts.

By suppertime, Flo was exhausted. She decided that as soon as they had eaten, and she had settled Mrs. Darnley down for the night, she would go to bed herself.

But her patient had other ideas. Mrs. Darnley got out of bed and began pacing up and down the room, calling for food and a fire to be lit in the hearth. She began railing against her husband who she said was never there and did not care whether she lived or died. It was only after a long fit of coughing that she consented to lie down again. When she finally quietened down, Flo turned down the lamp very low and tiptoed over to the small room she had been given across the landing from her patient, where she could hear if she called or rang the bell. It was in fact a storeroom which had only partly been cleared to make space for a bed, a small bedside table, and a wardrobe. She put her mother's photograph on the little table. It was becoming her talisman. "Mama," she whispered to it, "help me. Please help me."

It was the first night of her new life. Curled up uncomfortably on the lumpy old flock mattress she had been given, she felt thankful she at last had somewhere to live, at least for a while, and the prospect of earning some money. It dawned on her that she was no longer a daughter, a wife, or even a younger, help-seeking sister—she was now, for the first time ever, solely responsible for her own life. The premises were not good: she was at the mercy of a sick, half-demented woman—and heaven only knew how long that would last. As an outcast, she had the whole of society against her—and she had a young son to support. But at least she had allies. Mrs. Betts had become her friend and Mrs. Snodgrass had been so kind that she must become friends with her too. And then there was her other sister, the dear faithful Lizzie.

But then there was Godfrey. She missed him terribly and was sure he was desperately missing her and his brother. How cruel to take a child from his mother! She must try by every means possible to get him back. But how? And how could she keep him when she had to farm Cyril out to the Waifs and Strays? Crying bitterly and racking her brains for some solution, she eventually fell asleep.

She awoke the next morning feeling washed out, but calm, like the air after a storm. And strangely optimistic. *What a blessing,* she reflected, *that I found this post. Maybe the Lord meant it as a sign. Maybe He is giving me another chance. Please don't let me waste it this time.*

Chapter 6

What Emily had said was true: Flo, for all her flightiness, was an excellent nurse: caring, reassuring and cheerful. But Mrs. Darnley tried her patience to the utmost. Flo tried to persuade her to talk about her singing and for a short while she would chat pleasantly, but then she would start coughing and become bad-tempered and vicious again. She tried playing cards with her, or Halma and other board games. Sometimes it went well, but often she would end up sweeping the cards or pieces onto the floor in a fit of temper. Flo tried hard to remain detached and cheerful, but by the end of the week she was miserable and exhausted and seriously tempted to ask Dr. Willoughby if he had another patient for her.

That evening, however, delighted squeals and shouts of "Papa! Papa!" from below told Flo that the head of the house had returned. Her patient had been feeling slightly better, and she had persuaded her to get up for a while. Mrs. Darnley was reclining, warmly wrapped in shawls, on a green chaise longue by the fire in her room when her husband appeared in the doorway.

Francis Hunter Darnley was a tall, slim man with a shock of curly dark hair and an unruly moustache which half-hid an amused smile. He was wearing a formal, grey suit but had already loosened his stiff, high collar in anticipation of a comfortable evening at home.

"You must be Nurse Harris," he said affably to Flo as he entered. "It was so good of you to step in at such short notice. How is she doing?" And without waiting for an answer he went over to his wife. Flo discreetly left the room and closed the door.

After supper, Mrs. Betts was ensconced with Mr. Darnley in his study for a while then called Flo, telling her that her employer wished to speak to her.

She found him standing in front of the fire. He wore a navy-and-red velvet smoking jacket and a dark red kerchief knotted loosely round his neck. He was reading a letter. As she entered, he looked up and Flo found herself looking into a striking pair of pale-green eyes. *He must be in his late thirties,* she thought. He had a charming, slightly bohemian air about him that made her think of some French artist—not that she had ever met any.

"Well, Mrs. Harris, I can't thank you enough for responding so quickly after your predecessor left—and for the excellent care you are taking of my poor wife. I would be very grateful if you could stay with us, at least until a few weeks after the baby is born. Would that suit you?"

Flo was astonished. She hesitated, uncertain what to say.

"Please don't tell me you want to leave us," Mr. Darnley begged. "You might not believe this, but my wife is pleased with you, much more so than with the other nurses she has had. I do realise she is not an easy patient, but believe me, you seem to be doing her a lot of good, much more than you think. We really need you to stay."

Flo was even more surprised. But he looked so beseechingly at her that she had to give in. *At least he seems to understand her problem*, she thought.

"Very well, sir."

"Thank goodness. That is a great relief. I can offer you two guineas a week. I understand that is the usual rate."

"Yes, it is, sir." They also agreed that she would have Sundays free, apart from getting her patient up in the morning and putting her to bed at night, and would be off-duty between two and four o'clock all other afternoons.

"By the way," Flo added as an afterthought, "I shall need to go to the chemists to buy more medicines tomorrow."

"Mr. Longfellow will add them to our account. He sends us a bill every few weeks."

She was bid a courteous goodnight and left the room feeling reassured. Her employer was evidently a gentleman. He was friendly and he seemed to be on her side. He was also very attractive. Not, she told herself severely, that that mattered in the least.

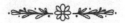

Flo decided that now that she had found employment, at least for a while, she must reach out to members of her family, to try and make her peace with some and to draw closer, if possible, to others. Her free time now would have to be devoted to letter-writing. She needed paper and envelopes.

"Ah, so you are the new nurse at the Darnleys'," Mr. Longfellow greeted her as she entered the chemist's shop, his eyes twinkling over his tortoiseshell glasses as he pushed aside his old brass pill-making machine and took her patient's prescriptions. "How are you getting on with Mrs. Darnley?"

Her patient's character seemed to be no secret, but Flo was not inclined to gossip. "Er, well, so far," she said.

"Good for you. She was such a splendid woman once, even though she was rather haughty. Such a tragedy."

On her way home, Flo stopped at the paper shop to buy writing paper and envelopes. As she re-entered the Darnleys' house she heard the soaring notes of an organ coming from Mr. Darnley's study. She stopped in his doorway to listen. He was swaying slightly to and fro, his hands flying over the keys, playing a tumultuous fugue. She stood for a while, listening, but as she finally moved off, she accidentally dropped the bag containing the medicines. He broke off and turned towards her.

"I'm so sorry, sir, I did not mean to disturb you, please go on. I just wanted to listen. What were you playing? It was so beautiful." She thought of the dreary hymns that Dave Philips had pumped out on the wheezy old harmonium in Josiah's chapel.

"It is the Fugue from Bach's famous Toccata and Fugue in D minor," said Mr Darnley. "You know, the one that begins …" And he turned round, pulled out a large number of stops, and launched into the dramatic first few bars. Even on his small house organ it sounded impressive.

"Oh yes, I know it," Flo said, "but I have never heard it played so wonderfully. How did you learn?"

"Actually, I studied music and became a professional organist. I was even attached to Chester Cathedral for a while. But I came to realise that it would be hard to support a wife and family comfortably on an organist's pay. So, I reluctantly became an auditor, like my father."

"An auditor?" said Flo, not certain what that meant. "Are you not a politician? Mrs. Betts said you were something in the government."

Mr. Darnley laughed heartily. "No! I'm afraid not! I work for the Local Government Board. I audit the accounts of county and town councils, to make sure that the public money is being spent correctly. It is dull work, unless I find someone lining their own pockets. It means I often have to be away from home. But it also gives me time between missions for my music. Are you musical?"

"Not really, but my son is. He has a lovely voice and was the lead chorister in our local choir."

"Your son? Where is he now?"

"He is here in Warley, but he is staying with friends for the time being." She was ashamed to mention the Waifs and Strays.

"Then let him come round. He can join in our singing lessons with Mary and Paul. Why don't you bring him when they come back from school this afternoon?"

Flo was overcome. How kind of Mr. Darnley! That would be fun for Cyril, and it would mean she could see more of him.

Mr. Darnley turned back to the organ.

⁕

"Who - killed - Cock - Robin?" intoned Mr. Darnley gravely, underscoring the question with a sonorous chord.

"I, said the sparrow, with my bow and arrow," piped five-year-old Mary. "I killed Cock Robin."

"All the birds of the air were a-sighing and a-sobbing …" all three children joined in the chorus.

"Now, Cyril." Mr. Darnley nodded to Cyril.

"I, said the fly, with my little eye," Cyril carried on in his strong, pure treble, "I saw him die."

"Aha!" exclaimed Mr. Darnley, almost to himself. "Paul, next …"

By the time the children had belted out the chorus together four times, Cyril's initial shyness on being fetched from the Waifs and Strays and thrust into a new and evidently well-heeled household, had evaporated. After a hearty joint rendering of "Bobby Shaftoe" and "London's Burning" as merry rounds, he was thoroughly enjoying himself, especially since he could tell he sang better than the others.

"Your son has a remarkable voice," Mr. Darnley said to Flo who had looked in on her way to the kitchen. "I'd like to hear some more." He sent the other two children away to play and motioned Cyril to come closer to the piano. He set him singing arpeggios, each a semi-tone higher than the last, to test his range.

"Can you sight read?" Cyril had learned to sight-read in the chapel choir. "If someone asked you to sing something, say for a concert, what would you sing?"

Cyril thought for a moment. "Perhaps 'Who is Sylvia?'"

Mr. Darnley struck up the introduction to "Who is Sylvia?" and Cyril launched himself into Schubert's beloved song.

"This is phenomenal," Mr. Darnley said when he had finished. "We must have him in the choir at St. John's, Nurse. That's the church where I play when I'm here. I'm not the choirmaster but I'm sure Mr. Fields would be thrilled to have him. Would you like that, Cyril?"

Cyril blushed and nodded.

"And I have another idea, but I'll talk to Mr. Fields about it first."

Flo had decided she must bite the bullet and write to tell her father that she would not be returning to Josiah. She agonised for days over how to break the news but finally composed a letter saying that they had "separated" and that no matter how hard she had tried, she and Josiah had regrettably come to the conclusion that she was not cut out to be a preacher's and minister's wife. They had amicably agreed to take one child each. She was now embarked on a life of nursing and ministering to the sick. She made no mention of Emily and John. After writing out several versions, she finally posted the one she thought most suitable and waited in a state of apprehension for his reaction. Several days passed before the postman finally delivered his reply and her hands were shaking a little as she slit open the envelope.

That any daughter of mine should leave her husband and the state of holy matrimony is abhorrent. You and your sisters have been brought up to respect the teachings of our Lord and our revered Founder and to contribute to the community into which you were born. Your mother, of blessed memory, would be heartbroken to know that you could ever be guilty of such a heinous sin. I command you to return immediately to your husband, seek reconciliation, and take up your sacred duties as his wife and helpmate. If you disobey me, you will cease to be my daughter. I will disinherit you and will never communicate with you again. Father.

Flo put the letter down. Tears welled up in her eyes. She knew she could hardly have hoped for anything else from her father but now she had lost both parents. Crusty though he was, she knew that deep down inside, he loved her and that it must have hurt him deeply to write that letter. But there was nothing she could do. Maybe with time ...

Her next task, almost as difficult as the letter to her father, was to try once again for a reconciliation with Emily, although she seriously doubted that she would succeed. Once again, she apologised humbly for her behaviour.

It was a terrible thing which I would never have done if I had not been so foolish as to drink too many cocktails, being unaccustomed to alcohol. Whether you forgive me or not, please know that I will never forgive myself.

As she feared, Emily did not reply.

Flo was constantly tormented by the thought of Godfrey. She was consumed by remorse. "Why did I not defy Josiah and take him with me?" she kept asking herself tearfully as she lay awake in bed at night. "How could I tell him that I would come back when I knew I wouldn't? The little imp, he must feel so betrayed. Abandoned and betrayed!" She had written him a long, tender letter telling him she loved him and asking him how he was, but he had not replied. Had he even received it? Josiah would surely not forbid him to write to her.

She had addressed it to him at the home of her sister-in-law Martha, whose husband, Ezekiel, was a senior Primitive Methodist minister and in charge of a big congregation in Aberdare in Wales, guessing—correctly—that Josiah would have taken Godfrey to live with her. At the same time, she sent a letter to Martha begging for information about him, although she knew that her sister-in-law had her hands full with seven children of her own as well as her work with Ezekiel's congregation and would have little time to write. Eventually, Flo received a hasty note confirming that Godfrey was now living with them, was well, and going to school with his cousins. Martha said nothing about his state of mind.

Much more comfortably, she wrote at length to Lizzie. Dear Lizzie, plain and dumpy but so loving and caring, had sadly been jilted by her one suitor and never married. She was now devoting her life to looking after their father in his cottage outside Sturminster Newton in Dorset. Although she would doubtless already have heard about it from their father, Flo told her about her "separation" and explained, cautiously, that she had found work but unfortunately was not able to have Cyril with her. Would Lizzie be prepared to take him? she asked. Flo was, in fact, sure that Lizzie herself would be only too happy to have him but was afraid that her father might object.

Lizzie was also Godfrey's godmother and Flo knew that with Emily now lost to her, it was important that she keep in close touch with her second sister who would now be her main link to Godfrey and the rest of her family.

Finally, Flo called on Mrs. Snodgrass. There were many things that she could not tell her, and she had to be careful what she said, but it was good to be able to talk to someone about her difficulties with Mrs. Darnley. Mrs. Snodgrass knew the Darnleys slightly, sympathised with Flo's problems, and generously showered her with motherly support and advice.

Flo soon settled into a routine at the Darnleys. She would get up at seven and have breakfast in the kitchen, then at 7:30 would wake Mrs. Darnley, draw the curtains, and have Nellie bring Mrs. Darnley breakfast in bed. She would administer her medicines, then get her up, help her wash, dress her, and sit her, well wrapped up, on her chaise longue while Nellie cleaned and tidied the room. When the postman came, she would bring her the mail and the newspaper which arrived on the doorstep early each day, and Mrs. Betts would look in to discuss housekeeping matters. Around mid-morning there would be a cup of tea and perhaps some biscuits; if Mr. Darnley was working at home, he would drop in for a chat, although Flo noticed that he did not linger long. There would be a visit by the doctor and occasionally a caller, but Mrs. Darnley did not seem to have many friends, at least not in Warley. Lunch was at one p.m., after which Flo would settle her patient down for a nap. In her two free hours she would write letters, rest, or, if Mr. Darnley was at home, she would go and fetch Cyril for his afternoon singing lessons with his children.

She would then have afternoon tea with Mrs. Darnley and try to entertain her and the children, playing board games or encouraging them to draw or paint. If her patient wanted to read, talk, or simply lie in bed quietly, Flo would sit in the room with her and knit or sew until supper time. On good days, if her patient was feeling up to it, Flo would take her downstairs to have supper with her husband in the dining room, but often he had to come upstairs and eat with his wife in her sickroom while Flo joined Mrs. Betts and Nellie in the kitchen. If she was lucky, Mr. Darnley would stay with her for an hour or two, if not, she had to keep Mrs. Darnley company until it was time to put her to bed.

It was a dull routine, Flo thought, but would be quite pleasant if her patient was a reasonable person. It was stressful to have constantly to navigate her ever-changing moods and cope with her whims. Things had improved slightly in one sense, she reflected, because her patient had come to respect her nursing ability and accept her authority in the sickroom. On the other hand, she seemed to resent, perhaps was even jealous of, Flo's good looks and vivacious charm, while her own beauty was draining away. Flo tried to make her feel better by making her look as attractive as possible, particularly when her husband was around. Meanwhile she was learning not to let herself be upset by her patient's insults and acidic remarks.

Chapter 7

ABERDARE, 1901

A couple of weeks earlier, Godfrey had appeared in the doorway of the Primitive Methodist manse in Aberdare in south Wales, clutching the grubby remains of a stuffed dog to his chest with one hand, his schoolbag with the other, and staring resentfully at his seven cousins. Behind him stood his father, Josiah, with Godfrey's few belongings in a small suitcase.

"It's so good of you to take him, Martha," he said to his sister with a sigh of relief. "I've been at my wit's end."

He had returned from the chapel in Pillowell that fateful morning to find Flo and

Cyril gone, as he had decreed, and eight-year-old Godfrey all alone in the house, crying hysterically.

"I want Mama! When's Mama coming back?" he kept on asking. Every time he heard a train whistle he would run out to the gate and wait to see if she and Cyril were walking back up the street. Josiah, hopelessly trying to cope with his work, look after the boy, and produce meals for them both, wrote to his sister Martha begging her, as Flo had foreseen, to take him. Exhausted by Godfrey's questions, he finally sat him down, held him by the shoulders, looked into his eyes and said firmly, "Listen, Godfrey. Your mother has done something very wicked and has had to go away."

"What has she done?" Godfrey was wide-eyed. The very idea of Flo doing something bad was inconceivable to him.

"One day, maybe I will tell you, but at the moment, you are too young to understand."

"So, when will she come back?"

"No, my dear, she is not coming back, ever again."

Stunned silence. Then a deluge of tears.

"Now I am going to take you to Aunt Martha's," Josiah continued once the boy had calmed down a little. "There you will have your cousins to play with and Aunt Martha and Uncle Ezekiel will look after you because, as you know, I have to travel a lot and I can't take you with me."

Silence again. Then, "What about Cyril? Will he come back?"

"I hope Cyril will come and visit us one day, but he will be living with Mama, and you will be living with Aunt Martha."

The merry, mischievous little boy was never the same again.

"Godfrey's more than welcome. The more the merrier," Martha said after ushering father and son into the house. She added two more chairs to the large dining table. She was a cheerful, motherly woman, adored by her children and her husband's congregation. "Sit down and have some lunch. Ezekiel, would you say grace?"

But it was as if a ghost were hovering around the table as the family sat down to the meal. Flo, always warm and lively, had been the life and soul of such get-togethers and her in-laws and their children loved her. Martha and Ezekiel had named their youngest daughter Florence—now Florrie—after her. But today's lunch was quiet and a little awkward, as the grown-ups did not want to discuss the situation in front of the children, and the children sensed that something was very wrong.

When they had finished, Martha said to them, "Run along now. Take Godfrey with you and go outside and play."

Ezekiel went to attend chapel business, leaving Martha and Josiah alone. "Tell me, what has happened, Josiah?" Martha began. "Where is Flo? You didn't explain anything in your letter."

"All I am going to say is that I have sent her away. She is not cut out to be a minister's wife. Don't ask me anymore. I am never going to speak about her ever again."

"But Josiah, I'm your sister, you can confide in me!" Martha insisted, but Josiah flatly refused to say any more. Her brother was obviously deeply shocked. Martha was dying to know more but did not press further. Many people had dark secrets they never revealed to anyone, not even those closest to them.

Outside, the children tried to coax Godfrey into joining in their games, as he had happily done in the past, but he preferred to be on his own, playing with the cats behind the woodshed. Five-year-old Florrie caught him there, quietly weeping.

"Don't cry, Godfrey" she said, and asked innocently, "Where is your mama?"

"I don't have a mama," he replied, sullenly.

"Of course you do! And we all love her very much, so much that they called me Florence after her!"

"I don't anymore. She's gone away."

Florrie, mystified but moved by Godfrey's misery, hugged him in sympathy. "Never mind, Godfrey, our mama can be your mama too, and we can be your sisters and brothers."

But Godfrey would not be consoled.

Chapter 8

WARLEY 1901

As Mr. Darnley had predicted, Mr. Field, the choirmaster, was delighted to have the gifted new treble join his choir. The Coopers were happy to let Cyril take part, as they were always anxious to keep on good terms with the local parishes. Flo had warned Cyril that the ways of the Church of England would be a little different from those of his father's Primitive Methodists, starting with the red cassock and surplice he would be wearing, but that he should just keep his eyes and ears open and do what the others did. She began attending Sunday service at St John's to give him moral support, but also because she was avoiding going near the Methodist chapel for fear of running into Emily and John.

St. John's was indeed very different from their chapel. The people were different, solid, comfortable, middle-class, healthier, and much better dressed than the miners, farm workers, and unemployed poor of Josiah's congregation. The parson spoke in calm, ponderous tones. His flock needed to follow the teachings of Christ and give money to worthy causes but otherwise, Flo had the impression, all was as it should be in the world. Flo had

had little love for the fundamentalist teachings of the Primitive Methodists, imposed on her first by her father and then by Josiah. Here, everything was more reassuring, much less challenging. Moreover, she felt somehow that here at St John's she had risen socially. Maybe she had joined the middle class. She smiled as she remembered how acutely aware Josiah had been that the Primitive Methodists, and particularly their clergy, were generally considered rough and uneducated and how he had spent so much of his spare time, poor man, studying Latin and Hebrew to prove that he was as cultured and erudite as his Church of England colleagues.

Cyril had only been in the choir a couple of weeks when Mr. Darnley called Flo into his study after supper.

"Frank Field says young Cyril is doing extremely well in the choir and is going to let him sing solos. He certainly would acquit himself very well, but we think he can aspire to more than that. We think you should apply for a place in Westminster Choir School."

"Westminster Choir School?" Flo gasped. "Do you really think he would stand a chance?"

"I certainly think he would, and so does Frank. I have a friend—we studied music together—who teaches at the school and who could put a word in for him. He would get a very good education there."

"Oh, how marvellous!" exclaimed Flo, clasping her hands together in delight. That would be a wonderful solution for Cyril and so much preferable to growing up with her father and Lizzie. Her heart swelled. From what Mr. Darnley said, it was clear Cyril would get an excellent education, one that she herself would never be able to afford and which would give him an excellent start in life. Besides, she thought thankfully, it would mean that he would be taken care of for much of the year, no more Waifs and Strays. She would just have to find him somewhere to stay for the holidays. Maybe Lizzie again.

But then her face fell, and she let her hands drop. "But no, I couldn't possibly afford it. A school like that must cost a fortune," she sighed.

"No, it doesn't. The school is largely financed by the Abbey; parents only have to pay for the boys' board and lodging, but there are bursaries for boys whose parents cannot even manage that. I strongly recommend that you apply for one of these."

"Oh, Mr. Darnley, what a wonderful idea, you are so kind! How can I ever thank you?"

"Nurse, it is such a pleasure for me to help a gifted boy develop his talent—but first let us get him accepted and obtain a bursary for him." He sat her down there and then at his writing desk and dictated the letter that she was to send to the head of the choir school. Then he wrote a brief letter to his friend and when he was finished, he put them in envelopes, addressed them and gave them both to Flo to post.

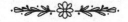

Easter was approaching and the choir was to sing Handel's Messiah in the church on Easter Saturday. Cyril was to sing two solos. Mr. Darnley would be playing the organ.

He devoted much time to practising with Cyril, either in the church or on his small organ at home.

When the day finally dawned, Flo put on her apricot-coloured dress, swept her hair up in the fashionable bouffant style, and put on her elegant matching hat. The weather was unusually warm, and she only needed a shawl, not her shabby navy cape. As the mother of a soloist, she wanted to look her best.

"You have really got yourself dolled up," Mrs. Darnley had commented acidly as she checked on her one last time before leaving for the church, but Flo did not care. As she was ushered to the place specially reserved for her on the front pew, she was thrilled to notice that heads were turning to look at her and people were whispering.

The church, full of spring flowers, was packed. The performance was an immense success and Mr. Field and Mr. Darnley, the soloists, and the choir were all given a standing ovation. Flo felt extremely proud.

Afterwards Cyril, now in his sailor suit, joined her outside the church. People gathered round to congratulate him—and her. "You must be so proud, my dear!" exclaimed Mrs. Snodgrass who had been able to tear herself away from her husband's parish for the occasion. There was Mr. Longfellow, the chemist, and a few shopkeepers she knew, but also strangers who, she could see, were curious to meet this lovely redhead who had joined the congregation.

"Well done, Cyril!" Mr. Darnley's voice came from behind their admirers. He moved forward to tousle Cyril's hair. He looked at Flo, then stopped. At first, he did not seem to recognise her, then stood for a moment as if transfixed. "Madame," he said finally, making a deep bow, "may I congratulate you on Cyril's remarkable performance."

Florence flashed him an enchanting smile.

From then on, it seemed to Flo as if Mr. Darnley's attitude towards her had changed. It was hard to pin down. He was as polite, kind and correct as ever. It was as though he saw her differently, not just as an employee but perhaps—she struggled to define it—as a woman.

The following week, a letter arrived inviting Cyril to an audition at Westminster Choir School.

"Much sooner than I expected," said Mr. Darnley. "I'll go with you, if I may. I'd very much like to see my old friend Tom Peters again."

Flo was grateful. She was not at all sure she was up to taking her son to such a prestigious establishment all on her own.

They set off on the same train she had taken with John what felt like years, rather than just a few weeks ago, but she pushed the embarrassing memories aside to focus on Cyril who, scrubbed and in his sailor suit, was pale and shaking with nerves.

Cyril had been thrilled at the idea of going to the choir school. He loved singing and it was the one thing he did well. But above all, he hoped with all his heart he would get a place and be able to leave the Waifs and Strays. Mr. Cooper was all smiles and kindness when talking to his mother, Mrs. Snodgrass, or other grownups, but Cyril soon realised that he and his wife had held a reign of terror behind their backs. Believing in the old saying "spare the rod and spoil the child" they would deal with the slightest misdemeanor, real or perceived, with canings, bed without supper, or confinement alone in a dark cellar. Cyril was spared such treatment, and he wondered if the Coopers were afraid he would tell Mrs. Snodgrass or his mother. He became sure of this when, on his second day, he became upset to see Mrs. Cooper caning a young boy he had befriended for accidentally knocking over a jug. Mr. Cooper took him aside. "Every child must learn to behave properly. Most of the ones we take in come from terrible circumstances and we have to help them to learn. But to spare them the shame, we never, never tell anyone outside this house what we have to do to teach them. If anyone does," and the look on his face and his tone of voice became threatening, "there will be serious trouble."

Cyril understood. He did not tell his mother what really went on until long after he had left.

With so much at stake, the boy was extremely nervous as he sat with his mother and Mr. Darnley on the train.

"Don't you worry, Cyril, you will be fine," Mr. Darnley reassured him, and began telling him funny stories about his own and his friend's experiences as music students. It worked and gradually Cyril began to relax and almost looked forward to the audition.

"You will probably be auditioned by Sir Frederick Bridge, the chief organist and master of the choristers," he told Cyril. "But don't be afraid of him, as he is a very kind man. He has done wonders for the standard of music in the Abbey, he has reformed the choir, had a new organ built, and I gather, he is now planning to build a brand-new choir school. He is excellent at training young voices."

Flo realised why a new school was needed when they arrived at the present one, housed in cramped quarters in a run-down area just behind the Abbey. It seemed too small to house the thirty-odd choristers who sang in the Abbey, but Darnley explained that many of them were not boarders but lived with their families in nearby boroughs of London.

They were warmly greeted on their arrival by the jovial Tom Peters, Mr. Darnley's friend, who was the sub-organist and a teacher at the school. "Come into the practice room straight away; Sir Frederick has to go to a meeting shortly, and he wants to hear this young man first," he said, hustling Cyril inside. "Ma'am," he said, turning to Flo, "would you mind waiting outside for the moment? We find it is easier for the boys if their parents are not in the room."

Flo obediently settled in a chair outside in the passage. At Mr. Darnley's suggestion, she was wearing her nurse's uniform, cloak, and bonnet, to underline her need for a bursary, although he stressed that the decisive factor would be Cyril's voice and singing ability.

As she surveyed her somewhat dingy surroundings, she could hear Cyril being put through the musical paces he had practised many times with Mr. Darnley. After a slightly shaky start he seemed to be doing very well.

After a while, Tom's head appeared round the door. "Would you like to come in now, ma'am?"

She walked in to see a small panel of three men, obviously teachers or examiners, and Tom and Cyril by the piano. The middle one on the panel, slightly hunched, bespectacled and grey-haired with a prominent moustache jutting out over his lower lip, was obviously Sir Frederick. He left his place and came towards her, shook her hand warmly and exclaimed, "Madam, may I congratulate you. Your son here has a heavenly voice, and I am sure he has it in him to become one of our best choristers. I am pleased to tell you that we would like him to start with us at the beginning of next term, which is now only a month away. I'm sure he will enjoy it here."

Flo was overwhelmed; she thanked him profusely and hugged the delighted Cyril.

The great man then said goodbye, leaving them to discuss further questions with Tom. Mr. Darnley, much more at home in this environment, began discussing what clothes Cyril should bring, visiting arrangements, and other details. As she watched him, still wearing his long, grey greatcoat, totally at ease, leaning on the piano negotiating a bursary and asking questions on her behalf, he seemed to undergo a miraculous transfiguration. She stared, spellbound. He looked just the same, yet seemed to be radiating some powerful force, like high-voltage electricity. Her heart started pounding. She looked at Tom to see if he had noticed anything and could not understand why he was going on talking as if nothing had happened. She began to fuss over Cyril to hide her confusion.

"Would you like me to show you where you will be living?" Tom asked Cyril. Flo followed in a trance as Tom, Cyril, and Mr. Darnley trooped round the small dormitories, the refectory, and classrooms, and finally into the Abbey itself. As though drawn by a magnet, she caught herself stealing glances at Mr. Darnley—Mr. Darnley leaning over the carved choir stalls, Mr. Darnley's curly head framed by the Gothic stone tracery behind them, Mr. Darnley looking up at the elegant, massed pipes of the organ. As she followed his gaze up the fine soaring columns high above her, Flo felt as if she could fly, up and up to the glorious fan-vaulted roof and out through the great stained-glass window to the sky. She felt intoxicated. *What is happening to me?*

Then, standing there in the main aisle of Westminster Abbey, she suddenly realised that she was in love.

That night, thrashing around in her lumpy bed, Flo relived rapturously, again and again, the moment that had transformed her existence. Then, in turn, she agonised about the journey home. She and Mr. Darnley had sat, as before, opposite each other in the railway carriage but she was so agitated and confused that she could hardly say a word. She could not bring herself to look him in the face for fear he would see the turmoil going on inside her. All she could do was thank him profusely—too profusely? too often?—for arranging the audition and preparing Cyril so well. When he spoke to her had her answers sounded silly? Would he have thought she was stupid? She tormented herself. She had tried to hide her confusion by fussing even more over Cyril, in a way she never usually did, and which irritated the boy who kept saying, "Don't, Mama."

It had never been like this. As a girl and young woman, she had flirted, had delighted in leading her admirers on, had revelled in their adoration. But now she was in deep awe of this man, almost frightened of him. There was one thing of which, in her ecstasy and torment, she was absolutely certain: he must never know. Nobody must know. *He's my employer, I'm basically just a servant. And I am caring for his wife! It's all completely impossible!* The memory of her expulsion from the manse and again from Emily's house had burned into her soul. She had made a vow. Never, ever must anything like that happen again. Ever.

The following morning, determined to keep her feelings completely under control, she resumed her duties. But nothing was the same. Mr. Darnley's visits to the sickroom sent her into an embarrassing fluster. The sound of the front door opening and closing as he went out and the key in the lock as he returned became major events of the day. The strains of the organ as he practised transported her to heaven. Miraculously, the harassment and insults from Mrs. Darnley no longer affected her at all; she felt that she was floating above it all. It occurred to her that she even felt happy that Darnley's wife was so unpleasant. *I would have hated it if she had been nice*, she thought. She began, for the first time, to wonder about the relationship between her employer and his wife. Normally, people got married and stayed that way for life—she was a rare exception—and it did not usually occur to her to wonder whether they were happy, or whether they even cared for each other. She did not dare broach the subject with Mrs. Betts for fear of betraying herself. But one day Mrs. Betts herself shed a little light on the matter when she remarked that "in the old days" —meaning the early years of their marriage—Mr. Darnley had tried to be away as little as possible and often brought piles of documents home to work on, whereas now, she suspected that he went away as often, and for as long, as he possibly could.

"And in fact," she added, "he is about to go away again."

Flo was flattened by the news, although at the same time slightly relieved that for a while she would not have to be constantly on her guard not to betray herself.

That evening, Mr. Darnley looked round the door of his wife's room and beckoned Flo out into the landing. "I have to be off tomorrow to work in Norwich," he said. "I don't like to leave Mrs. Darnley so close to the expected birth, but I know she will be in very good hands. And Norwich is not so very far away, if there are any problems, please send for me immediately. I have left a note on my desk with instructions as to how I can be reached."

"Don't worry, sir, I'll take care of her. I'm sure she will be fine," Flo replied.

He gave her a grateful smile and went in to break the news to his wife, while Flo leaned against the doorpost, afraid her knees would give way.

"You can't! You can't go and leave me! I'm going to die, I know it! How can you do this to me?" Mrs. Darnley shrieked as he told her.

Flo moved away and went into her room but could still hear Mr. Darnley trying to reassure her. "I have to go; I can't abandon my work. But it will only be for a short time, and I won't be so very far away. Nurse Harris is here so don't worry now, just rest."

But Mrs. Darnley continued to scream and cry, and Flo wondered whether she should not go in and give her some drops of laudanum, but then her husband, normally so gentle and controlled, lost his temper and began shouting too. She stayed put.

She could hear a blazing row which ended with him storming out and slamming the door. A little while later, he began playing the organ, but not the kind of music he usually played—it sounded bitter, tormented, full of loud, crashing cords, and wild runs. By this time, Flo was back in her patient's bedroom, trying to pacify her and counting out drops of laudanum, but at the sound of the music Mrs. Darnley became distraught again. "That Liszt is driving me mad!" she croaked. "Tell him to stop it! Go down and make him stop it!"

Obediently, Flo went downstairs and knocked on the study door. There was no response, so she gently opened it and walked in. She stood by the organ but, deep in Mr. Darnley's tortured music, he still seemed unaware of her, so she put her hand on his arm. He started, stopped playing and looked at her. His eyes were wild and he looked extremely unhappy.

"Sir, your wife asks if you would please stop playing that piece," she said quietly. "She is calming down now."

He said nothing and seemed to be trying to compose himself.

"Shall I bring you something to help you calm down too, sir?" she asked. "Some chamomile tea, perhaps?"

He relaxed and smiled. "No, thank you, though I think a glass of whisky might be a good idea."

"I'll get it for you," Flo said. She went over to the decanter which stood on a small table near the fireplace and poured him a small glass.

He took a large gulp. "I should not have lost my temper," he confessed. "I know she is sick, and I should be more patient with her."

"It is not easy, sir," Flo said sympathetically. She felt safe in the role of the ministering nurse. He needed calming down too and she could do that.

"Why don't you play something really soothing?" she suggested. "I think it would do you both good and it might help her to sleep."

He thought for while then turned to the keyboard, adjusted some stops, and began playing a few quiet arpeggios on one keyboard with his left hand, then with his right hand, on a lower one, picked out the most beautiful, tranquil melody. It sounded as though it were being played on a flute.

"It's called 'Meditation;' it is an intermezzo from a recent opera by a French composer called Massenet," he explained as he played. "He wrote it for a solo violin and orchestra, but I like the way it sounds on the organ."

"It's beautiful," Flo agreed. She listened for a few moments then reluctantly moved to leave the room.

"Stay a while, Nurse," he begged, smiling at her.

Flo hesitated. She longed to stay but she sensed danger. "Sorry, Sir, but I really must go and see to Mrs. Darnley. Goodnight," she said, and returned upstairs, the melody following her as she went.

She was to hear him play the melody again and again in the following days and sometimes wondered whether it could be a secret message to her. Then she pushed the thought away. *Impossible*, she told herself angrily. *Don't be so foolish.*

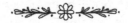

Shortly after Mr. Darnley left for Norwich, his wife's condition began to deteriorate rapidly, and Flo became seriously alarmed. Her face, which had become so gaunt, had begun to swell up, as had her hands. She was suffering from bad headaches and complaining that even the dimmest light bothered her. And she seemed to have developed a deep sense of foreboding and dread of the approaching birth.

Perversely, she refused to let Flo call Dr. Willoughby. "He's useless; he can't do anything about it. I'm just going to die," she would moan. But one evening, after she began vomiting, Flo ignored her protests, roused Nellie, and dispatched her urgently to fetch Dr. Willoughby. At the sight of her patient, the good doctor was visibly shocked. He told Flo to send Nellie to wake the chemist and tell him urgently to mix a certain medicine which she must take as soon as possible. He would summon a colleague, a specialist, from London to give his opinion. Flo must not leave Mrs. Darnley alone—at the slightest sign of a seizure she must send for him instantly. Flo brought her mattress and bedding and laid it out on the floor in her patient's room. From then on, she stayed constantly at her side.

Late the following day, the specialist, a young, towheaded Welshman, arrived from London with a curious piece of equipment, a kind of cuff that he placed round Mrs. Darnley's arm and inflated by the means of a rubber bulb, while listening to her heartbeat with his stethoscope. When he had finished, he muttered something to Dr. Willoughby and Flo caught the words "pre-eclampsia," which she did not understand, and—to her horror— "caesarean," which she certainly did.

Dr. Willoughby beckoned Flo out of the room and in a low voice explained that Mrs. Darnley had a condition that was very dangerous to expectant mothers and the sooner the baby arrived, the better. The next few days would be critical. Flo was to watch her constantly and send to the chemist's for chloroform and disinfectant. He would be back the next morning.

"Should I send for Mr. Darnley?" Flo asked in trepidation.

"Yes, certainly."

Flo realised that she would have to take charge of the situation. Kindly Mrs. Betts, so efficient in her household routine, seemed paralysed by the thought of the crisis they could be facing. There was no knowing when Mr. Darnley, who she had immediately cabled, would arrive. There were no relatives within reach. It was up to her.

She persuaded a kindly neighbour to take the children so that they would be well out of earshot. She asked Dr. Willoughby for the name of the best midwife in the area and sent word that she would soon be needed. She instructed Nellie to make sleeping arrangements in the attic for Mrs. Betts, rolled up her own bedding during the day, and cautiously rearranged the furniture in the sickroom so there was more space around the patient's bed.

She'd done so not a moment too soon. In the early hours of the next morning, she was awoken by screaming and gasping and ran into Mrs. Darnley's room to find her with her bedclothes thrown off, sweating, and writhing in pain. She counted out a few drops of laudanum and gently coaxed Mrs. Darnley into swallowing them, wiped her face with a damp cloth, covered her again, and tried desperately to soothe and calm her. But after a short lull, she erupted again like a woman possessed.

Did it last for days or just hours? From then on everything merged into a phantasmagoria of convulsions, screams, vomiting, delirium, the doctor wielding a syringe, surgical knives being laid out, more screams, the sickly odour of chloroform, the smell of gin on the midwife's breath, blood and more blood. Mrs. Betts was rushing about with clean linen and Nellie was heaving in pitchers of hot water. Mr. Darnley, in shirtsleeves, was hovering all the time, pale and agitated, outside the door. After what seemed an eternity, out of the chaos emerged a tiny being which whimpered quietly, was washed, wrapped up, and handed to Flo. Exhausted, dishevelled, sweaty, and her uniform smeared with blood, she carried the baby to their father. He stood there, not looking at the baby, his green eyes riveted instead on her face as if hypnotised. Flo could not think what to say. Finally, she stammered helplessly, "It's … he's … a boy."

Darnley looked down at the newborn at last and stroked its tiny cheek. "Luke," he said, and, "Thank you, Nurse."

She turned back to see Laura Darnley lying immobile on the bed, her eyes half-open. For a moment Flo was afraid she was dead. The doctor, who evidently had the same thought, was taking her pulse. He nodded. "She's asleep. She's exhausted, but we've saved her, thank God. She'll be quiet now, just let her sleep as long as she can. I'll be back again in the morning." He left with the midwife.

Once the baby was settled in his cradle and the room had been cleaned and tidied, Flo told Mrs. Betts and Nellie to go to bed. She went over to her room, took off her uniform, let down her hair, and put on her nightdress. She felt more than exhausted but still tense after the day's events and longed for a relaxing glass of warm milk. All was quiet, everyone would be asleep by now, so she wrapped a shawl around her and went down to the kitchen.

The door from the kitchen to the garden was slightly open. "Mrs. Betts must have forgotten to close it," she thought. When the milk was ready, she stood at the door, sipping it and breathing in the perfume of some night-scented flower on the warm summer air. Still holding her glass, she strolled slowly out into the dark garden.

"A lovely night," a voice said from behind her.

Flo jumped, dropped the glass, and nearly fell over. "Mr. Darnley! You gave me such a fright!"

"I'm so sorry, Nurse, I didn't mean to startle you."

"*I'm* sorry, I didn't think anyone was around." Clasping her shawl tighter around her in embarrassment, she moved to go back into the house.

"Don't go, Nurse, you deserve to relax; it has been such a long, hard day for you. Why don't you sit down here for a while and enjoy the wonderful night air." He picked up the fallen glass and gestured towards a small white table and two ornate garden chairs that she could just make out in the darkness. She felt his hand on her elbow, gently guiding her to the table. "Come and chat for a few minutes, Nurse, I need to relax a little too."

She obeyed. She became aware of another smell, strange and aromatic. She deduced from the tiny glowing dot by his left hand that he was smoking a Turkish cigarette. He thanked her again profusely, and they talked a little about the birth.

It was becoming lighter. She looked up and saw the moon sliding over the crest of the trees at the bottom of the garden.

"What a night!" he said softly. "Do you like poetry?" and without waiting for a reply he went on:

The moon shines bright. In such a night as this
When the sweet wind did gently kiss the trees
And they did make no noise, on such a night

Troilus methinks mounted the Trojan walls
And sighed his soul towards the Grecian tents
Where Cressid lay that night.

"How lovely!" exclaimed Flo. "Who wrote it?"

"Shakespeare. *The Merchant of Venice.* Does it not capture perfectly a night like this?"

"Absolutely. What a wonderful perfume there is, where is it coming from?"

"That is probably those night-scented stocks over there," he answered and began reciting again:

I cannot see what flowers are at my feet
nor what sweet incense hangs upon the bough ...

Florence was enraptured. She could make out his green eyes looking at her with an unnerving intensity. She could have stayed all night listening to him, but she felt her shawl slide from one shoulder and abruptly remembered, to her embarrassment, that she was in her nightdress. And that he was her employer. And that he was married to her patient. And that she had made a vow ...

He was still talking, but she could not hear for the turmoil inside her. What should she do?

A tiny cry issued from the house.

"The baby has woken up. I must go!" she said jumping to her feet. She tripped on the hem of her nightdress and stumbled. He leapt up and steadied her, grasping her by both shoulders. He held her still for several seconds, looking deep into her eyes. She thought he was about to kiss her. Then he gently let her go.

"I'm sure he will go back to sleep again soon. Goodnight, Nurse."

"Goodnight, sir."

Chapter 9

I t was the first day of term and a bespectacled teacher was filling in the details of new boys in the school ledger. "Father's occupation?" He looked inquiringly at Flo and Cyril.

"My husband is deceased," Flo replied, hesitantly.

Cyril was puzzled. As far as he knew, his father was still very much alive. Why did his mother keep saying things that were not true? His father had taught him that this was wicked, but if his mother did it, surely it could not be so wrong, could it?

"Age?"

"Ten."

"Address?"

Flo gave the address of the Darnleys' house.

Their parting was lacerating. Cyril's excitement at joining the Choir School had turned into panic. Another separation: he had been torn from his home, then from Aunt Emily's, dumped in a grim orphans' home—and now his mother was abandoning him again. He felt terrified of being left alone once more among complete strangers. He tried not to cry in front of the teacher and other boys but clung desperately to Flo's cape as she tried to go.

Flo was astonished. She could not understand this sudden change in her son. "But my darling, you are going to love it here! You will sing, you will get a good education, and you will make lots of friends," she said as she unpicked his fingers from her cape. "And I'll be coming to see you soon. I'll not be so far away. Be brave!"

As she rode back on the train, happy at Cyril's good fortune, her thoughts turned wistfully to her lost younger son. "Oh, Godfrey! If only some miracle like that could happen to him! If only I could have him back!" She would even be content just to see him again, just to talk to him. She wrote to him often, but he never replied to her letters. Good-hearted Martha, out of pity for her beloved sister-in-law, wrote that she kept them in case one day Godfrey would change his mind and want to read them, but it seemed that that day had never come. Many a time, Flo had been tempted to write to Josiah and beg to have him back, but she knew it would be useless. Even if Josiah were to relent—which she knew he never would—what life could she offer the boy? The Waifs and Strays? He lacked Cyril's divine voice, and he was almost tone deaf; there would be no hope for him at the Choir School. She sighed and stared out of the carriage window at the darkening countryside. The loss of Godfrey, she mused, was even more bitter than her banishment from her home.

Cyril gritted his teeth and tried to remember his mother's words as he lay face down in the mud on the rugby pitch. The pain in his left leg after a vicious kick and a shove from someone in the scrum was almost unbearable, and he wondered if it was broken. The kick had been deliberate, he knew. It had taken only a few days to realise that the danger in the school came not from the masters, as at the Waifs and Strays home in Brentwood, but from other boys. The masters were strict, but they were kind, fair, and good-humoured.

Cyril had been at the school two weeks and was desperately unhappy. From the start he felt he was an outsider, though he could not understand why. Although a group of boys obviously came from wealthy, privileged families, most came from a wide variety of backgrounds, some, like his, were very modest. What was it that made other boys dislike him? Why had there been titters and nudges at the beginning when he let slip that he had previously sung in a Methodist chapel? Was that something to be ashamed of? Could it have been because he would go bright red and clam up when asked what his father did, where he lived, or where he had last been to school? He could not tell anyone of his pain at being wrenched from his home and separated from Godfrey, or about the frightening scenes at Aunt Emily's or the even more frightening night in the church at Brentwood. Would they ever be able to imagine what it was like being hungry and having no home, or the shame and terror as a child in the Waif and Strays? He just kept silent and became sullen and withdrawn.

Someone grabbed him by the collar and heaved him bodily out of the mud and set him on his feet. It was Tom Peters. "You'd better get Matron to look at that leg," he said. "Then scrub down and be quick about it, we are practising for a special concert in half an hour, and I want you to be there."

Tom had kept his eye on Cyril since his first day at the school, not only because he was a friend of Darnley but because the boy had a rare voice and he wanted to start working on it. For the moment, Cyril was still a probationer in the lowest ranks of the choir with little chance to shine. But Tom was training a small group of half a dozen boys to sing madrigals in preparation for a concert of Renaissance and Baroque music and saw that this was his chance.

It proved a blessing. Before long, Cyril realised that his path to acceptance was to become an excellent chorister and with Tom Peters' training and encouragement he worked hard at his singing. As he began to succeed, and as Sir Frederick began to notice him and pick him out for solos, his self-confidence grew and the bullying gradually subsided. He slowly adjusted to the school routine, early breakfast followed by choir practice, then lessons, so many of them religious instruction that he was eventually to turn against religion for the rest of his life. Then came games and more lessons, choir practice again, evensong. He sung Eucharist on Sundays and other feast days, special rehearsals for occasions including, the most unforgettable of all, singing with other massed choirs for the Coronation of the King, Edward VI. Bit by bit he began to settle in and even to feel that he belonged.

Chapter 10

Flo was being torn apart. Rationally, she knew that she would have to leave the Darnley household if she was to avoid yet another disaster. But the thought of not seeing Mr. Darnley again, hearing him play, or even just being near him was unbearable. She was scarcely able to eat, night after night she lay awake, agonising over what to do. In the end her head won, and she made up her mind that she had to leave. She gathered up courage and went to see Dr. Willoughby.

"I will just tell him I cannot work for her anymore," she said to herself. "He knows what she is like, he will understand."

The good doctor did understand. "I'm very sorry you have decided to leave because you did Mrs. Darnley a lot of good, even though she might not admit it. I do have another patient who needs constant care, an elderly gentleman who has had a severe heart attack. Sadly, I fear he might not be long for this world, but it would be a good position for the time being and would certainly be easier than the present one." Flo needed no further details. She agreed to start the following Monday.

That evening, after she had put Mrs. Darnley to bed and made sure that she was fast asleep, she went downstairs and knocked

TRAIL TO TREASON

nervously on the study door. She had rehearsed a little speech: she would say she had come to give notice and if she was asked for a reason, she was going to say diplomatically that she felt Mrs. Darnley was not satisfied with her.

He was sitting, staring into the fire, neither reading a book nor working. His face, which had looked pensive when she opened the door, lit up as he turned and saw her.

"Mr. Darnley," she began, her voice trembling. "I have come to give my notice. I-I-I shall be leaving on F-f-friday."

"What?" He leapt out of his chair and came towards her. "Why? You can't do that, you can't! Why?"

"I-I can't stay …" Whatever she had planned to say had gone straight out of her head. She put her hands to her face and began to cry. "I can't stay!"

Mr. Darnley went over to the door and turned the key in the lock. He came back, took her hands and gently pulled them from her face. "What's the matter? What has happened? Has Mrs. Darnley offended you?"

She shook her head.

"Has someone offered you a better position?"

She shook her head again.

"Are you not happy here?"

Stammering, she finally began, "You have been so kind but …" and stopped.

"But what?"

Silence.

He slowly dropped her hands, walked to the fireplace, and stood for a few moments looking into the flames. He turned back and took her hands again.

93

"Florence ..." He had never used her first name before. "You are the angel of this house. I don't need to tell you all you have done for my poor wife. But what you don't know is what you have done for me. My life, my happiness had turned to a pile of ashes, and you have brought me joy, beauty, light ... I think of you every moment of the day and night. I have to confess I could not bear it if you left."

Flo looked up at him in astonishment. "And I, er, think of you too," she stammered. She paused, then went on, "all the time. That's why I have to leave." She paused again, then blurted out brutally, "You're married."

He was silent for a while. "Yes, I'm married," he said slowly and miserably. "That is the burden I must bear, as there is nothing I can do about it. But please, please don't leave, I need to know you are near me, I need to see you, to hear your voice ... Stay, Florence, if only for a while."

He had taken her face in his hands. He was stroking off her nurse's cap and caressing her tumbling red hair. Her whole body was going into a slow burn. He bent his head to kiss her—and at that instant came the sound of the bell and a hideous screech from above. "Nurse! Nurse! Where are you?"

They both froze. "I must go." Flo pulled away and ran for the door.

"Where have you been?" Mrs. Darnley demanded when Flo entered the room. "Where's your cap?"

"What is the matter, ma'am? Can you not sleep?" Flo asked, fussing over the bedclothes and ignoring the question.

"Where were you? You were not in your room!"

"Ma'am, I started getting ready for bed and then decided to go downstairs to make myself some hot milk. Are you in pain?"

"Where is my husband?"

"I don't know, ma'am, although I did see a light coming from under his study door."

Laura Darnley said nothing more, but Flo was alarmed. A seed of suspicion seemed to have lodged in her patient's mind. All the more reason to leave, as it was getting dangerous.

After what seemed like an eternity, Mrs. Darnley finally drifted off to sleep again, and Flo crept back to her own room. On her pillow lay her cap and a note. "*Please* stay. I love you."

The next day, too embarrassed to tell him herself, she sent Nellie with a note to Dr. Willoughby saying that she had been persuaded to stay on at the Darnleys' for a while and regretting any inconvenience she may have caused.

She had grave misgivings over her decision but promised herself that she would not give her patient the slightest cause to dismiss her.

Mr. Darnley was also being very careful not to give any hint in front of his wife or the staff of what had passed between them. A few days later, he came into his wife's room while Flo was brushing her long, black hair and said, "I very much regret to tell you, my dear, that I have just received urgent instructions to conduct a special inspection in the Isle of Man, of all places. I will have to be away for three or four weeks, and, because of the distance, it is unlikely I will be able to get home for the weekends. I am so very sorry, Laura, but I know you will be in the best of hands with Nurse Harris here."

His wife broke into a storm of tears, accusations, and reproaches, becoming almost frantic. While Mr. Darnley sought to calm her, Flo seized the first opportunity to slip out of the room and go and fling herself on her bed, trying desperately not to cry for fear of betraying herself.

After supper, Mr. Darnley formally asked Mrs. Betts to send Flo to his study, saying he wanted to make arrangements for her pay for the next few weeks. When they were alone, he asked quietly, "Will you be going to the Abbey on Sunday?"

Flo frequently used her free Sundays to go to London to hear Cyril and the choir in the Sung Eucharist. After she had got Mrs. Darnley ready for the day, she would walk quickly to the station to catch the train which would get her there for the eleven o'clock service. She and Cyril would have lunch and a short stroll together before he had to go back, and if the weather was fine, she would walk in St James' park, visit a museum, or look in shop windows before taking a train back to Brentwood.

She nodded.

"Then meet me outside the north entrance of the Abbey, opposite Parliament Square, at five to eleven."

"But—but I thought you said you were going to the Isle of Man?" Flo asked, bewildered.

"I will explain everything then. Needless to say, you must not breathe a word."

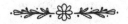

96

The train had been a few minutes late, and Flo was out of breath as she found him, in an elegant frock coat, outside the great Gothic portal looking anxiously at his watch. Visibly relieved, he doffed his hat, bowed, then took her gloved hand and pressed it to his lips. "Come," he said, "we must go in, Tom has reserved us two good seats."

There was no time to talk. The music, a mass by Palestrina and a motet by William Byrd, followed by a Bach prelude and fugue on the organ, was sublime. Sitting next to Mr. Darnley in the front row, Flo felt she was living a dream, her heart soaring once again towards the great fan-vaulted roof. Afterwards, they chatted briefly with Tom Peters, Mr. Darnley invited Flo and Cyril to lunch at a good restaurant. It was only after they dropped Cyril at the Abbey for Evensong and strolled towards the Embankment that they were finally alone, and Flo was able to vent her curiosity. "I thought you were supposed to be on the Isle of Man!"

He took her arm. "You see how love makes a liar of a man. No, the work I spoke of is actually here in London, a big court case. But I chose one of the remotest places I could think of in our bailiwick in the hopes of spending Sundays, not in Warley, but with you here in London."

Florence gasped. "But Mr. Darnley …!"

"Francis. Please call me Francis. And please think of me not as your employer but simply as a man who has fallen passionately in love with you and who would give everything just to be near you, to see you, and talk to you for a few precious hours."

Flo said nothing. She stopped, turned, and leaned against the granite wall of the Embankment, her mind in turmoil. Propping her head in her hands, she looked out over the grey Thames, blind to the boats chugging past. She had made a vow. But she could not tell him—and she certainly could not tell him why.

"Francis …" she began, then stopped. "Francis …" she tried again. "Oh, if only! I can't imagine anything more wonderful! But I can't! If your wife ever found out—if she ever had the slightest suspicion—she would throw me out in an instant, you know she would. I would be completely disgraced. I can't, I can't, Francis." She sobbed. "I'm a respectable woman!"

Mr. Darnley offered her his handkerchief. "Of course you are a respectable woman, Florence. And there is nothing disgraceful about running by pure chance into your employer when you go on a Sunday to hear your son singing in the Abbey. Indeed, it is I who would be less than respectable for saying I was in one place when I was in quite another."

Flo laughed. "But she can't throw you out!"

"No, my dear, she can't, but don't worry, there is absolutely no reason why she should ever know. She does not have any friends or relatives who live in London and, as you know, she hardly sees anyone. We are completely safe. Come, I've heard the flowers are wonderful along there in the Embankment gardens, let us go and see them."

Flo still hesitated.

"Come!" pleaded Darnley again.

She will never know, Flo thought to herself. *There surely can't be any harm in it.* Throwing her qualms to the wind, she set off on Darnley's arm, laughing and flirting merrily as they strolled through the gardens, fed the pigeons, and sat chatting on benches. And when the time came for her to head reluctantly to the station, they embraced in the back of a cab on the way to the station, abandoning themselves to long, passionate kisses.

All week she was walking on air, counting the days and the hours till the next Sunday, humming and singing to herself as she went about her duties.

"What is there to be so cheerful about all of a sudden?" asked Mrs. Darnley, moodily.

"It must be the wonderful weather," answered Flo, gaily. "The sun is shining, the birds are singing, it's wonderful outside, Mrs. Darnley. It really lifts the spirits. If you would only allow me to take you out, even just into the garden for a few minutes, it would do you a world of good."

"Don't be stupid, it would kill me. Maybe that's what you want."

"Ma'am, how can you say such a thing?" Flo was genuinely shocked.

Laura Darnley was recovering from the birth of little Luke, but she was still very weak. They had engaged a wet-nurse for the baby who fortunately cried little and rarely woke them at night. Flo had proposed that they buy a wheelchair so she could take Mrs. Darnley and the baby for strolls round the neighbourhood, but Mrs. Darnley would not hear of it. She was appalled at the idea that people should see her being pushed around in a wheelchair like an old lady, baby or no baby. Flo was, however, permitted to take the baby for walks in his pram if the weather was good, which was a blessed respite from the rest of the day when she was confined with her patient to the dark, stuffy sickroom where she was only rarely allowed to let in a little daylight, and even more rarely, fresh air.

The following Sunday, Flo was even more deliriously happy than the last. In the Abbey, and later at lunch with Cyril, it was a struggle—and appeared to be so for Mr. Darnley too—to behave as if they were simply employer and employee. She wondered if Cyril noticed anything.

Later, as they were sitting on a bench in St James' Park, tossing crumbs to the many-coloured ducks, Darnley reached into his inside pocket, pulled out a little parcel and gave it to her. "Florence, I want this to be a reminder, no matter what may happen, of these wonderful hours we are having together and of my undying love for you."

Flo opened it. It was a beautiful gold locket with an elegant double "F" engraved on the front. "Francis and Florence" she murmured, tears of joy welling up in her eyes. "How exquisite! I shall wear it always—even under my uniform." And amid raised eyebrows among passers-by she threw her arms around him and kissed him.

"I must have a photograph of you in it!" she exclaimed, disentangling herself. "No, maybe not," she went on, "that might be too dangerous. But a lock of your hair! Will you snip a piece off and give it to me next time?"

Darnley promised.

On the third Sunday, the warm, sunny weather had vanished, it had turned cold and gloomy. Flo arrived in London to see ominous black clouds hanging low over the towers and spires of Westminster and cursed herself for not thinking to bring an umbrella. In the Abbey, she was alarmed not to see Cyril in his usual place in the choir stalls and noticed that there were altogether fewer choirboys than usual.

Mr. Darnley shot a questioning look at Tom Peters several rows away who put his hand on his forehead to signal that Cyril had a temperature. Another parent sitting behind them whispered that more than a dozen boys had come down with the flu. They were being kept away from the others in the hopes of preventing it spreading, and parents were being asked not to visit. At that moment, thunder crashed outside, competing with the organ, followed by another and another. By the time the service was over, it was raining torrentially. She and Darnley, along with many others of the congregation, waited in the entrance for it to let up, but it only rained harder.

Flo was bitterly disappointed. "What shall we do?" she asked Mr. Darnley, shivering.

"You're cold," Mr. Darnley said, concerned. "I'm thinking. My lodgings are only a couple of minutes from here in Old Queen's Gate. If you can bear to make a dash for it, we could warm up and shelter there for the time being."

It seemed much longer than two minutes, although they were almost running. Mr. Darnley's umbrella blew inside out, and they arrived soaked to the skin at the large, flat-fronted house where Mr. Darnley pulled out his keys and let them in.

"Let me take your cape," he said as they reached the flat and hung it up next to his own coat. Flo looked around. The flat, on the second floor, was roomy and comfortably furnished but impersonal. And it was cold.

"It belongs to an old friend on the Board who lives downstairs," Mr. Darnley explained. "He lets it out to colleagues when they have to be in London on Board business." He was crouching down putting a match to the fire. "Thank goodness the maid always makes sure there is a fire laid, just in case."

Flo's teeth were still chattering.

"Your dress is soaked right through!" he exclaimed, straightening up.

"And so are my boots!" Flo added. "Would you think me very rude if I took them off?"

"Just a moment." Darnley went out of the room and came back with a thick robe. "Why don't you go into the bathroom, take off all your wet things, and put this on while they dry. Otherwise, you'll get your death of cold."

Flo obeyed and returned, laughing and tripping over the robe which was much too large for her. "My hair is sopping too," she said, unpinning it and sitting down on the floor in front of the fire to dry it.

Darnley, now also in a bathrobe, settled down on the floor beside her.

"This is all very improper," she remarked in mock disapproval.

"But delightful." He laughed.

"You promised me a bit of your hair to put in the locket," she reminded him.

He fetched her a pair of scissors and she snipped off a curl, took off her locket, and he put it in. He fastened it back round her neck, stroked her neck, then kissed her face, her shoulders, and slowly slid his hands down under her robe to her naked breasts, then down and down …

Chapter 11

The Manse, Aberdare

The end of Cyril's first term at Westminster Choir School was approaching, and with it, the problem of where he should go for the holidays. Although Mr. Darnley would have been happy for him to stay with the family at Warley, he and Flo knew his wife would never countenance it. Cyril had pleaded with Flo not to send him back to the Waifs and Strays. So, after a flurry of letters to-and-fro, it was decided that he would go and stay with Martha and Ezekiel in Aberdare where he would be reunited with Godfrey for the first time since he and Flo had left home. Lizzie, Godfrey's doting godmother, was to accompany Cyril from London, while Zachary went to stay at Emily's.

Cyril had been looking forward immensely to seeing his brother again, his beloved playmate and partner in mischief. But when he and his aunt arrived at the manse, with Cyril still in his school uniform, bright and chirpy, Godfrey took one look then ran up to the boys' bedroom and locked himself in. Efforts to coax him out again failed; it finally took a stern command from Ezekiel to bring him down, glowering, to the table for the family supper.

It was only a few months since they had last been together, but the events of that morning and their consequences had changed each of them. Outwardly they still looked very similar, tall, goodlooking boys, each with a curious coiffe of light brown curls over his forehead that they were said to have inherited from Zachary, although Zachary, now balding, had none left to prove it. Neither really understood yet the full reason for their mother's and Cyril's ejection from their home, but the ominous silence that surrounded it all was traumatic enough. It had left deep wounds.

No-one was able to say afterwards quite how the trouble started, but the next morning yelling, banging, sounds of punching, and shouts of "bastard!" came from the boys' bedroom. The older cousins ran up and found the brothers locked in a vicious brawl. Cyril was bleeding from the nose and had a swollen eye, and Godfrey, winded, was gasping for breath. They were still shouting insults as they were physically dragged apart. The cease-fire was only temporary. Fights and quarrels broke out again and again until the exasperated grownups agreed that they must be separated.

Lizzie wrote to Flo.

My dearest sister,

I am deeply distressed to inform you that your two boys, once such loving companions, have developed a bitter enmity, to the extent that they cannot bear to be under the same roof. We have done all we can to calm their spirits and effect a reconciliation, but in vain. I will spare you a description of their fights and the injuries and insults they have inflicted on each other, but Martha, Ezekiel, and I have decided that for the sake of the family and themselves they must be separated forthwith. I therefore intend, without waiting for your approval, to leave with Cyril first thing in the morning for Sturminster where he can stay with father and myself for the remainder of the holidays. I know that if you were here you would agree with us entirely that this is the only course of action.

It has been impossible to extract from either boy a coherent reason for their falling-out, but from their shouts and from the accounts of the other children, Martha and I have deduced that Godfrey regards you—dear sister, I am extremely distressed to tell you this—as an evil woman while paradoxically resenting the fact that you left him behind and took Cyril with you, promising, but failing, to return. We believe that Cyril, on the other hand, feels that his father rejected him and condemned him to a life without roots or a home, while Godfrey at least has the warmth and security of a family.

It is all extremely distressing, but I can assure you that Cyril will be in good hands with us, as of course Godfrey is with Martha.

The next day, Lizzie and Cyril set off for Sturminster Newton, where Zachary, somewhat surprisingly, welcomed him warmly. Cyril was the one child in his family who had shown a genuinely keen interest in his stories about Germany and in actually learning something of the language.

"Komm, mein Kind," he said affably. He put his hand on Cyril's shoulder, steered him outside to a little shed next to the chicken coop, and unlocked the flimsy wooden door. Cyril stared in amazement. The shed was crammed with piles of books about the country Zachary had left so mysteriously in his youth. Pictures and maps of Germany hung on the wooden walls. Drawings of Fokker aircraft, dirigibles, hot-air balloons, and dreadnought battleships were piled up on a stool.

"You might like these," said his grandfather, handing him a small pile of Karl May books, in English as well as German. "They are really exciting adventure stories, the Wild West, the Sahara …" The boy was riveted and from then on spent as much of his holidays as he could in Zachary's shed where, in an almost conspiratorial fashion, over a rickety wooden table, his grandfather would often regale him with tales from German history, show him pictures and tell him about famous places and teach him German words and phrases. He would sing the praises of the great Kaiser who was about to make Germany more powerful than Britain and would one day dominate the world. If the British were foolish enough not to ally themselves with this great, new power, there would inevitably be a war. Would not it be wonderful if, instead, Germany and Britain could join together and lead the world with their culture, science, civilization, and all the other wonderful things they had in common? Cyril absorbed like a sponge everything his grandfather had to tell him.

He was so happy that Flo was easily persuaded to let him stay with Zachary and Lizzie during all his holidays.

As for Godfrey, Lizzie's description of his resentment towards her shook her to the core. She tried to blame Josiah, but in her heart of hearts, she knew that she had largely brought it on herself. Would there ever be any hope of a reconciliation with the poor boy? With an aching heart, she had to realise that there very likely was none.

Chapter 12

WARLEY

The court case that Darnley had been working on ended, and he returned to Warley. Mrs. Darnley's condition appeared to have improved somewhat and though still very weak, she was often able go downstairs and sit by the fire in the parlour, glancing listlessly at newspapers and magazines that Mr. Darnley had brought home. But Flo was becoming alarmed at her state of mind, as she would alternate between fits of feverish agitation and mental confusion and periods when she was aggressively lucid. Paler than ever and alarmingly thin, she had taken to wandering around the house like a ghost, for no clear reason.

Unnerved, Flo and Mr. Darnley rarely dared to steal even a few moments alone together. One day, however, having made sure his wife was asleep in her chair in the parlour, Francis took Flo into his study and whispered that he would shortly be called to London again, the case had gone to appeal. Flo immediately began to dream of another Sunday together when an ear-piercing screech came from the parlour. "Francis! Francis! You liar! You scoundrel!"

Mr. Darnley dashed into the parlour.

"You told me you were working on the Isle of Man, you ..!" she screamed, shaking a copy of the *Times* in his face. "But here you are in London, giving evidence in court!"

Darnley took the paper. There was an article about a mayor and a couple of councillors from a town in Leicestershire who had appealed against a jail sentence for siphoning off public funds. It mentioned evidence given in court by Local Government Auditor, Frances Hunter Darnley.

"Yes, that's me," he said calmly.

"But you told me you would be on the Isle of Man!"

"I *was* on the Isle of Man, my dear," he lied, "but I was called back for a couple of days to give evidence in court. Then I came straight back to Warley. It was all perfectly normal. I didn't bother to tell you because I know you are not interested in my work. For which," he added with a sympathetic smile, "I don't blame you."

His wife continued to rage but, to the others' relief, appeared to have accepted the explanation. Two weeks later, Darnley set off again, this time ostensibly to Llandudno, and Florence began counting the hours till she would see him in London.

The following night she was wakened by strange sounds in her room. She sat up with a jerk and switched on the light, her heart pounding. There was Mrs. Darnley in her nightdress, poking around in her wardrobe.

"You gave me such a fright, ma'am! What are you looking for?"

Was she sleepwalking? Flo got out of bed and took her arm, intending to lead her gently back to bed. But the woman pulled away.

"Don't touch me!" She continued poking around. "Where have you put my blue evening dress?"

"Your dresses are not here, ma'am, they are all in the big cupboard on the landing where you keep them."

She was not sleepwalking, Flo realised, but she was obviously confused. She started looking around the little room, touching Flo's things. Then her eye fell on the locket that Mr. Darnley had given her, lying in its open box on her bedside table. She picked it up.

"It's very pretty. How come I've never seen you wear it. Who gave it you?"

"It was my mother's," Flo replied.

She tried again to lead her away but now Mrs. Darnley was looking at the box which bore the name of a London jeweller. Then she opened the locket, looked at the lock of curly hair inside and snapped it shut again.

"Very pretty," she repeated, and allowed herself to be led away to bed.

The next day, Flo was having lunch with Mrs. Betts and Nellie as usual in the kitchen when they heard shrieks coming from upstairs, then objects being thrown around. "Whore! Bitch!" Mrs. Darnley screamed. "I'll kill you!"

"Come with me," Flo said to Mrs. Betts, and they hurried upstairs. Flo's clothes were flying out of her room on to the landing, followed by her boots, Bible, and hold-all. Inside was her patient, screaming, shouting, and flailing around her like a woman possessed. "Get out of here, you whore! Get gone this very instant!"

Flo immediately sensed the reason for her outburst but said to Mrs. Betts quietly, "She's having a fit of hysteria, we've got to calm her down." Then, to the patient, soothingly, "There, there, Mrs. Darnley, everything's all right, don't you worry. We're here. Let's take you into your room, and I'll give you something to calm you down."

But the woman turned on her, wild-eyed, and clawed ferociously at her face while Mrs. Betts tried to pull her away. "You slut, you seduced my husband! You think I don't know? It's all clear now—that locket—your mother's—ha ha! It's new, the box is new, you've been in London with my husband. Do you think I don't know?"

"That's nonsense," said Flo, trying to remain calm and professional. "You're imagining things. Let me take you back to bed."

"Imagining things—any fool can see: FF—Francis and Florence! Look!" She had the locket in her hand. "And the hair inside is curly!"

"My mother's hair was curly, and her name was Faith," Flo said in an irritated tone. "Now, come with me …"

The woman seized the photograph of her mother. "Curly? That is curly?" Her mother wore a lace cap in the picture but what hair could be seen certainly did not look curly. She flung the photograph into the corner of the room, smashing the glass.

At that, Flo exploded in fury. "That's enough!" She snatched the locket from the woman's hand and, gripping her arm so tightly that she squealed, dragged her forcibly across the landing, and pushed her into her room, slamming the door and locking it from the outside. "I've never been so insulted in all my life!" she shouted through the door. "How dare you! I am leaving this instant!"

She handed the key to Mrs. Betts saying, "I'm sorry, but as you see, I can't stay after this. She's going from bad to worse, but I'm afraid someone else will have to look after her from now on."

Mrs. Betts, trembling and weeping, threw her arms around her. "Don't go, please don't go, Nurse. Whatever will we do without you?"

Still shaking with rage, Flo picked up the photograph of her mother. It was still in one piece, but its thin metal frame was badly bent. The glass was in smithereens. She put the photo and the frame in her hold-all, retrieved and packed the rest of her things, and put on her cape and her hat. Sadly, she bade affectionate farewells to Mrs. Betts and Nellie, who were both weeping profusely and begging her to change her mind. As she headed for the door, she was pleased that she was leaving them thinking that she was the innocent victim of an employer who was fast going mad.

So, this is the third time, she reflected as she stepped out into the street. The third time she had been cast out for adultery. The thought was so painful she refused to dwell on it. She had broken her vow. But it was different this time, she told herself. There was Francis. She loved him and he loved her. She must find him quickly. He would save her, somehow.

"Florence! Whatever are you doing here?"

Flo turned round, immensely relieved. She had been standing at the door of the house in Old Queen's Gate perplexed, as there was only one bell. It had no name by it but was almost certainly not his. "Francis,

thank heaven you are here! It's happened! Your wife …"

"Oh, no! What happened?" He dropped his briefcase to fiddle with his keys and stared at her in dismay. "Come inside and tell me all about it." He was looking very distinguished in the formal clothes that he had been wearing in court.

Upstairs, she chokingly spilled out, blow by blow, the scene that afternoon. "So, it's all over, Francis. I was so afraid that would happen and now it has," she concluded tearfully. "Whatever will become of me?"

Mr. Darnley pulled her to him and held her tight for several minutes without speaking. Finally, he said, "My dearest, don't be afraid. I will find a solution which enables us to see each other as much as possible until such time as … as we can finally be together."

It was the first time either of them had acknowledged, even indirectly, the fact that Laura Darnley would not survive her illness.

Mr. Darnley returned to Warley but almost immediately it became clear that they would not be able to meet up frequently in London as they had planned.

My dearest,
Laura's condition has gone rapidly worse. She is prey to the wildest

hallucinations and, although extremely weak, roams the house at all hours of the day and night, raging confusedly against the world, the staff, and particularly against you and myself. Baby Luke now cries continuously. One nurse left after a day, the present one can hardly cope and is likely to follow her soon. I am at my wit's end but cannot bring myself to entrust her to some institution. Dr. Willoughby has ordered some particularly powerful sedative. I pray to God it will help. But for the present, at least, I am not able to leave her. Pray for me, my precious one, you know only too well how I am suffering. I love you and long for you every hour of the day and night.
Your Francis.

Flo was heartbroken, but gradually found a certain consolation in the fact that her daily life was now much calmer and pleasanter than in Warley. Mr. Darnley's colleague, the owner of the apartment in Old Queen's Gate, had taken a liking to her and engaged her as a live-in nurse-companion to his aged and nearly blind mother who lived just up the street. Her duties were light and generally dull but two weeks later she made a discovery which both shocked and delighted her. She was pregnant.

It was less than a year since she had left Pillowell, and her life was being turned upside down yet again. But this time she felt curiously serene, as she trusted Darnley completely. They wrote to each other almost every day, but she decided she would not tell him yet, as he had enough to deal with for the moment. Instinctively, she felt that their problems were destined to come to an end; it was only a matter of time. In the meanwhile, her present life of quiet and seclusion, punctuated only by visits to the Abbey, suited her new situation admirably. She settled down to wait.

Six months later she received an urgent, hastily scribbled note from Darnley:

Dearest—Laura is critically ill with pneumonia. She wandered out of the house in the middle of the night and was found in the road in the pouring rain, unable to find her way back. Doctor is here. Yours forever, F.

For three days she heard nothing. Then came a telegram.

LAURA DIED LAST NIGHT.

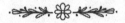

Two months after the death of Laura Darnley, in a London establishment catering to ladies who desired the utmost discretion, Florence Ada Harris gave birth to her widower's child, a boy.

They christened him Francis Hunter Harris—if he could not have his father's surname at least he could have his Christian names. Thereafter they called him Frank.

Part 3

Storm Brewing

Chapter 13

Littlehampton, Sussex 1910

Looking back, it seemed as though those years were one long summer. Littlehampton had become a fashionable and thriving watering-place. Elegant gentlemen in straw hats and ladies in long skirts, sweeping hats, and parasols paraded down Pier Road to the shore. Bands played for holidaymakers on the Esplanade. Families would gather on the quay opposite the Nelson and Victory pub, children chattering excitedly while their parents bought tickets for a day trip across to France on the *Worthing Belle*. Others would sail toy boats on the former oyster pond. The sea breezes wafted whiffs of oysters and fish from the fishermens' stalls, and tar and boat smells from the river. Seagulls squawked as they circled over the row of bathing machines on the beach, while braver visitors braced themselves for a dip, and children, under floppy sunhats, collected shells or shoveled the sand to make castles and moats. Trouble might be brewing in the world outside, but here in Littlehampton unbothered holidaymakers were enjoying summer at the seaside.

Around five one July afternoon, a figure in a crisp, pale-blue-and-white nurse's uniform could be seen tripping down the steps of No. 31 Pier Road and hurrying in the direction of the beach. Nurse Harris was by now a familiar figure in Littlehampton, dispensing injections, changing dressings on wounds, washing the bedridden, making sure old people took their medicines, all the while careful to not to encroach on the preserve of the doctors on whose approval and recommendations she depended. Red-haired, vivacious, aged around forty but still remarkably attractive, she was said to be a widow, while some townsfolk gossiped about the role of the tall, curly-haired gentleman who seemed to be more than an occasional guest and who her four young children evidently adored. And some wondered how she could have become the owner of No. 31 on what she earned from her ministrations. But her uniform and her role as an angel of mercy made most feel that she was a respectable woman and suspicions about her private life would be out of place.

Turning left along the promenade, she soon spotted a little knot of children around a crumbling sandcastle.

"Come on everyone, it's tea-time and do you know what? Mr. Darnley is here!"

"Dada, Dada!" The children leapt up joyfully, grabbed their buckets and spades, and without waiting to put their sandals on, scampered off excitedly in the direction of home.

As she followed them with an armful of sandy footwear, it seemed to Flo that life had never been so good. She could not be happier, she thought, or more precisely: she could not be happier under the circumstances. She and Francis had four lovely children and still, she believed, loved each other even though—or perhaps because—they were unable to live together.

It had not always been thus. She preferred not to think of the moment after Laura died, when he had proposed, and she had to tell him she was not a widow after all. He was deeply shocked, even though she had not told him the real reason she had left Pillowell. For a while, she was afraid he would leave her. But he recovered and devised a way that they could be near each other. It was not entirely unusual for a gentleman to discreetly maintain a second family, but Mr. Darnley knew that his position as a civil servant would be seriously endangered if he was known to have a mistress and an illegitimate brood. So every couple of years, when he was posted to a different town or city, he would find her and the children lodgings in a nearby town, near enough to be convenient but far enough away not to raise eyebrows. Eyebrows, nevertheless, were raised, as Flo found out to her cost, decidedly and often.

She was in a very difficult situation. As one baby after another came into the world

she could hardly continue claiming to be a widow and, when necessary, she would speak of Mr. Darnley as "my husband." The children grew up calling him "Dada," which sounded reasonably convincing but had to be discouraged from calling him "Papa," because of their different surnames, and in fact they were growing up not entirely sure who their real father was. As it happened, bureaucracy was light in those days and documents were rarely required, which was fortunate because even the children's birth certificates were fabricated. Their father appeared as Francis Harris and his profession appeared variously as "clerk" or "accountant." Her maiden name she gave as Isobel Wyles or Wylie, flights of fancy which she would come to regret later on.

Nevertheless, eventually some people would guess that all was not as it should be, and she would become aware that neighbours were avoiding her, and women were gossiping that—as she happened to hear one day—she was "no better than she should be" or even a "fallen woman."

She steeled herself to ignore the knowing looks and snide remarks which would come her way and thought up sharp retorts to use if people became offensive. But she was unable to protect the children at school or at play, and her heart bled when they came crying because they had been called "bastards" or "brats" and bullied by other children. Sometimes landladies would indignantly demand that she and the children leave. Other times, hostility was such that Flo would move the whole family out of her own accord. She was no stranger to the nomadic life for as a child they had often had to move from one place to another when her father's dogmatic and cantankerous nature became too much for his landowner employers. But with her own growing family, their frequent changes of address had become exceedingly tiresome.

She longed more than ever for acceptance and stability. Whenever she could, she tried to arrange light nursing and first aid work, at least it paid for a part-time maid-cum-childminder, and she found that her nurse's uniform gave her a certain air of respectability and even authority.

In 1908, Mr. Darnley's father had died, and Francis decided to use a sizeable part of his inheritance to buy Flo a new row house in Pier Road. It was a little further from Worthing than would have been handy, but he thought life at the seaside would do the children good.

"I want you all to have a home of your own," he told her. "It will give you security, in case anything should happen to me."

Flo was delighted to have her own home and began to believe that at last she had the stability and acceptance that she had longed for. It was true, though, that in the past year Mr. Darnley's visits had become fewer and shorter. He said he had been promoted and that as a result, he had been given much more work. He often seemed distracted and when he left the house to go back to his work and family, he no longer turned to wave at her as she watched from the window.

She tried not to be suspicious. It was normal, she told herself. They had known each other for nearly ten years, they were getting older, and their relationship was bound to change. But she assured herself that it was solid, and she was well provided for. She was safe and no longer had to fear for the future. The trajectory from that violent shove out of the door in Pillowell had ended here as softly and happily as on a pillow. Hadn't it?

When she arrived back home, she found pandemonium in the kitchen where the children were milling around Francis, trying to tell him their latest adventures and Margie, the maid, hopelessly unable to keep order.

"Stop, stop, stop!" Flo's voice rose above the melee. "Margie, take this lot upstairs, and see that they get washed and dressed properly." The little herd thumped noisily up the wooden stairs.

"Where's Cyril?" Darnley asked, as peace returned.

Chapter 14

Cyril, as it happened, was on the other side of the river, escaping. He had rowed across in the small boat Mr. Darnley had given them, heading for the golf links on the other side. He was at yet another turning point in his life, his thoughts and feelings in turmoil, and the presence of Darnley in the house, on top of the chaos generated by his young siblings, was too much. He needed peace and quiet to think about what to do next. He needed to find work and, if at all possible, create a normal, stable life for himself.

He might not have believed it at the time, but now he could look back on his years at the choir school as the happiest and most serene since he was uprooted from his boyhood home. It had been sheer joy to send his pure, strong, treble voice up to the highest vaults of the Abbey, to receive praise and admiration. He still was not popular with the other boys; however, he had covered up his uncertainties by becoming a cocky know-all. Then, in his fourth year, just as he seemed to have reached the peak of his singing abilities, disaster struck.

It was Ash Wednesday and, as was the tradition, the choir was to sing Allegri's exquisite *Miserere.* It was one of the beautiful but also most challenging choral works because one of the solo parts had several high C's, practically the highest note in any choral music, and there was much friendly rivalry each year to be chosen as that soloist. Cyril had been in the running in previous years and this time, it being his last year at the school, would be his last opportunity. They had rehearsed intensely in the previous weeks and finally, almost at the last minute, the name of this year's Sir Frederick announced his choice, and it was Cyril.

Cyril, as he often did, got goosepimples as the choir began, "Miserere mei, Deus ..." while the congregation silently filed up to the altar rail where a priest marked a cross in ashes on the forehead of each one. He loved this work, partly because of the story that it was originally sung only in the Sistine Chapel in Rome as the Popes thought it so beautiful they forbade anyone to write it down so it could not be sung elsewhere. But Mozart, during a visit to Rome with his father when he was fourteen—Cyril's age—heard it and, back at his lodgings, transcribed it, returning a few days later to check that he had got it down correctly.

Cyril was excited but confident. His voice soared once, then twice, to the celestial note and came cascading down again. But the third time instead of the high C out came a strange rasping noise. Cyril froze. The other boys saw him go white. Sir Frederick, who was conducting, paused for a split second then smiled at him encouragingly and gestured him to carry on regardless. Terrified, Cyril forced himself to go on singing. Luckily, he managed to finish without further mishap, but he was trembling violently and trying hard not to choke. When the service was over, he fled into the lavatory and cried bitterly. His voice was breaking. His days of glory would soon be over and soon he would be a nobody again.

"Harris! Harris!" It was Tom Peters come to look for him. Tom steered him out of the cabin and sat him down in a quiet corner. He fetched him a cup of tea from the staffroom.

"I don't know what happened. It's never done that before." Cyril blubbered. "I could not stop it."

"Don't take it so badly, Harris, it can happen to anyone," Tom tried to cheer him up. "Look, if your voice is going to break how many people in this world can say it broke in the middle of a *Miserere* high C?" Cyril did not appreciate the joke and cried even louder.

"Harris, it was just damn bad luck that it happened to you at that moment," Tom tried again. "But don't give up, you can still sing in the choir. You are very musical and a splendid singer and, if we take care of your voice and train it carefully you could become a really good tenor."

"I don't want to be a tenor." Cyril sobbed. "I just want to go away. I want to get out."

It was all Tom, Flo, and Mr. Darnley could do to persuade him to stay on until the end of the school year, when he would be leaving anyway. Then they had to decide what he should do next. Although he had learned several instruments he was not interested in a future in music, he did not want to sing any more, and was horrified at the

thought of one day teaching it. His marks were not good enough to get him into a senior school, and in any case, Flo would not have been able to afford it. He would have to learn some trade. At Mr. Darnley's suggestion, he joined the Navy as a boy seaman.

His grandfather, Zachary, was furious when he heard of it.

"How could you do such a thing? If you become a sailor in the Royal Navy, you may well soon have to be fight Germany and betray me and everything I have taught you about your great heritage. Resign immediately and find some other apprenticeship.

But it was too late and, in any case, Cyril had no intention of quitting even if he could. He was learning a useful trade—he was being trained as an electrician, which he knew would practically guarantee him work in the outside world as factories, railways, households, and cities everywhere were becoming electrified. When he reached eighteen, instead of signing on for ten more years, he left. Now that he had a good qualification, it was time to decide on his future.

Cyril knew that Mr. Darnley wanted to discuss this with him during his current visit, and he was hoping to avoid him. His feelings about Mr. Darnley, and indeed about his mother, were becoming ever more complex. He knew he should feel extremely grateful to Mr. Darnley for steering him into the Choir School and for his many kindnesses. On the other hand, he could not help resenting the fact that he had usurped his own place as the man in his mother's life and affections. Not that he unconditionally adored and trusted his mother as he had when he was a little boy. In fact, he thought of her now with affectionate cynicism. As he grew older, he had gradually become conscious of the web of secrets and lies which surrounded her and her family. He now fully realised that he was illegitimate, as were his four younger siblings, and therefore socially somehow inferior. He had grasped the reason why his mother and he had been thrown out of the house that morning in Pillowell and out of Emily's house as well. Still deeply imprinted by the stern moral teachings of his father and grandfather, he could not help feeling he was born in sin and was somehow surrounded by it. It gave him a deep, subconscious sense of alienation.

Then there was the pack of half-siblings, but he dismissed them as if they were a litter of puppies, with their childish nonsense and their failure to give him the respect that he, now a tall, goodlooking young man, felt he deserved. No. 31 was altogether too full and too noisy. This was the moment to explore the old, ruined fort that lay across the river in one corner of the golf links and which no one seemed to know anything about except that it had never been much use militarily, even in its heyday.

As he scrambled over the weed-covered remains of the old fort, he realised that part of it, perhaps the former barracks, was still standing and that something was going on inside. And in the courtyard stood two large, wooden-and-canvas contraptions which he instantly realised to his amazement must be aeroplanes. Two young men were working on them.

He clambered down into the courtyard and peered through the glassless windows into the grimy building. It looked a mess. There were untidy stacks of wood everywhere, tools, trestle tables, and rolls of canvas. Hammocks hung from the rafters, empty beer bottles, paper bags, and the remains of bread rolls littered one corner. In the middle stood a portly, bearded man in plus-fours who spoke with a slight foreign accent and seemed to be in charge. He was deep in discussions with a much younger man who also seemed knowledgeable and confident of what he was doing.

"Hello," called one of the men working on the plane. "Looking for something?"

"Are you building aeroplanes?" Cyril asked shyly, feeling that it was a stupid question.

"We are assembling them," the man said. "This one here is Elsie," he pointed to the nearer of the two, "and that one is

Sylvia. All being well we are going to try out Elsie on the beach tomorrow morning."

"Ooh!" exclaimed Cyril. "Can I possibly help?"

The man scratched his head and looked at the others.

"Have you got a boat?" asked the older man.

Cyril nodded.

"Then look," he said, fishing in his pocket and bringing out a handful of coins, "could you go over to the shops and get us a crate of beer, a good lot of sausages, bread rolls, and anything else you see that would do for our supper. We are camping here, and our stores are running low."

Cyril, thrilled to be involved, did as he was asked. When he returned, staggering under the weight of the provisions, dusk was falling, a fire had been lit in the courtyard, and blankets laid out to sit on.

"Since you have brought the stuff would you like to join us?" asked the younger man. "By the way I'm Fred—Fred Handley Page. The boss," he said with an affectionate smile, "is Mr. Weiss. And these here are Gerald, Eric, and Gordon."

Gerald got busy with the frying pan, and before long, they were tucking into sausages and beer.

As they sat round the fire, Cyril and Fred discovered that they both had had electrical training. "But I have given that up now," said Fred. "I have started my own company, and I am going to build aeroplanes."

"You're very brave," remarked Cyril.

"I almost had to." Fred laughed. "I got sacked from the electrical engineering firm for experimenting with aviation technology instead of doing what I was supposed to be doing. So, I decided to start out on my own and build planes using some of Jose's inventions."

Jose, he explained, was French—"his family come from Alsace, actually, that's why he has a German name"—but had lived in England for many years near Arundel, not far away, and was naturalised British.

"He is actually a landscape painter, quite famous in fact, but his great hobby is finding out how to make things fly. He started by making copies of birds, then models—gliders. Every time he wanted to build a new one and experiment with it, he would sell a painting or two. They got bigger and bigger, and now I have persuaded him to put engines in them and someone inside to steer them. Tomorrow it will be Gerald's turn.

"The War Office are very interested, and they keep on sending someone to watch. They think aeroplanes could be very useful if war breaks out. But it seems like every time they come, it rains, and the canvas shrinks on the wings and pulls them out of shape. Nothing has come of it yet."

It was late by the time Cyril stumbled back happily to the boat, but he was back again early the next morning in the hopes of giving a hand in the great event.

He helped the others carefully pull the plane out onto the beach which had been left flat and firm by the outgoing tide. There was much hanging about and fussing over details, and then suddenly there was a roar and a cloud of smoke rose from the engine's exhaust. The propeller whirred. Everyone stepped back and, with Gerald at the controls, the plane leapt forward on its flimsy wheels. It slowly rose from the ground and, skimming only a few feet above the sand, flew a couple of hundred yards before bumping down onto earth again. Cyril and his companions were ecstatic.

Weiss and Handley Page made various adjustments, and Gerald several more tries. Then Eric took over the controls but as the plane was racing down the sand it suddenly veered violently to one side, overturned, and landed upside down, with Eric trapped in his seat. They rushed to free him; luckily, he had no injuries other than a big graze on his face, but the plane was quite badly damaged.

The group were deep in discussion about the incident.

"What went wrong?" asked Cyril.

"Not stable enough; we need to widen the undercarriage," said Mr. Weiss. "It will take us several days to sort this out."

Cyril hurried home, bursting to tell everyone of his experiences and fired up, despite the crash, with the idea of a future in flying. Fred had suggested he join his embryonic company but made it clear that there would be no pay until it started making money—if it ever did.

When he got back to the house, he found a letter waiting for him. It was from a fellow seaman who had trained with him in the Navy. The London United Tramways, which had been spreading its electrical tram network all over the capital, was hiring electricians. "I've applied, why don't you?" he wrote. "Do it as soon as possible. See you there!"

Cyril told Mr. Darnley and Flo about Weiss's experiments and how he would love to join Handley Page's company and build planes.

"I can see that," Mr. Darnley said after a while, pulling on his pipe. "It is all very exciting, but what would you live on? This flying business is all very risky and very expensive, no one knows if there is any future in it. Handley Page no doubt has money behind him, but I'm afraid your mother and I would not be able to support you while you tried it out. Cyril, if I were you, I would apply for a job with the Tramways. They are expanding very fast and will always be needing qualified electricians. I think that would be much, much safer."

Cyril felt utterly deflated. He went to bed in a sour mood but by morning had come round to Mr. Darnley's point of view. He needed a safe, steady job. He wrote to the tram company and applied to be taken on.

Chapter 15

DERBY, 1912

"For heaven's sake, just this once, Godfrey. Go and tell your mother you are leaving for Australia. Just this once! Do you realise it could be your last chance ever to see her again?"

"I don't want ever to see her again! She never wanted to see me. She never tried to get me back. She dumped me and that's that. And now she has a brood of illegitimate brats by that man! As far as I am concerned, she does not exist."

"Then at least write to her and tell her you are emigrating. That's the least you can do."

"No! Aunt Lizzie, no! No! No!" he was shouting now. "*You* write and tell her if you want. I'm not going to."

Godfrey was very fond of Lizzie, his aunt and godmother, but she really could be exasperating at times. She had never given up hope that one day she could reconcile him with his mother and here they were, going round and round in one of their everlasting arguments. She should know by now it was a hopeless cause; he not only would never forgive Flo for abandoning him and taking Cyril with her, but he also strongly disapproved of her—what was by all accounts highly immoral—way of life, one that went totally against the family's Primitive Methodist principles. He never wanted anything to do with her again.

Lizzie had been horrified when she received a letter from Godfrey announcing that he was about to emigrate to Australia and had immediately taken a train to Derby where he was living with Ezekiel and his cousins. Tearfully, she tried to persuade him to change his mind—how could he leave his family, his father, herself, knowing that he may never see them again? Had he not thought of the sorrow he was inflicting on them? And his poor mother? It was only slowly and reluctantly that she was persuaded to see Godfrey's argument that Australia could offer him a much better life than he would ever be able to expect in England, that it was the country of the future, where thousands of young Britons like him were emigrating in response to a campaign by the Australian government itself to attract settlers. They would pay for his voyage and would give him land and help him establish himself. He was going to become a farmer. He would have huge amounts of land! He might even make his fortune!

"But you know nothing about farming, you silly boy," she had objected. "And you don't know a soul out there."

"I can learn to farm, Aunt Lizzie; it can't be that difficult. And, didn't you know we have relations out there? Uncle John, Aunt Emily's husband—his sister and other members of his family live out there in Brisbane and have written they will help me get settled."

Even though she had finally come round to the idea, Lizzie was still heartbroken. She

loved Godfrey more than all her other nephews and nieces, not just because he was her godson, but also because she felt sorry for him and in a curious way, he needed her. Who knew if she would ever see him again? "If only I could come with you," she said wistfully, although at that point neither of them took the remark seriously.

Godfrey could not wait to leave England behind and start afresh far away where nobody knew him. Like Cyril, he had grown up always feeling something of a misfit. It was true that he had learned to rub along with his cousins, but he had never really felt one of the family. The warmhearted Martha had been like a mother to him, but when he was fourteen, she had died tragically of cancer. Ezekiel's new wife, Bertha, who he had quickly married to run his house and look after his large family, was only a few years older than Godfrey, not at all motherly, and unable to deal with the reserved and sensitive boy. Josiah had dutifully visited from time to time. Their relationship was correct but, Josiah being Josiah, not warm. After leaving school, Godfrey had done an apprenticeship and qualified as a gunsmith then, prompted by growing talk of an impending war with Germany, signed up as a volunteer in the territorial army. It was during training there that he heard from comrades about the opportunities in Australia. Thrilled, and without consulting anyone, he had applied to emigrate himself. His future had priority over a war. He was looking forward immensely to his new life.

Chapter 16

Littlehampton 1912

It was time for Mr. Darnley to leave again. That evening, after the children were tucked up in bed, he and Flo strolled to down to the end of the pier and stood, leaning on the railings, looking at the moon and the path it had laid across the sea in the direction of France. It was a mild evening, with just a gentle breeze.

"I'm so very, very happy" she murmured. "I think it is impossible to be happier than this."

Francis put his arm round her.

"You have every right to be happy, my dearest," he said. "But I've been thinking … in case anything should happen to me …"

"What could possibly happen to you, my love?" Flo broke in. "You are fit and well …"

But Mr. Darnley persisted. "As you know, I bought you the house so that you and the children could have a home of your own. But if anything did happen to me you could make some money by letting two, or even three of the rooms to holidaymakers. The children could sleep up in the attic, it's big enough for all of them and Margie."

"Don't talk like that!" Flo said again. "You frighten me! What do you think might happen to you? You are not ill, are you? Is it that you think there will be a war?"

"Yes, I'm beginning to think there could be a war, Flo. But don't worry, I'm too old to be called up to fight. No. It's just that … you never know."

Somewhat disconcerted by Francis's remark about a war, Flo began to take a more active interest in the world beyond her home, family, and work. Ever since she had come to Little-hampton, she had been dimly aware of talk about a growing threat from Germany which seemed to have replaced France as a potential enemy. It did not occur to her that anything might actually happen. Whatever her father might say, she did not feel even partly German. She had forgotten much of the language and most of the songs and fairy tales she had learned as a small girl; like their Primitive Methodist beliefs, it was something that had been drummed into her by her father at an early age, but which she had been happy to slough off once her old life had ended. But now she kept her ears and eyes open and realised that it was true: people in the shops and tearooms, the doctors' waiting rooms, and on the beaches were constantly talking about the threat from Germany—and from Germans themselves, of whom there were many living in England. People seemed to be sure of it—Germany was planning to invade and conquer Britain.

"They will take over and make slaves of us!" One elderly patient was almost panicking as Flo arrived to give her an injection.

Some time back, Mr. Darnley had given Flo a book, *The Riddle of the Sands*. It was a very popular book, but not being a keen reader, she had put it on the shelf and forgotten about it. Now she took it down. It was a wonderful, gripping story of two young Englishmen who, in the course of a sailing holiday along the north German coast, stumble upon secret preparations for a massive invasion of England's east coast by a fleet of tiny barges. It all seemed highly plausible. Could it be true? Could it really happen?

She lent the book to her next-door neighbour, Klaus Frantzen, a kindly, older German watchmaker whom the children adored, not least for the abundant supply of sweets which he would distribute over their common garden wall. Frantzen had come to Britain as a young man to work for an uncle who had a jewellery business in Hatton Gardens in London, had fallen in love with a young English girl and, once he had learned his trade, started a small jewellery shop in Littlehampton, which was his wife's hometown. For nearly thirty years he had sold the townsfolk engagement and wedding rings and mended their clocks and watches. He had served for a time on the town council and practically everyone knew him. His wife, June, occasionally suggested he should apply for naturalisation as a British subject, but he kept putting it off. There really was no need, he thought.

"A wonderful story, my dear, but complete nonsense," was his verdict on the book. "Imagine the Royal Navy and our coastguards not noticing thousands of men in hundreds of barges being towed by tugs all the way across the North Sea! The Kaiser certainly is a dangerous man and is doing dangerous things, trying to build up Germany as a rival to Britain. But I'm sure the Navy is perfectly capable of fending off an invasion."

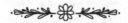

Soon after, Flo started reading the *Daily Mail* which was full of cartoons of monstrous-looking Germans in spiked helmets and articles about the "German Menace" and the "Hidden Hand" of Berlin, which was capable of anything, from surreptitiously seeking to destroy the Empire and dominate the world to sneaking dreadful ingredients into German sausages to poison British consumers. One day her eye was caught by a poster outside the newsagent's advertising a lecture entitled "The German Menace" by one William Le Queux.

"Is that the man who wrote *The Invasion of 1910* which they printed in the *Daily Mail?*" she asked the newsagent.

"The very one," he replied. "It's going to be interesting, why don't you go and hear him?"

"I'm curious; I think I will," said Flo.

The hall was packed that evening. Although she had gone early, Flo only found, with difficulty, a seat near the back. People were discussing how to pronounce the speaker's name, some thought it should be "Le Ker," more or less as the French would pronounce it, others "Le Kwex." When he finally appeared on the podium the person who introduced him called him "Le Kew."

"We are honoured to have here in Littlehampton this highly distinguished writer, traveller, diplomat, and expert in international military matters and who is almost alone in opening the eyes of his countrymen to the dire dangers facing them and about which their government is doing nothing," he declared. "Thousands of German spies, agents, and saboteurs are lurking in England, preparing the ground for the German invasion. Many of you will have read his brilliant book *The Invasion of 1910* which appeared in installments in the *Mail* and which has been translated into twenty-seven languages and has sold over a million copies.

Now he is here to warn us in person of the real danger which is facing our country."

Le Queux was a distinguished-looking gentleman with a moustache and monocle who exuded an air of authority.

"Ladies, gentlemen, fellow Britons," he began. "As an Englishman and a patriot, the last thing in the world I want is to be standing in front of you tonight."

A slight stir arose among his listeners.

"I must warn you that our country is sleepwalking into the gravest danger. Germany is preparing to invade. Thousands of troops will soon land on our eastern coast and take control of the country. A vast network of at least five thousand spies and agents are swarming over Britain, gathering information and preparing to sabotage our strategic installations to assist the onslaught of their hordes." People in the audience gasped. Although they had heard such warnings before, coming from such an authoritative-seeming personage they felt so much more real.

Le Queux declared that he had travelled extensively on the Continent, had been given audiences with kings and prime ministers, had many friends and acquaintances in high places in Germany, had travelled around Britain, and had heard and seen it all for himself. And now he was in possession of an amazing collection of documents which proved it without a doubt Germany was carrying out a "clever and dastardly plot" to conquer Britain.

He had even warned members of the British cabinet, but the government would not listen, he declared. "They say Germany would never dare to go to war. The Kaiser is half English and speaks English like an Englishman, the king is his cousin. But no—I tell them that I am in possession of a secret report from the heart of the German government. His ambition is for Germany to dominate the world. Only first he must conquer Britain and France, then the way is open to him. But our elected representatives, our leading newspapers" —by this he clearly included the sceptical *Times*— "don't want to see this. Like ostriches, they bury their heads in the sand.

"His spies are all around us. How else would they know how many horses there are in a given area? What are the supplies of fodder? The direction of the telegraph wires? The location of railway intersections and tunnels to be blown up? On the coast particularly, in places like Littlehampton as well as great naval ports, they are sketching our fortifications, watching our ships, and signalling at night from the cliffs and beaches. And no-one is stopping them.

"Colonel Mark Lockwood, the member of Parliament for Epping, asked in the House of Commons if the government knew about spies operating in Essex. He was snubbed."

By far the greatest danger, Le Queux warned, was a German by the name of Steinhauer who he described as the chief of the German spy system and a close personal friend of the Kaiser. Steinhauer, "the man of a hundred disguises," was also a man "of charming manners, excellent education, undoubted ability and unquestioned daring," he said. At vast expense he had set up an extensive network of naval and military spies in every dockyard and garrison town. "Every town along the coast has its agent or agents recruited by him."

Flo shivered.

"And who are these spies?" he asked. "They are mostly, but not all, German." There are thousands of Germans in Britain, he said, shopkeepers, hairdressers, waiters, tradesmen, governesses in the households of important men, businessmen, teachers, doctors, even members of high society. Many are married to English men or women. Many have lived here for years, are well known and trusted in their communities, many are even naturalised British. But that makes no difference.

"The heart of a German is always German, no matter what papers he may sign," he declared. "Every German resident should be considered a spy, ready at all times to assist the Fatherland."

"Beware!" concluded Le Queux. "Be alert! Spies are all around us. Responsible citizens must unmask and report them before it is all too late."

Thank goodness no one here knows that I'm half German, thought Flo. *People might think I was one of them!*

As Flo left, she noticed a table on which Le Queux's books were laid out for sale. She leafed through *Spies of the Kaiser* and noticed that the frontispiece was a picture of an attractive young lady apparently signalling on some radio or telegraphic device the movement of a battleship visible from her window. A woman spy.

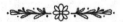

That evening, just as she was dropping off to sleep, she was abruptly awakened by the sound of a loud crash next door, glass falling, and someone running away. She

flung on her dressing gown and went round to find the Frantzens, also in their nightclothes, in a state of shock. A large stone had been lobbed through their main sitting-room window. Broken glass lay all over their furniture and carpet. The words "GERMANS GET OUT!" had been chalked on their wall.

June Frantzen was sobbing. "How could they! How could they! Just because Klaus was born in Germany!"

Chapter 17

On board the Kieler Förde, June 1911

The glorious Kiel regatta week, the Kieler Woche, had just ended. Hundreds of sails had skimmed through sheets of spray, trophies had been handed out, balls had been whirled, crowned heads spotted, and admirals saluted. The Kaiser, a dominating presence throughout, was dwindling to a tiny spot on the deck of the imperial yacht Hohenzollern as it steamed off up the förde towards the Baltic Sea. His bearded younger brother, Prince Heinrich, Grossadmiral and patron of the Kiel Yacht Club, was saying farewell to important guests in his August residence in the Schloss. Gentlemen in white ducks and ladies with lacy parasols turned to preparations for the last parties or for the journey home.

By a quiet stretch of the shore a sleek yacht, the *Sirene*, lay moored, alone. On board stood two men, tanned from the week's wind and sunshine. One was the owner, a senior admiral, the other his guest from London and they were watching two more men—like them, in civilian clothes—arriving on board a launch steered by a young naval rating.

"Welcome aboard!" the admiral greeted them jovially. "I wonder if you know Captain Handke who is our naval attaché in

London." They did, and handshakes and comradely greetings followed. "Do sit down. Benningsen," —this to the sailor— "bring up plenty of beer and pretzels or whatever you have, then you can go off for an hour."

Commander von Schiller, the head of the imperial naval intelligence unit, the Nachrichtenabteilung, which the initiated referred to simply as "N," and his deputy, Captain Boehnke, settled into canvas chairs on the deck with the others and set about lighting their pipes.

"Gentlemen, I do sincerely apologise for calling you at this time and in this highly unorthodox manner," the admiral began. "Fortunately, our service is newer, and therefore, we are not as tradition-bound—I will not say hidebound—as our comrades in the army. I know you have much better things to do than drink beer with your chief."

Murmurs of dissent issued from his guests.

"But I am anxious to discuss a very tricky problem which concerns 'N,' which has so far not been recognised as it should, but which could have dire consequences for our armed forces and for the country. And I thought I would seize the opportunity to discuss it away from Berlin, as informally and inconspicuously as possible, while taking advantage of the presence of Captain Handtke here who is over from London for the regatta.

"Soon I will have to bring it up it officially in the appropriate quarters but the, er, different pressures and, er, sensitivities inside the government and the naval High Command, of which we are all aware, make it difficult to discuss with the frankness that it deserves." He paused for a few moments while Benningsen served the beer then let himself down into the launch and headed off.

"So, I am asking you, my colleagues and fellow officers," he went on, "if you will give me your honest, unvarnished opinion, so that when the time comes, I can try to deal with the question in the most effective possible way. I know that—all of us being men of honour—not a word spoken in this meeting, in fact no word of the meeting itself, will be uttered beyond this vessel."

A muttered chorus of "of course" and "goes without saying" arose amid spirals of pipe smoke.

"I am very proud to head the Admiralstab[1] during this extraordinary build-up of our navy and the expectation that before long, we will rival the greatest navy in the world—that of our friends here." He jerked his pipe stem

towards the grey sterns of three British warships which were disappearing up the förde after paying a friendship visit.

"As you know, included in the plans was that our great new navy should build up the necessary intelligence network to provide the information it would need on the movements of other, potentially hostile, forces. The army has one and you will agree it is essential that the navy should have its eyes and ears too, or we will be unable to draw up plans for a war, let alone conduct one. I hardly need to say this is most necessary in the country which is most important to us and could well be our enemy in a future war—Britain. Reading the British newspapers is not enough!"

His guests laughed their assent.

"Three times the Kaiser approved my plans for this unit, but unfortunately they were repeatedly thwarted by other, er, departments" —his listeners knew perfectly well he was referring to his

---

1. Naval staff

archrival, the all-powerful Admiral von Tirpitz— "and it is only after his intervention that we were even able to set it up at all. But in all this time we have only recruited a handful of agents and even fewer really useful ones. If there is a war, and it is very possible there could be one soon, we would be fighting almost blindfold."

"The British don't think that, sir!" laughed the attaché. "They are convinced that the country is swarming with thousands of German spies and secret agents, preparing for the moment when we supposedly stage a massive invasion from the east. Newspapers are whipping up no end of public hysteria. And books—a ridiculous writer called Le Queux, in particular, is making a fortune with books full of lurid scare stories."

"Maybe it is not a bad thing that they should be frightened," ventured Captain Boehnke.

"On the contrary," replied the attaché. "The people behind it are couple of retired generals and a few Conservative politicians who are convinced that the British people are too complacent, that the country is not prepared for a war. They are sounding the alarm—and it is working. While there are people in the government who perfectly understand the situation and who realise that their propaganda is all a lot of nonsense, public pressure is strong. So they don't want to be seen to be doing nothing. They are already putting together a counter-espionage unit to keep an eye on our fellows."

"The fact remains, however, that our intelligence network in Britain is pitiful," said the admiral. "We must increase it substantially, by whatever means we possibly can. We do not have time to lose. What do you propose, Commander?", he asked, looking at "N"'s director.

"It will come as no surprise to you, sir, that the main problem is money," von Schiller said bluntly. "Without adequate funds, it is impossible to build up an effective intelligence network. As you know, we are operating on less than one-tenth of the budget you asked for and this is being systematically reduced every year."

The admiral nodded grimly.

"We are asking people to take enormous risks—even to risk possible execution—for a mere pittance. We had, of course, hoped that we could use our naval attachés around the world to help set up networks in their country. They are on the spot, and it would at least have saved us money," said the commander with a meaningful look at the attaché.

"Seen from Berlin, that would appear logical," mused the attaché, pausing to relight his pipe. He knew this argument only too well.

"In practice, things are not so simple. As members of an embassy, we have to be seen to be working for cooperation and friendship with our host country, not scheming behind its back to prepare for war. In fact, if they found out, there would be a colossal stink and London could well break off diplomatic relations. My ambassador takes a very dim view of me going off to make contacts in important ports."

"But are there not a lot of Germans there who would want to work for us out of patriotism?" asked the admiral.

"There are certainly a lot of Germans in Britain—we think about 60,000 of them, though of course, many do not live in places where they could be of any use. But the problem is that most of them are fully integrated. They have married Britons, for instance, or have businesses there, some have even taken refuge there for political reasons. It is extremely difficult to persuade them to betray the country that has become their home. We have had very little success with German citizens.

"And thirdly," he went on, "even if I were able to set up a nice little spy network, people forget that the minute war broke out, I would be recalled to Berlin and then what would happen? Who would pay them? How would they get their information out?"

"Nevertheless, we do have a small number of people—spies—in Britain," objected the admiral. "Did you recruit them? If not you, who?"

"Most were recruited by Steinhauer. He is a naval man himself and a remarkable character, very flamboyant, very full of himself. He uses the most amazing disguises and stories to conceal his identity—you would think he was something out of a boys' story book. He learned a lot of his tricks at Pinkerton's Detective Agency in Chicago and speaks very good English. Knows the country well.

"He has been more successful in recruiting spies than anyone, especially with people who are neither German nor British, although I have to say there are some pretty dubious characters among them. And there are still no more than a couple of dozen. He picks up a great deal of useful information himself. He has spent some time as one of the Kaiser's bodyguards and his Imperial Majesty thinks very highly of him."

"Where is Steinhauer now?" asked the admiral.

"He's on his way back from a tour of Scotland," said the attaché.

"Is there no other solution? Do you not have any other ideas, gentlemen?"

His guests looked at each other uncomfortably then shook their heads.

"Then all we can do is send Steinhauer back again and tell him to redouble his efforts. I insist that we must have a fully-fledged espionage network; one that can function in time of war. It is essential! I don't mind if he recruits shady figures so long as they produce the right information. He could even recruit women. I would have nothing against that under the circumstances, and they would probably arouse less suspicion. We desperately need more people. I will try once again to squeeze more funds out of the powers-that-be, but Steinhauer will have to be much more inventive.

"Gentlemen, have some more beer."

Chapter 18

HEREFORD/LITTLEHAMPTON 1912

It was a wedding of "considerable interest" in the city, according to the Hereford newspaper. Alas, it reported, the weather was behaving its worst, but the pouring rain did not prevent a large number of townspeople from gathering at St Mary's Church for the "full choral" service in its flower-decked interior. The bride, the daughter of the church's organist and "much esteemed for her work for the church and Sunday School," was radiant in an ivory, satin dress, a wreath of orange blossoms, and a veil of old Brussels lace. She wore a diamond ring and carried a bouquet of white, perfumed flowers, both given to her by the groom. The two bridesmaids wore pale-blue silk. The list of wedding presents was lengthy: silver vases, serviette rings, tableware. The happy couple left for their honeymoon in "Shakespeare country." The bride was Henrietta Robson, twenty-two. The groom, an organist colleague of her father, was Francis Hunter Darnley, forty-six.

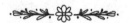

"Sorry, Nurse Harris is not well. She is very sorry, she can't come," Margie had to say several times a day to the emissaries of patients needing injections, massages, and assorted ministrations. At No. 31 Pier Road, it was as if someone had died. The mistress of the house was shut up in her room, refusing to eat or see anyone. The children, frightened and disoriented, tiptoed around the house, the older ones, Frank and Mollie, keeping order while the younger ones frequently burst into tears themselves.

They had been aware that some kind of bombshell had exploded when a registered letter arrived at the house. Flo, puzzled, signed for it, opened it, read it, and nearly fainted. Margie had to almost carry her to her room.

My love, this is the most painful and difficult letter I have ever had cause to write in my whole life," the letter began. *"I have long racked my brains, but I had to come to the conclusion that there is no gentle way of breaking the news. I would have given anything to spare you the pain that I know it will bring: it is my duty to inform you that tomorrow I will be joined in holy matrimony with a lady who I love and esteem and who comes from a family I know well and greatly respect.*

I thank you from the bottom of my heart for the love you have given me during these past years, for all the happy times we had together and for our four lovely children. It grieves me greatly to part with you all, and believe me, it is not a step I have taken lightly. But perhaps you will understand that it is desirable for my children, particularly little Luke, to have someone who will be a mother to them and to live once more as a complete family, an outcome which was tragically denied to us. It is essential to their future happiness that they never become aware of your existence or that of our children.

I hope you will understand that in view of my new family obligations, I will very regrettably only be able to send half the usual sum towards the support of our children. I comfort myself with the knowledge that you have the house and potential income which can be earned from it as we have discussed before. The remittances will continue until the children are all of an age to earn their own living but will cease instantly if you or they were ever to contact my new wife or in any way seek to inform her of your and their existence.

My dearest one, my heart bleeds to have to write these lines. I pray that you will one day forgive me and just carry in your heart memories of the love we shared. May you find again the happiness that you deserve. Francis.

Her life was at an end. After hours of weeping, Flo reached for her phial of laudanum and was about to pour its entire contents down her throat when the sound of her children whispering outside her door made her pause. *No.* She threw it across the room and flung herself back on her tear-soaked pillow.

How could he? Scenes from their years together flitted through her mind: the way he had looked at her after little Luke was born, their meetings in London, their sensual and passionate lovemaking, his love for the children, his smile when he presented her with the deeds to the house he had bought for her. The house—at least she had that. She now understood why he had spoken of it the last time they were together.

How long had he been planning to leave her? She tormented herself wondering what she could have done wrong, why his love had cooled, why he had done such a terrible thing. How could she possibly live without him?

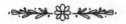

It was lunchtime two days later when Flo finally emerged, pale, exhausted, her eyes swollen, and her hair unkempt. She sat down limply at the kitchen table, telling Margie to make her a cup of tea and that she did not want anything to eat. Little Joanna climbed into her lap and the others looked at her in expectant silence.

"Listen, my darlings, I have two things to tell you. Mr. Darnley won't be coming to see us anymore."

"But why not?" Frank asked, alarmed. Mr. Darnley had been particularly fond of his first-born, and Frank of him.

Joanna started weeping.

"He has other things to do now. I'll tell you all about it when you are older and can understand," Flo said. "The second thing is that from now on we are going to have to take boarders, visitors who come here on holiday. So, you will all have to sleep up in the attic with Margie. You will have to be quiet and well-behaved and very nice to our guests."

A burst of chatter broke out. Frank and Mollie were not happy about giving up their beds to strangers but Prue and Joanna, the younger ones, were excited at the idea of sleeping up in the attic with its sloping roof which had always held an air of mystery and adventure.

"When will the boarders come?" asked Prue.

"Soon, I hope, but first I will have to advertise in the newspapers."

Thus, Flo grudgingly joined the ranks of Littlehampton's boarding-house landladies. It was considered a respectable way for women to earn an income, and after their husbands died, many widows had taken in boarders to make ends meet. With Little-hampton becoming ever more popular as a holiday resort, they usually had plenty of customers.

With Margie's help, Flo set to and rearranged the house. They turned three bedrooms into bed-sitting rooms, put a breakfast table in a corner of the parlour, and set up camp beds for the children in the attic. From now on, the family would have to spend much of their time in the basement kitchen.

Flo was just setting out to register No. 31 as a boarding house when another letter arrived. It was from her father. Flo could not believe her eyes.

"No! What can he possibly want? I can't deal with him now—now, of all times!"

Flo had not heard from her father directly for years. According to Lizzie, he had never ceased to rant against her for leaving Josiah—even though, mercifully, he had never discovered the true reason—and was outraged that she had a family by a man to whom she was not married. He was over eighty now and apparently still sprightly, despite his wooden leg, but Lizzie had never mentioned any desire on his part to speak to her again.

His letter was blunt.

I will be arriving in Littlehampton at 3:30 on Tuesday next where I intend to stay for one or two days. I trust you can accommodate me. I have a matter of great importance to put to you.

What could the "matter of great importance" be? He had already disowned her and cut her out of his will—it seemed highly unlikely that he would have changed his mind, *welcome though that would be at this time*, she thought to herself wryly.

She spent another sleepless night weeping over Francis's betrayal, racking her brains as to how to make ends meet, dreading the arrival of her father, and wondering what on earth his motive could be.

In the morning another letter arrived. This time it was from Lizzie.

My dearest sister, Papa has just told me he is going to visit you, and I am as astonished as I am sure you are. All I can tell you is that his decision seems be the consequence of a secret meeting with his German friends—these things nowadays have to be very hush-hush, as you can imagine. When I asked him the reason, at first he would not say, then he murmured something about being an old man and that he did not know if he would ever see you again. Though I can assure you that despite his age, he is in the best of health.

Dear sister, you know his temperament—and yours. I beg you to humour him. If possible, seek a reconciliation. Do not provoke him or let yourself be provoked, try not to enter into any dispute. Be kind to him, for when all is said and done, he is the victim of his own character. Your loving sister, Lizzie.

Flo put on her cape and her hat and went out for a stroll to the end of the pier. Lizzie's letter and the fresh sea air calmed her and cleared her head. Dear Lizzie, she thought, so loving and kind. The one member of her immediate family who had remained faithful. And so sensible—that was good advice. She would do as she suggested. No, even better, she would make a big fuss of her father.

"The prodigal father comes home!" She laughed to herself.

She made a detour to the post office and sent him a telegram:

YOU ARE WELCOME.

The elderly, balding gentleman with white sideburns who descended from the 3:30 train with some difficulty, owing to his wooden leg, was at first surprised, then amused and a little disconcerted, by the small group waiting for him on the platform. Three small girls in their Sunday best presented him with little posies they had picked themselves, curtsied, and said their names. The boy, a little older, bowed and called him "Sir." Then, a still attractive, red-headed woman in a nurse's uniform stepped forward, kissed him, and said, "It is so wonderful to see you again, Papa. How was your journey?"

The boy took his bag. and the little group walked him back to Pier Road, the girls chattering and taking it in turns to hold his hand, fired up by Flo in advance at the thought of having a real-life grandfather of their own, just like other children. They were fascinated by his wooden leg but studiously avoided staring at it, which Flo warned them would be rude.

After tea, the children showed him round the house, then took him out into the garden. Over the low wall they saw Mr. Frantzen tending his beloved roses. Zachary was introduced and on hearing their neighbour's name said, "Guten Tag. Sind Sie Deutscher?"

"Well, I was born in Germany," their neighbour replied in English, "but I have been here for so many years that one could say I have become more English than the English. I have no longer any connection to Germany, not even close relatives there anymore."

"Hmm," said Zachary pensively, adding, "splendid rose bushes you've got there," over his shoulder as he was being pulled away by the children who were demanding that he come and see the sea.

Well, so far, so good, thought Flo as she watched her father buying ice cream for the children by the beach. *Please God, let it stay this way*, she prayed.

But once supper was over and the children tucked up in bed, his mood changed.

"To think I, who have led an upright, God-fearing life, should have a daughter who is little better than a prostitute and four illegitimate grandchildren, sweet, innocent creatures though they may be," he growled. "It is a blessing that your saintly mother never lived to suffer this shame."

Flo clenched her teeth and forced herself to stay calm. "Papa, you said you have an important matter to discuss. If that is all you have come to say to me, I shall go to bed now and you can leave first thing tomorrow morning. I have worked hard to gain a respected position in this town and to make a good home for my children. I have nothing to be ashamed of, and I never want to hear such talk ever again!"

Zachary looked as though he might explode but made a visible effort to control himself. After a few moments' silence he stood up and looked down at her. "There is one way you can redeem yourself after your sinful life. Before long Britain and Germany will be at war ..."

"Papa, do you really think so?"

"I know so. I have friends who know well what is going on behind the scenes. There will be a war. Germany must win and rule over this decadent and benighted island and bring order and its great Kultur to Britain and make it at last a truly great country. I am doing what I can, but I am too old now to be of much use. But you, with our German blood in your veins, you must work to achieve this great goal."

"Papa! What are you talking about? How could I possibly? Even if I wanted to." *Which I never would*, she thought.

"No, you must. As your father I demand it of you."

"But what on earth would you want me to do? I am merely a mother and a nurse, what difference could I make?"

"Listen to me. You have heard, no doubt, much talk of the possibility of a German invasion. That, of course, may happen, but first Germany must defeat Britain on the sea. The German navy will soon be as powerful as the British navy, with new Dreadnoughts, battleships and so on. But what it needs is not just great ships, it needs intelligence, information about British naval movements, ports, defences.

"You are living in one of these ports. In fact, I could hardly believe my luck when I realised that you live close to the entrance to the river, behind the harbourmaster's office, and can see all the ships coming and going. You must keep watch and report."

"Papa, you want me to be a spy! But there are already supposed to be thousands of German spies in the country ready for when war breaks out! Why should they need me?"

"That's all nonsense. Pure hysteria whipped up by that man Le Queux and others. We don't have all those spies, and we need people who will quietly inform them about ship movements ..."

"But I don't know anything about ship movements! And suppose I was caught! Think of the children!"

"You wouldn't get caught. Who would ever suspect a nurse and housewife? Does anyone here know you are German?"

"Half German," Flo corrected him. "Only Mr. Frantzen next door, and I don't think he would ever tell anyone."

"There you are. And think of the honours that would be showered on you when the Germans have taken over! You would be a heroine!"

Such a prospect seemed so absurd that Flo nearly laughed. "No, Papa. I can't see myself doing it. It would be too dangerous. I'm sure the Germans could do perfectly well without me."

"You must. You would be earning money too. I am going to send somebody to arrange it all and teach you what to do. Don't worry, you will be perfectly safe and from the 3:30 train just think—you will be serving the Fatherland!"

He never will realise that "the Fatherland" doesn't mean to us what it means to him, Flo thought to herself wearily. She thought of his efforts to have them learn German when they were small. Their sweet, gentle mother, a Dorset woman born and bred, had no say in the matter. But since no-one else they knew spoke German, and there was no talk of ever going to Germany, the exercise seemed pointless, and Flo had long since forgotten most of what she had been taught. Now, the idea of earning money, well ... she certainly could do with it. But not at any price, she decided. This was nonsense.

But her father was not going to take no for an answer, so she tried to humour him. "Well, let's see. I'll think about it," she said.

"I'm going to write to Cyril too. He has to play his part too; you must tell him that."

"Yes, Papa," she replied dutifully, knowing she was not going to do anything of the sort.

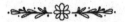

Before long, Flo had boarders, occasionally men with business in the town but mostly holidaymakers from the cities who pronounced themselves delighted with their accommodation and Margie's service, as well as the charms of Littlehampton.

Among them was an elderly couple from Birmingham; a woman who was asthmatic, and her husband who was recovering from severe bronchitis. Flo found herself ministering to them both and the doctor, after a couple of calls, took her aside and said, "You know, Nurse Harris, you could do worse than turn your house into a small nursing home. People recovering from pneumonia, or who have asthma like this lady here, need the sea air and would be only too happy to have an experienced nurse looking after them. And they would pay more than mere tourists."

"A nursing home! I never thought of that!"

"Of course, you would have to register and follow certain standards, but that would not be too difficult. And you would need a doctor to provide medical supervision, when necessary, but if you like, I could do that for you."

"That sounds an excellent idea, doctor! I will certainly think about it."

With the smaller amount Darnley still sent, her nursing activities around the town and

the income from her guests, she was just about managing to make ends meet. But if she turned No. 31 into a nursing home she could charge more and also keep open all the year round instead of just in the holiday season.

She set off for the town hall to enquire about the necessary formalities, and when she returned, Margie met her at the door saying that a "Mr. Rymers" had asked if he could stay. "I said I yes because the two ladies have just left, and the back bedroom is free. Shall I get it ready for him?"

"Yes, dear. Where is he now?"

"He has gone for a stroll by the port."

"The port?" *Odd,* Flo thought. Most new visitors made a beeline for the seashore.

The new guest turned out to be a youngish, fresh-faced, slightly portly gentleman with a dark bushy moustache and eyes that were narrowed as if he were permanently amused. He was jovial, exuded self-confidence, and spoke with an American accent.

"Good afternoon, my lady. Rymers is the name," he said breezily, handing her his card.

Flo saw that his name was spelt Reimers and that he was a commercial traveller in optical instruments.

"What a charming place this is, as charming as its mistress," he remarked as she showed him to his room. She sensed that he was scrutinizing her more closely than his surroundings and, despite his words, not in a manner that made her feel flattered.

Reimers was soon making himself popular in the house, flirting with Margie, charming the other guests, and playing with the children. The latter reported that they had seen him hovering around at the shipbuilders' yards on their way home from school. And once, Flo thought she spotted him over at the old fort across the river.

One day, Reimers came down into the kitchen saying he had seen from his window that their neighbour had beautiful roses in his garden. He was a rose fancier himself, he said, and asked if he could go out into the garden to meet this neighbour. Flo could see through the window that he seemed to strike up a friendship with Mr. Frantzen and after a couple of chats was eventually invited inside next door for tea.

After some time, Flo heard the Frantzens' door slam loudly and saw Reimers return looking shaken and angry. He went straight up to his room.

Flo did not concern herself much with the doings of her guests, but this one puzzled her. *He's rather odd,* she thought. *I wonder what he is doing here.*

Late that evening, as she sat in the kitchen mending a pile of children's socks, there was a knock on the door. "May I come in?"

It was Reimers. He was carrying a bottle of port and two small glasses which he put on the kitchen table.

"Would you care to join me in a nightcap, dear lady?" he asked. "When I'm on my travels, far from home, I find there is nothing more comforting than a quiet chat and a glass of something before turning in."

Flo, who had been about to go to bed, perked up at this sudden arrival of this affable gentleman. "What a delightful idea! Do sit down."

Reimers first poured two glasses of port and put one in front of her. After taking a small sip as he toasted her health, Flo left hers untouched. Her downfall at Warley had made her wary of alcoholic drinks.

He settled down comfortably at the table as if he was a member of the family and, leaning forward over one arm with a slight smile on his face, looked at her intensely. "Mrs. Harris—or may I call you Florence?" he began.

Flo, flustered by his gaze and the sudden intimacy, found herself nodding.

"Florence, then," he went on, "I have something important to tell you. I am not the man I seem to be. I am here on a mission, and my mission is directed at you." His smile grew broader, he was clearly relishing the mystery he was creating.

"Me? Whatever for?"

"I am not a commercial traveller or anything of the sort. I am an emissary of the Kaiser."

Flo stared at him incredulously, tempted to laugh.

"No, it is true. We know that you come from a family with deep German roots, and I am here on behalf of the Kaiser to urge you to help the Fatherland."

Papa said he would send someone, and I didn't take him too seriously, thought Flo. *What do I do now?*

"I saw the Kaiser once. He smiled and waved at me," she said, attempting to change the subject.

It was Reimers's turn to look surprised. "Did he? When was that?"

"It was when he came to see the old Queen, just before she died." She recounted how during her visit to London with John, she had stumbled almost into the path of his carriage, and he had waved at her.

"Aha!" he said, his eyes lighting up. "I was with him on that very visit. In fact, I can say that was when I helped save his life."

"Save his life?"

"Indeed. I was in charge of the Kaiser's bodyguard and soon after I arrived, I met up with my old friend William Melville, then the Superintendent of Scotland Yard's Special Branch, to discuss security arrangements. He told me there were rumours that anarchists would seize the opportunity of the state funeral to assassinate the Kaiser, but he begged me not to speak a word of it to the Kaiser or his entourage. 'The Prince of Wales fears that if the Kaiser hears of them, he may very well not attend the funeral, which would have severe consequences for Britain's relations with Germany,' he told me.

"The Queen died the following day. While we were still at Osborne preparing the funeral, Melville received a message from his office in London. He immediately came to me, clearly very agitated, and said 'Tonight I am going to arrest three of the most dangerous anarchists in Europe. I would like you to come with me; it is not something one can leave to subordinates. But do not say a word to the Kaiser, the new King has expressly forbidden it.'

"We set off for London, and on the train, he told me that three Russian anarchists had recently arrived in London and were hiding at an address in the East End, planning their attack. We went first to his office where he gave me a pistol, although I already had one on me, and a black scarf to hide my white collar which would be visible in the dark.

"Melville was a reserved, laconic man, not given to exaggerations, but he asked me if I had made my will—which I had—and said he had written a letter which was only to be opened at the time of his death. He suggested I do the same, and I took his advice. He even joked that the Kaiser would erect a statue to me if things turned out badly."

"Weren't you afraid?" Flo asked, entranced by the story.

"I have to admit I was very much afraid. However, at eleven o'clock that night, we set off in a cab for an address near London Bridge station where Melville got out and came back shortly afterwards with a woman—an Italian, it turned out—dressed in a dark raincoat. She guided us to a poor, dirty part of London that I did not know. The cab stopped in a dark alley, and she led us through a maze of dark, smelly streets—we, following a few yards behind her—to a house. She went in, then returned, signalling to us to follow. It was pitch dark, I could see nothing, but I could hear her going up the stairs. We clutched our pistols.

"Suddenly there was a flash, a shot, and a woman's scream. Then they started shooting down at us. We fired back, there was a shout and the thud of a body falling, and the shooting stopped. We rushed up the stairs. There was no light, but we could just make out two figures, one was the woman and the other was one of the anarchists, lying on the floor, moaning in pain. The others had vanished—obviously they had jumped out the window, which we saw was open. Melville quickly handcuffed the man, and we raced out in pursuit of the fugitives. We thought we saw them jump into a cab, but the cabbie said that only one had got in, and soon after leapt out again, while the other had made off on his own.

"It was futile to pursue them further. We returned to the house—by that time a crowd had gathered, alarmed by the shooting—and found the room empty! The culprits had evidently returned, freed their accomplice, and made off with him and the woman."

"Did you find them?"

"No, they vanished. However, some time later a colleague in the Russian Secret Police told me in Berlin that a couple of Russian anarchists who had been in London had been hanged. It sounded as though they could have been the same ones."

"And the woman?"

"She had been Melville's informer. She had had a love affair with one of the Russians and he had thrown her over. She wanted to take revenge, so she went to Scotland Yard. It cost her dearly. Her body was later found in the Thames. She had been murdered."

Flo shivered. "I never heard about this."

"No one did. We made sure that it did not get into the press. You are one of very few people who I have told about it."

Flo felt immensely flattered, and somehow complicit. "Did you tell the Kaiser about it?"

"Of course—but only after he was safely back in Berlin. He was very appreciative and is going to give Melville and me medals for it. 'We need heroes like you,' he said."

He drained his glass and poured himself another.

"And talking of heroes, Florence," he went on, "here you have a wonderful opportunity to become one yourself. The Kaiser needs your eyes and ears here in Littlehampton; his navy needs to know about ships that come and go, about any maneouvres you may see in the Channel, movements of troops, even the appearance of aeroplanes or airships."

"So, there *is* going to be a war?" Florence asked, shivering.

"I hope not," Reimers said. "The Kaiser does not want one, nobody does. This talk of plans for an invasion is complete nonsense. But he is building up a great navy, which will soon be as great as the Royal Navy. And any navy needs information on what the other is doing. And you are perfectly placed to do this for him."

Flo was silent for a moment. "Mr. Reimers, you want me to be a spy."

"No, not a spy," Reimers said soothingly. "We are not at war. Let's say—a source of information."

"Listen to me," Flo said firmly. "You have no idea what a scare there is here about German spies. I went to a talk by a Mr. Le Queux the other day, and he was warning us that there are thousands of them in hiding here, preparing the way for an invasion. People are being arrested or reported to police simply for being German. Even poor Mr. Frantzen next door has had some nasty moments."

"That Le Queux fellow is talking utter nonsense; you shouldn't listen to him," retorted Reimers. "He is a dangerous fabulist, and it is all the product of his imagination. I can assure you, because I know the Kaiser and his armed forces well, that there exists neither an army of spies nor any plans for an invasion.

"It is true I am half German," Flo went on, "but I am half English too. I feel English, this is my country, and I have lived here all my life. Why should I want to betray it? And in any case," she said, pointing to the pile of socks on the table, "I have four young children – and two older ones, as it happens. I cannot possibly take such a risk. What would become of them if I were caught?"

Reimers, like her father, insisted that no one would ever possibly suspect a woman who was English, a mother, and a nurse. "I omitted to say," he added, "that you would be well remunerated, not on a princely scale, but nothing to be sneezed at."

Flo paused again. She stood up. "I'm very sorry but this is something you can't ask of me. It is too dangerous. I can't do it."

Reimers saw he could do no more. But he remained seated, pulled a pencil from his

pocket, tore out a page from a small notebook and started writing.

"First of all, will you promise me that you will not say a word to anyone of what has passed between us this evening?"

Flo nodded.

"And Florence, one day you may change your mind. If you do, contact this person. He will tell you exactly what to do and how to do it and will also make sure you are generously paid. He will know who you are. Trust him." He gave Flo the paper.

She glanced at it. On it was the name Peter Hurst and an address in Forest Gate, near Epping, Essex. Shrugging her shoulders, she put it behind the clock on the mantelpiece. "I'll think about it."

"Tell him Steinhauer sent you."

"Steinhauer?" Flo gasped. Everything that Le Queux had said suddenly fell into place.

"Gustav Steinhauer. At your service, ma'am."

With a flourish, he clicked his heels, bowed, kissed her hand, turned, and left the room.

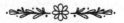

"Has that dreadful German gone yet?" Klaus Frantzen appeared the next day, somewhat agitated.

"You mean the one calling himself Reimers?" asked Flo, pouring Frantzen a cup of tea.

Frantzen had come round with a bunch of his prize roses and clearly wanted something more than an over-the-garden-wall chat.

"He left this morning. Why do you ask?" Flo added.

"That is a very dangerous man," said her neighbour. "He is a German secret agent. He tried to persuade me to spy for them. He said once a German, always a German, and that it was my duty to keep the German navy informed about naval movements around here. The blackguard!"

"What did you say?"

"I sent him away with a flea in his ear. I told him I would never dream of doing anything so dishonourable. I would never betray my adopted country. I was an army officer once. If there is a war, a soldier—no, any decent German—would see it his duty to face the enemy and, if necessary, die in battle. Not to sneak around in the shadows, live a double life to steal and betray the country you love."

"You were quite right," said Flo, wondering whether she should tell him that Steinhauer had attempted the same with her. She had promised not to tell anyone, but what was the value of a promise to a foreign secret agent? Anyway, Klaus had not yet asked.

"It is heartbreaking, though," her neighbour sighed. "For over thirty years I have lived among the people of Littlehampton, they have welcomed and trusted me and, if I may say so, they have liked me. I have always been regarded as one of them. Never has anyone objected to the fact that I was born in Germany—until now, with these people spreading this poisonous propaganda. And now, suddenly they think I'm the enemy. Many, even some of my customers, turn away from me. They no longer come to my shop; they don't speak to me. They don't even greet my poor wife."

"It is so unfair. So un-Christian," said Flo. "But I went to the talk by that man Le Queux the other night, and he really made people frightened. He sounded so convincing."

"He's a terrible man, whipping up hysteria like that," said Frantzen. "I think the government know it is all nonsense, but I suppose they can't stop him."

"Anyway, Klaus," said Flo, laying a hand on his arm, "you know you have good friends here. We know you and we trust you and we always will." Frantzen put his hand on hers and smiled wryly.

Though he has a point, she reflected. After Le Queux's talk, even she had begun to wonder about her neighbour. It was the memory of the angry look on Steinhauer's face after speaking to him that convinced her that Frantzen was telling the truth.

She did not know quite why, but something told her to keep her conversation with Reimers/Steinhauer to herself.

She did not intend to write to her father about it either. He would only badger her to take up Steinhauer's proposal—worse, he might even come again and give her no peace until she did. But that possibility evaporated a few days later when she received a letter from Lizzie saying that their father was very ill in hospital. He had had a stroke.

Flo was deliberating whether to leave the children with Margie again and go to see him when Frank came down with the mumps. The next morning all four children had it, so she had to stay. She cabled:

ALL HAVE MUMPS. LOVE AND BEST WISHES TO
FATHER.

The telegram crossed with one from Lizzie.

FATHER DIED LAST NIGHT.

Part 4

War

Chapter 19

LITTLEHAMPTON

By March the following year, Flo was becoming seriously worried about money. Since her puritan childhood, she had been accustomed to living very frugally and even in the halcyon years when Francis was largely supporting them, she had always been very careful. Now that his remittances were considerably reduced, she had to rely on her little nursing home to make up the shortfall. For all her bitterness at his remarriage, she had come to appreciate his foresight in putting the house in her name. But it had not solved her problems as she had hoped. Although the sea air was supposed to be more healthful in the winter than the summer, few patients stayed long when the skies were dark, the grey sea churned, and the rain lashed down on the promenade. She had learned to set aside the money she made during the busy summer months to keep them going in the winter, but now this was running out, and she was struggling to feed and clothe the four growing children. And she could not dismiss Margie, whose help was essential.

The remittances always arrived punctually at the beginning of each month. On April second, she went to the bank as usual to collect it, but this time Mr. Stopes, the old teller, scratched his head and checked through his papers. "It doesn't seem to have arrived yet, Nurse." He went into the back room and checked again. "No, it's not here. It'll probably come by tomorrow."

Flo returned the next day, and the next, and the next. Still, it had not arrived. By the end of the week, she had become seriously alarmed. She was frustrated because she was unable to contact Mr. Darnley; he had been careful not to let her know his address or even his general whereabouts, presumably—Flo thought—to avoid his new wife ever finding out about her and their illegitimate family. She knew only that the money came from a bank in Stafford. Seeing her increasing anxiety, the kindly Mr. Stopes suggested she might ask Mr. Fawcett, the bank manager, to make enquiries with the branch which had always sent the money. "I'll see what I can do. Come back at the end of next week, Nurse, and maybe we will have heard something," said Mr. Fawcett.

The following Friday, she returned to the bank. Mr. Stopes appeared engrossed in some accounts. Mr. Fawcett, looking grave, beckoned her into his office, closed the door behind her and asked her to sit down.

"I've received a message from my colleague in Stafford," he began. "I very much regret to tell you he has informed me that the sender of your remittances, Mr. Francis Hunter Darnley, is deceased."

Florence went white.

"My colleague wishes me to stress that what I am telling you now is unofficial, merely for your information. He believes that the cause of death was pneumonia. And the gentleman has left everything in his will to his wife and three children."

She continued sitting, immobile, her mind a blank.

"Are you all right, Nurse?" asked Mr. Fawcett, concerned. "I'm so sorry to have to give you this news. Would you like a glass of water? Is there anything I can do to help?"

Flo did not hear him. Slowly she stood up, turned, and walked shakily out of the office.

Still in a daze, she walked in a straight line down to the promenade and sat on a bench, staring unseeingly at the distant line where the grey sea met into the grey sky.

Francis was dead. The love of her life, the father of her four young children. The man who had given her the closest thing to happiness that was possible for a woman in her situation. Dead. The pain and bitterness he had inflicted on her by remarrying suddenly dwindled in comparison with the memory of the years with him. His laugh, his curly hair, his music, his kindness …

Then the grim reality struck like a punch in the stomach. No more remittances. How would they be able to live? The black, almost forgotten terror resurfaced: once again she had that terrible feeling of being naked and helpless, as in the kitchen in Pillowell and the church in Brentwood. *No! No!* she screamed inwardly. *It can't happen again!*

It was some time—she had no idea how long she had been sitting there—before she realised she still had the house and her nursing home business. But it would not be nearly enough to support them all. She would have to take on more nursing work if she could find it, particularly when the season ended in the autumn.

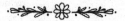

As summer approached, though, she began to get enquiries from would-be patients about vacancies. Soon she was busy again, the income from her invalids and convalescents kept them afloat for the time being, and her worries subsided somewhat. She had little time to pay any attention to the news. The billboards outside the newsagents blared news about Irish Home rule, strikes, and the scandalous behavior of suffragettes. While Flo would have liked to know more about the suffragettes, she had neither the time nor the spare cash to go in and buy a paper. Nor did she bother when they announced the assassination of some foreign Archduke by a wild-eyed Serb in a far-off place called Sarajevo.

But her patients, with time at their disposal, were growing alarmed. Captain Tillotson, a large retired naval officer with a red face and huge white moustache, began making it his business to buy newspapers and hold forth to the others over breakfast about the turmoil in the chanceries of Europe following the assassination.

"Austria is going to have to retaliate against Serbia, and the Russians won't like it. So, they will mobilise, and there will be war. And then Germany will have every excuse for jumping in with both feet."

The captain's wife, a pale, emaciated woman who was convalescing after a near-fatal attack of pneumonia, fluttered her hands nervously. "My dear, please don't say those things, you are making us all frightened."

At the next table the Bowker sisters, in their forties, both afflicted with asthma, were more than frightened. "They say the Germans are preparing to invade, and that there are thousands of German spies here just waiting to blow up our bridges and railways. Whatever would become of us?" wheezed Agatha, the elder sister, nervously twisting her long string of jet beads.

"Don't you worry, Miss Bowker, the Hun will never come here, you can take it from me," the captain reassured her. "The Navy would quickly put a stop to any nonsense

of that sort. If England goes to war, we will fight on the Continent, and a good thing it would be too. It is time someone gave the Kaiser a bloody nose; the Germans are getting altogether too big for their boots."

"My son can't wait to volunteer," came a deep voice from the third table. It belonged to Mrs. Robinson, a very large, amiable woman from Wolverhampton with a face that—people noticed, though refrained from remarking upon in her presence—looked exactly like to that of the little pug dog she carried around with her everywhere. "He thinks it would be an enormous adventure, but I can't say I share his enthusiasm. He could get killed."

Flo, who had come in to give her patients their various morning doses of medicine, paused. Young men volunteering to fight? To risk getting killed? Suddenly the talk of war, which had seemed even more distant than the Irish Home Rule question, became more real. What about Cyril and Godfrey? Would they have to go and fight?

Her nurse's instinct to calm and reassure her patients took over. "I would not worry if I were you, I'm sure it will all blow over. Why don't you all go to the concert on the seafront this afternoon? It's such a lovely day, and the outing will do you a world of good."

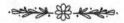

As the summer wore on, suspense mounted. Flo and Margie would join her patients at breakfast to hear Captain Tillotson's résumé of the previous day's events. Even Frank was allowed to listen in. Austria had made up its mind to avenge the assassination, Russia was arming in support of the Serbs, Germany was declaring war on Russia and France. Then, in July, the dam burst. German troops were marching into neutral Belgium, heading for France. The Prime Minister, Mr. Asquith, issued an ultimatum to the Germans: stop, or Britain will declare war. "And rightly so," the captain declared. "Teach the Hun a good lesson."

The Bowker sisters were almost frantic, whether from excitement or fear the others—and even they themselves—could not tell. "We must go home at once!" insisted Prudence, the younger one. "Please, dear nurse, could you prepare us our bill quickly?"

"Remember, it's a bank holiday, the trains may not all be running," warned Mrs. Robinson.

"I want to go and fight!" clamoured Frank.

"You'll do nothing of the sort," snapped his mother.

"They won't take you, sonny. You have to be eighteen before you can join the army," said Captain Tillotson. Frank looked dejected.

The bank holiday, the captain informed them, was being extended three more days. Three days! It was because many people were taking their money out of the banks and the banks were risking collapse, he explained. Flo had no savings to take out.

The next morning, the captain was not at breakfast. He had gone early to await the arrival of the newspapers to see if war had been declared. He found a sizeable group of people outside the newsagents waiting anxiously too. They waited and waited. Finally, the papers came, and he returned to No. 31 with the news. "We are at war."

Some of Flo's friends and neighbours were euphoric at the prospect of war. Young men in Littlehampton were queuing up to volunteer. But others, particularly tradesmen and boarding-house keepers like herself were worried whether their businesses could survive.

Mrs. Robinson was the next patient to go. "I'm so sorry, Nurse, but I really feel I should go back to help my married daughter. Her husband is in the army, and they are mobilising. She will be so worried about him. But I'm sure I'll be back again next year."

Her patients were not the only ones to leave. The crowds of holidaymakers on the promenade had thinned visibly.

The captain, however, was still in high spirits and relished his daily walk to the paper

shop for the latest news. Two days later, as he was expounding on the latest developments, he mentioned in passing that as soon as the Prime Minister declared war twenty-one German spies had been rounded up and put in prison. Flo was stunned. Casually, she asked the captain if she could look at one of his papers. It was true. On orders from the Home Secretary, police had raided houses in the principal ports and arrested twenty-one spies, one of them a woman.

She went quickly to her own room and sat on the bed while she recovered from the shock. What a blessing, she thought, that she had not taken up Steinhauer's offer, as she could be in prison now. Maybe even facing a sentence of death!

It was Frank who noticed a number of naval vessels engaged in some activity off the coast. He told the captain. "What are they doing, sir?" he asked. The captain walked down to the pier and had a look, then dropped in at the harbourmaster's office.

"They are laying mines. They are laying mines so that German ships can't come here," he explained when he got back.

"Laying mines, here?" gasped his wife. "The war is coming here?"

The captain tried to insist that the mines were intended to stop the war coming to Littlehampton, but she worked herself up into such a state that she could not sleep or eat. She started coughing badly and demanding that they leave instantly. The captain had no choice but to give in.

Flo was left with no patients, no bookings, and four young children to feed. With a heavy heart, she told Margie to go home.

Chapter 20

Headquarters of the Admiralstab, Koeniggraetzerstrasse 70, Berlin

"You're back, Steinhauer," growled Captain Boehnke as the master spy walked into the Nachrichtenabteilung after returning from a mission to Denmark. "Brace yourself. All hell has broken loose. You should be damn glad you were not here on Monday."

"What on earth could be the matter?" asked Steinhauer sarcastically as he dropped his travelling bag on the floor of the captain's office and took off his cap. "I can't possibly imagine."

"Oh, nothing really," the captain said, echoing his sarcasm. "Only that your entire spy network in England got arrested and thrown into jail the minute Asquith declared war! Only that an entire British Expeditionary force has embarked, crossed the Channel, and landed in France without us knowing a thing about it—let alone being able to stop them! Now the Army has to completely rethink its plans. The Kaiser held a top-level meeting at the Kriegsministerium. He was beside himself with fury.

"As I said, it was a good thing you weren't there. He ranted and raged for the best part of two hours. He called us incompetent and useless. 'Am I surrounded by dolts?'" the captain barked, imitating the Kaiser. "'Why have I never been told that we have no spies in England? Who is responsible?'"

"Did anyone tell him that it was the fault of you-know-who, who would not give us enough money to run a proper secret service?"

"Of course not. We all sat around with long faces, shuffling our feet and wishing he would stop. Eventually he came to an end saying, 'We must have network of first-class spies in England, Germans whose patriotism can be relied upon.'"

"As if it was that simple." Steinhauer snorted. "I have been warning you all for a long time that our network in England could break down the minute war was declared. And I would have told the Kaiser too, if I had been there—respectfully, of course. I would have told him that you can't set up a serious, professional secret service in a foreign country without sufficient funds. But the people he listens to," he dropped his voice to a near-whisper, "are those high-up bootlickers, pompous, opinion-ated asses who only tell him what he wants to hear. Let's face it," he added pensively, "His Majesty was never one to appreciate the truth.

"So now I've got to conjure up these 'first-class spies,' God only knows how. But there are still one or two agents in England who haven't been rounded up and I'll

prod them to get busy. We also have to work out some better, more secure way of getting the information out."

"It didn't help that you had them all sending their reports to a couple of German barbers in London," complained the captain. "The English were on to that well before war was declared and were just waiting for the moment to arrest them all."

"Well, I couldn't have them writing to addresses outside England, could I? That would have aroused even more suspicion. And what else could I do? If we had had the money, we could have bought radio transmitters—who knows, we could possibly even have used submarines. With enough money, we could certainly have recruited better-quality agents."

"Well, the Chief will tell you that somehow or other we have to find people who will report, not only from the big naval ports, but also on further troop movements across the Channel. The British are bound to send many more troops out to fight, and the Army needs to know the numbers that it will be facing."

"I'll see what I can do, but it's a bit late now. They should have thought of all this a long time ago. Is the Chief in?"

"Yes, and he wants to see you."

Chapter 21

Littlehampton, 1914

When her patients had gone, Flo went to Dr. Richards, who had suggested her opening the nursing home and figured as its medical officer, and poured out her troubles. Dr. Richards was sympathetic.

"I know, we're in difficult times. I'm afraid it is quite likely you won't have patients of your own for the time being, and without our usual holidaymakers there are far fewer people needing attention," he said. "But we are now at war, and I am afraid there will be wounded soldiers who will need treatment, so nurses will be very much in demand. The Red Cross is already setting up a hospital here in Littlehampton, you should go and speak to the matron. The Voluntary Aid Detachment is getting mobilised too—of course it is mostly made up of non-professional volunteers but does have a quite number of professional, paid nurses. I think you would have no trouble finding work."

Full of hope, Flo went in her freshly washed and pressed nurse's uniform to the local Sailor's Institute where nurses and helpers were setting up beds. It was tiny, she saw, as there were only five or six beds, and she wondered how many nurses they would need. The matron, a young, severe-looking woman with a long, horsy face and dark hair pulled back under her starched white cap, looked at Flo's uniform and immediately asked, "Where were you trained?"

Flo had been dreading this question, but hoped she had a good answer.

"I was taught by Dr. Alfred Willoughby in Warley, near Brentwood, and by Dr. Richards here. I have a lot of experience treating their patients. In particular, I spent months caring for a consumptive lady who developed pre-eclampsia but gave birth to a healthy child and survived. And until the war broke out, I was running my own nursing home in Pier Road. Dr. Richards and Mr. Willoughby can certainly vouch for me."

"So, you have never had any proper training in a hospital?"

"No, ma'am. When I started it was not customary, and in any case, my husband had died suddenly, and I had to start working immediately to be able to feed my children."

"Well, I'm afraid our organisation takes a dim view of domiciliary nurses like you," was the curt reply. "My superiors believe that many of them bring the profession into disrepute and are campaigning for a system of registration so that only ladies with the right training and qualifications will be allowed to call themselves nurses." The matron seemed to have felt she had been too harsh because she went on more gently,

"I'm very sorry, you may have had a lot of experience, probably more than the girls who have recently qualified, but I can't offer you work here, it's against the rules."

Flo was floored. She had not expected the slightest problem. She went back to Dr. Richards and begged him for a written reference to show at her next interview.

"I did hear that there is a big controversy in the nursing world about qualifications and registration," said the doctor as he wrote out a glowing letter. "But I had not imagined it would have come to this. Anyway, take this," he said, blotting the letter and handing it to her, "and go and talk to the VADs.[1] Good luck!"

The local office of the VADs had quite a different atmosphere. Well-dressed women speaking in cultured tones were bustling around, sorting sheets, uniforms, bandages, and other equipment. Lady Grenville, an elderly woman in a high-necked, lacy blouse and grey skirt, who was evidently in charge, was much more sympathetic than the Red Cross matron.

"You seem to be just the kind of person we want, as you obviously have plenty of experience," she said, smiling encouragingly as she read Dr. Richards's reference. "The Red Cross is opening auxiliary hospitals and nursing homes all over the country and we badly need volunteers such as you."

"Volunteers?" repeated Flo, slightly alarmed. "I am a professional nurse."

Lady Grenville looked at Dr. Richards's letter again. "The doctor does not say anything about your training, though. Do you have any qualifications?"

Flo was forced to repeat the argument that failed with the Red Cross.

"My dear, I am very sorry, of course we have paid nurses on our staff, but they have to be qualified. Those are the rules. What we need—and what you would be really ideal for—is volunteers

---

1. Voluntary Aid Detachment, an organisation of civilian volunteers caring for military wounded at home and abroad

who will act as assistants, orderlies, who will make bandages and so on."

Flo's heart sank. "Lady Grenville, I am a widow and have four young children to feed. I cannot possibly afford to volunteer; I need paid work here." She picked up her gloves and her bag and, having received Lady Grenville's best wishes and promises she would be accepted as a volunteer if ever she changed her mind, and went home. *Change my mind!* Flo thought to herself. *As if it was that simple. She has no idea!*

All she had now was the money from her last patients, and she knew that would not last more than a few weeks. She made enquiries with all the chemists and the other doctors in the town but with no results. Volunteers, yes, paid nurses, no.

The war was turning her life upside down. And not only hers. She began to wonder about her two older boys, both of whom could be called up and have to go and fight. Godfrey was now in Australia and presumably safe. But she was worried about Cyril; she must write and ask what he was doing.

She was spared the trouble. When she got home Cyril was there, unannounced as usual, boasting to Frank about something.

"Cyril's going to be a soldier, Mama!" Frank announced enviously.

"What's this?" Flo asked, her heart sinking.

"I've volunteered," Cyril said. "A lot of the lads from the London Tramways have. Some recruiting officers from the London Electrical Engineers came round and said they needed trained electricians. We'll be operating searchlights. Everyone was very keen."

Flo sat down to try and take it all in. "Does that mean you will be sent away to the war? Will you have to fight?"

"Don't worry, Ma. Our job will be to defend the ports here, to watch out for enemy ships. We will have huge searchlights, you can't imagine how big they are, that can pick out ships miles away at sea."

"Well, thank the Lord you are not going away to fight," said Flo, greatly relieved. "When do you start?"

"We are doing our training now and, in two or three weeks, they will assign us to our various batteries. With luck I might not be too far away from here."

❦

Late that evening, returning from the pub after a drink with some old friends, Cyril found his mother still up, struggling with her accounts.

"You look worried, Ma," he said. "Is everything all right?"

"No, it isn't," Flo said. She had not intended to burden Cyril with her worries but found herself pouring out her woes. "As you see, I have no house patients anymore. And when Francis died, the money he sent stopped. I have tried to get work nursing in the places they are setting up for wounded soldiers, but now they will only take nurses with these newfangled qualifications."

"Could you not go back to being a live-in nurse?" asked Cyril.

"Well, I could. People are still advertising for them, but who would look after the children? I couldn't take them with me, and to pay someone to look after them would probably cost more than I could earn."

"Well, I could try to help you out, but it would not be anything like enough—assuming we get paid at all in the L.E.E."

188

"Did you really have to volunteer, Cyril? Could you not have stayed in your job as a switchman?"

"Well, I could, but it was sort of expected of us. Everyone of my age is doing it. But, Ma, I thought it was better to do that and stay here in this country than perhaps be called up later on and have to go and fight the Germans."

Flo looked at him. That was very revealing, she thought. Cyril had always been very attached to his grandfather. She wondered if Zachary had, in fact, written to him and suggested he become an agent for Germany, but she hesitated to ask him directly.

"You were always a better disciple of Grandpa than I was." She laughed. "You even learned more German than I ever did. Did he ever talk to you about the possibility of a war?"

"Well, yes, and if there were to be a war, of course he would have been on the German side," Cyril replied. "He would have wanted the Germans to come and take over the country and run it as he thought it should be run. You know what he was like."

"And what do you think?"

"Between you and me, I think he was right. There is a lot that is rotten in this country. All the lads are so patriotic and so keen to fight for King and country, but why? So many people are desperately poor—think of the ones in Papa's congregations. Even those with jobs can hardly feed their families while the rich flaunt their money.

"I know people are shocked that Germany invaded Belgium and is attacking France. But Germany has enemies all around it, especially Russia and France, and if it didn't attack, sooner or later it would have been attacked by them."

"I see your grandpa must have given you a good talking-to," Flo tried a little harder. "Did he want you to ... er ... do anything about it?"

Cyril was silent. "He ..." he began, then stopped.

"He what?"

"Well, if you must know, he wrote to me suggesting I do something like that," he admitted.

"For heaven's sake, Cyril, you mustn't!" Flo exclaimed. "It would be so dangerous. You could get into the most dreadful trouble! And please don't even talk like you just did to anyone else, people are so terribly suspicious nowadays!"

"Of course not, Ma, I'm not stupid. I'm just keeping my head down and doing what I'm told."

It was the longest and frankest talk that she had ever had with Cyril, and she felt that it had somehow brought them closer. Cyril had always been a difficult boy—or more precisely, he had become difficult since she had put him in the Waifs and Strays home in Brentwood, and then at the Westminster choir school. He hadn't had an easy childhood, being shunted around from one place to another, she had to admit. The four younger children had much happier, sunnier natures. She was pretty sure he was too sensible to follow his grandfather's wishes.

Then there was Godfrey. By all accounts, he had changed much since she left Pillowell. According to Lizzie, he had turned in on himself, become uncommunicative and, like Cyril, had few friends. And now he was on the other side of the world anxious, so Lizzie said, to make a totally new life for himself. *I will probably never see him again*, she thought sadly. *But at least*, she consoled herself, *he was far, far away from the war.*

Chapter 22

Enoggera Barracks, Brisbane, Australia

"So, what's your trade, mate?" The recruiting officer scrutinised the young farmer who had reached the head of the long queue of volunteers keen to go to war with the newly formed Australian Imperial Force.

"Gunsmith in England," replied Godfrey, "but now I'm a farmer."

"When d'you get here?"

"Two years ago."

"Date and place of birth, military experience if any, criminal record if any, religious denomination?" The officer rattled off the questions mechanically. Then, "Next of kin?"

Godfrey was silent.

"Next of kin? We need to know who to contact if, er, anything happens to you."

Godfrey still hesitated.

"Father? Mother?" The officer was getting tetchy.

"No mother. My father emigrated to Canada recently, and I don't know where he is."

"Well, who should I put, then?"

"Put Captain Angus Sinclair, Prospect Terrace, Brisbane. He's my uncle."

Well, a kind of uncle, he told himself later as he queued again, this time for the medical examination. Captain Sinclair, who had been skipper of a ship in Queensland's embryonic naval defence force, was related by marriage to John Norton, Aunt Emily's husband. More importantly, the captain, his only contact in the whole of Australia, had welcomed him warmly when he arrived, taking him into his family and helping him get settled on his land at Milmerran, some 150 miles west of Brisbane. He would not mind in the least being considered the next of kin.

Despite Godfrey's ardent desire to start a completely new life in Australia, like many settlers, he still felt a strong tie to the "old country" and when war was declared he decided without hesitation to go and fight. But volunteering solved another problem for him: he liked farming, but after a while he had to see that it was not going well. He had trouble adapting to the hot Queensland climate, in his inexperience he had made many mistakes, and he was losing money. Reserved as he was, he found it hard to ask neighbours for advice. By volunteering, he was able to put the problem on ice for a while.

Because of his training as a gunsmith, he was immediately appointed Armourer Sergeant and three months later was on a troopship heading to England for training on Salisbury Plain. But en route, plans were changed and instead the Queenslanders found themselves disembarking at Alexandria in Egypt, travelling by train to Cairo, and then marching out into the desert where a huge camp was still being hastily created for them.

"You won't believe this, Aunt Lizzie," he wrote a few days later, "looking out of our tent I can see the Pyramids of Giza and the Sphinx! They are amazing! Join up and see the world! The training here is really tough, marching miles

and miles in the sand in full kit with heavy backpacks, digging trenches, practising attacks, six days a week! And it's hot! A whole lot of New Zealanders have joined us; we can't wait to get to Europe and fight!"

But Godfrey was soon disappointed when it dawned on him that for all the training, he was destined to be a non-combatant. As an armourer sergeant, he was to be involved in the supply, distribution, care, and repair of pistols and rifles, mostly at headquarters. He learned all about administering supplies and equipment but was deeply frustrated. His hopes rose when they received orders to embark—not for Europe as they were expecting, but to Gallipoli in Turkey. Their mission was to reinforce the ANZAC troops who were fighting alongside the British for control of the strategically vital peninsula, and with it, the Dardanelles, the narrow strait which would give their Russian allies' warships access from the Black Sea to the Mediterranean.

Here, he was seconded to ordnance—yet another disappointment, though he soon found out that it was almost as dangerous as fighting up on the craggy ridges. He was landing, storing, and distributing crates upon crates of shells, bullets, and grenades, often in the dead of night and mostly among deafening artillery, rifle, and sniper fire, and always with the knowledge that some mishap could send it all sky high, and him with it. So, this was war—the sickening stench of rotting corpses, the pestilential clouds of flies, the thirst, the sickness, the graves, the lack of sleep, the inadequate and barely edible rations. After a couple of months, he was finally allowed to join his unit and, lugging his kitbag and his gunsmith's toolbox, he clambered in the footsteps of a guide up perilous goat tracks and through a maze of dugouts until he reached his unit.

They had changed since they had landed under a storm of Turkish gunfire. Their skin was sunburned to a dark leather, and miserable rations and repeated doses of dysentery had left them thin and haggard. They had become tough warriors but were nevertheless weary and disillusioned after the bitter fighting through the blazing hot summer which, in the end, had gotten the Allies nowhere. Godfrey quickly realised that there was only a handful of men that he knew, as so many of his young, keen Queensland mates had been felled by Turkish bullets or bayonets.

Autumn had arrived. The worst of the fighting had subsided, but Godfrey still had his work cut out, repairing their jammed or broken Australian-made Lee Enfield rifles, bayonets, and pistols. The squalor, the flies, the mud, the cold, the constant barrages of shooting made life at the front even worse than on the exposed beaches.

Unknown to them, the horror and futility of the campaign was finally being recognised in London and at the end of the year, grieving for the dead comrades they were leaving behind but also with immense relief, their turn came to slip away by night and board waiting ships. Little did they imagine, as they sailed back to Egypt, that the hell they had left in Gallipoli was mild compared to what awaited them in France.

Chapter 23

LITTLEHAMPTON, 1914

"You must be joking, Mr. Roberts! Eight pence for a loaf of bread? That's almost twice as much as it was last week!" Flo was furious.

William Roberts, the baker, looked a little taken aback but stood his ground. "There's a war on, Nurse. Shortage of flour. I'm having to pay a lot more for it than before."

"Nonsense!" bellowed a large lady standing next to Flo. "The town council promised us that there were enough supplies for several months—probably to last us through the war. You wouldn't like us to think you were price-gouging, would you, Mr. Roberts?"

Mr. Roberts went red in the face and stepped back as if something had hit him.

"You know I wouldn't do something like that, Mrs. Barlow. A lot of other shopkeepers are having to do the same thing, too."

"And they are profiting from the war as well." The redoubtable Mrs. Barlow continued her attack. "It's a scandal. We will have to talk to the town council about it."

She, Flo, and two other customers left the shop and gathered in a little knot of
indignation outside.

"You are right, Mrs. Barlow, they *are* profiteering. It's outrageous," said one of the other customers.

"And what makes me so angry is that there are people with money buying up stacks and stacks of food and hoarding it in case there are shortages later on. Which means that there is practically nothing left for those of us who can't afford to."

"It's got to be stopped," declared Mrs. Barlow. "I am going to talk to the mayor. Does anyone want to come with me?" She and one of the other women stormed off in the direction of the council offices.

The fourth woman, Sally Hines, was a widow who ran a boarding house, and who, like Flo, was in financial difficulties for lack of guests.

"Fat lot of good it will do complaining," she said to Flo as they headed back in the direction of Pier Road. "We have been telling the council we can't manage any longer without guests and they said the town clerk had written to the War Office suggesting that troops could be billeted in the boarding houses here. Not the same thing as holidaymakers of course, but better than nothing. But nothing came of it. The Army chose other towns along the coast instead."

"I just don't know what I'm going to do," confided Flo. "I've got four growing children to feed."

She was getting desperate. Everyone seemed sure that the war would be over in a few months, by Christmas at the latest, but she had calculated that the money from her guests and what little she now made with nursing services would not even last until then. Her heart breaking, she took the gold locket Darnley had given her to the pawnshop, knowing that she was unlikely ever to be able to redeem it. The proceeds scarcely lasted them a week. She had sent Frank out fishing with a friend after school and they had indeed brought home some small but very welcome fish, but then she had to sell the rowing boat, and such fish as the boys were able to catch from the riverbank were fewer and smaller.

Under the guidance of her neighbour, she had dug up her back garden and planted vegetables, but it was too late in the year for them to produce much and it was a poor consolation when Frantzen assured her that they would be excellent the following year.

"After all these years I'm back where I was with Josiah," agonised Flo as she lay sleepless at night, her pillow and handkerchief soaked with tears. She had never been well-off, but she had believed that never again would she and her children go hungry.

⋘⋙⊱✿⊰⋘⋙

In September, to her horror, little Joanna fell ill. She had a raging sore throat, a high temperature, and a bright red rash all over her face and body. Was it measles, chickenpox, or that terrible killer, scarlet fever? Flo put her in a bed in one of the guest rooms and forbade the other children to go near her. She tried coaxing her to sip some soup, but the child would only push it away. When, on the second day, Joanna became semi-comatose, Flo made up her mind. She had to call Dr. Richards.

"Scarlet fever, Nurse," was the grim verdict. He did not need to tell her how many children died every year from the dreaded disease.

"There is a serum now which has proved effective in many cases," the doctor went on. "But now there is a war on, I don't know if it is possible to get hold of it, and even if I can, it will be very expensive."

"Oh, please try, Doctor," Flo begged. "Please, please try." She did not know how she would pay for it, but she would sell the house if need be to save the child's life.

The doctor promised to do what he could, and after two anxious days, sent word that he had found it and would be there as soon as it had arrived. The serum helped, and Dr. Richards was able to pronounce Joanna to be out of danger, but she remained very ill, and he warned that recovery would be long and difficult. He did not charge Flo for his services but the serum cost almost all the money she had left.

That night, Flo dreamed that she was begging Mr. Fawcett at the bank for a loan but couldn't pay it back and the next moment was shut up in a debtor's prison. She had

sold the house and she and the children were sleeping under a bridge. She had got a job in a factory and come home to find all the children gone. She woke and, when reality sank in it felt almost as bad as the dream. She sat up, slid her feet into her slippers, went down to the kitchen, and opened the back door to let some air in. She drank a glass of water, filled it again, and sat down at the table.

All she had in the world was the house. She could try and sell it, though who would want to buy it at the moment? The war had turned life upside down. Many men were away, and people had very little money. And what would happen when that money she got for the house ran out? No, she decided, No. 31 was her rock, her anchor, the one solid fixture in her life. And it was not just their home, it could again be a source of income when—if—life returned to normal.

She sat for hours, her head in her hands, vacillating. The first light was creeping in through the back door when she finally stood up and fished out the piece of paper with the address that Steinhauer had given her from behind the clock on the mantelpiece. As she did so, her mother's faded sepia photograph caught her eye. She stared at it for a few moments. "I have no choice, Mama," she said. "What would you have done?"

She fetched a sheet of paper, a pen and ink and began writing.

Chapter 24

The next day, as she was returning home after posting the letter at the post office, she saw in the distance four or five policemen who seemed to be at her house. Alarmed, she walked faster and was at first relieved to see that they were next door at the Frantzens' house. But then, to her horror, she realised that they were taking Klaus Frantzen away and leading him to a police car. She ran and pulled one of the policemen by the arm. "What are you doing that for? That's Klaus Frantzen, the jeweller. You know him! You can't take him away!"

"Sorry, ma'am." The policeman looked embarrassed. "We have our orders. Aliens Restriction Order. Enemy aliens must be interned. He can appeal, though don't ask me who to."

June Frantzen was standing at her door, crying bitterly.

Flo went and hugged her. "We've got to get him back! It's ridiculous! Come with me!" She dragged June off on an exhausting round of offices, the police, the town hall, and the local army headquarters but found no one who could help them. They did learn, however, that he had almost certainly been taken to a camp near Frimley in Surrey and that June would probably be allowed to send or take him clothes and extra food.

June's brother, a wealthy Littlehampton businessman, had an open Lagonda motor car, and the next day the three of them set off on the fifty-mile journey to Frimley with a suitcase full of warm clothes and blankets and a bag of Klaus' favourite chocolates and biscuits. As they rolled up Frith Hill, just outside Frimley, they could hardly believe their eyes. Forbidding barbed-wire fencing with guards posted on look-out platforms enclosed a huge area of heathland where people moved between rows upon rows of white tents, huts, and campfires. In one part, they could see men in military uniforms, evidently German and Austrian prisoners of war, while in another part, the inmates wore civilian clothes, and many were at the fence talking to people in the crowds which had collected on the near side.

"How dreadful! It looks like a zoo!" Flo said to June as they walked over to join them and ask for Klaus Frantzen. A young man, who until a couple of days earlier, had been a waiter in Camberley, ran off and found him. Waving, Frantzen shouted to them to bring his things to the entrance where they could hand them over.

A friendly guard, after a cursory look at the contents of the suitcase and bag, allowed them to talk.

Frantzen did not want his wife to worry about him. "I must say, I feel safer here than I have done in Littlehampton recently," he joked. "And it's a bit like those scout camps, it would be quite fun if I was younger. The others in my tent are all good chaps. There's Hans Schwarz—you know, the doctor—and several musicians who we hope will play for us when they can get their instruments sent to them. It won't be much fun when the weather gets bad, though."

"But when will they let you out?" June asked.

"I've already applied, and you must apply as well, my dear. Here's the address of the office to apply to," he said, fishing in his wallet. "Listen: forty years' residence, married to you, a British subject, a spell as town councillor, a son in the Navy. But perhaps the most important point—remember—is my age. They only intern people up to fifty-five and I'm fifty-four so if all fails, I hope by my next birthday at the latest …" He held up crossed fingers on both hands.

"But that's not till next May," June protested. As they talked, a large column of prisoners-of-war were being herded around them into the camp and, in the confusion, the three of them were ordered to leave.

"Why?" moaned June again and again as they drove back to Littlehampton. "Klaus loves England. He's never done anything wrong. Why? Why? Why?"

Chapter 25

REQUEST SINGLE ROOM FIVE NIGHTS FROM TUESDAY
30TH STOP HURST.

"Reply's paid," said the telegraph boy, who was anxious to be off.

"Just a minute," said Flo and wrote out, "CONFIRM BOOK-ING" on his form and gave him a coin.

So, he was coming. Steinhauer's man. Flo was terrified, but it was her only hope.

"Mama, there's a gentleman for you!" Frank called through the open door. The three older children had been playing on the steps of the house when a tall man with white hair and moustache walked up and asked if this was where Mrs. Harris lived.

"Peter Hurst, good afternoon," he introduced himself to Flo as they met at the door. "Are these your children?"

Flo immediately sensed he did not just ask out of politeness, but replied, smiling, "Yes, this is Frank, that is Mollie and that is

Prue." The girls stood up and curtsied. "My youngest, Joanna, is poorly at the moment. Let me show you your room."

At closer range she could see that the man was younger than his white hair made him seem. He had blue eyes, smooth, fair skin and had obviously once been very blond. He was much more direct than Steinhauer. As soon as the children were out of earshot he said, "We must talk. But we need to be quite alone."

"I'll have the children in bed by about seven-thirty. Would you like supper here or will you be eating out?" To her great relief he said he would have a look round the town and find a place to eat. Her larder was almost empty, as was her purse.

⊱⋆⊰ ❀ ⊱⋆⊰

"I am very glad you finally got in touch with me," Mr. Hurst began. The children were safely in bed, and they were sitting at the kitchen table, as she had with Steinhauer.

"Gustav Steinhauer told me you would be excellently placed to help us and that your nurse's uniform and activities would be a first-class cover for you." There was something slightly odd about his speech, Flo thought. It was perfectly correct, yet somehow not quite English.

"Are you German?" she asked.

"Let's say I'm Danish," he replied evasively. He certainly looked Scandinavian. He was being very charming, she thought, but she sensed that it was a charm which could be turned on and off when it suited him. There was something about his cold grey eyes and his voice which suggested an icy will. "But I spent many years here in my youth. That is why Steinhauer asked me to come back, because I know the place and the people. Officially, I am a commercial traveller for a Danish beer firm, which enables me to travel around the country without arousing suspicion.

"I understand you have German blood and are well disposed towards the Fatherland. Are you sure you want to work with us? We are not asking you to do anything dangerous at all, just to collect some information for organisational purposes. Would you be willing to swear an oath of allegiance to the Kaiser?"

"First of all, you might tell me more about what I would have to do," said Flo, a little proud of her new-found caution.

"Of course, ma'am. You see we ..."

At that moment they were interrupted by the sound of the front door opening and a man's voice calling, "Hello, anyone at home? I'm back!" It was Cyril.

There were footsteps on the stairs, and Cyril appeared at the kitchen door sporting a brand-new khaki uniform. Flo's heart sank.

"Well, aren't you pleased to see me?" Cyril asked his mother, a little disconcerted not to get the reception that he had expected. "What's going on here?" He looked suspicious.

Flo got up and kissed him. "This is all so sudden, Cyril! I wasn't expecting you. And this uniform—does it mean you're in the army now?" Then, remembering her manners, "Mr. Hurst, meet my eldest son, Cyril. Cyril, this is Mr. Hurst, er, our new guest."

Her visitor, who had been looking distinctly irritated at the interruption, seemed suddenly galvanized. He sprang up, shook Cyril's hand, and looked admiringly at his uniform. "What regiment is that?" he asked, squinting at the shoulder tab.

"Not a regiment—the London Electrical Engineers," answered Cyril. "A volunteer unit. A whole lot of us from the tram company have joined up. We are being trained as searchlight specialists. My unit is being posted to Dover to keep a watch out for enemy ships."

"Dover! Are you really?" Hurst exclaimed excitedly. "That's splendid! When do you go?"

"The day after tomorrow," said Cyril. "I just came to let you know, Mama, and to collect some things. I'll tell you how you can reach me. I'll be going back early tomorrow morning."

The visitor was riveted. While Flo made Cyril a cup of tea and two slices of bread and dripping for his supper, Hurst started peppering him with questions, but suddenly Cyril gasped and hit his forehead. "Sorry, but I have just remembered—we have been told not to say anything about it. It's a secret. I shouldn't even have told you I'm being posted to Dover. Please don't tell anyone; I would be in real hot water."

Hurst fell silent and watched as Cyril ate his meagre supper. *He's noticing that we have next to nothing to eat*, Flo thought.

They heard agitated children's voices from upstairs. "Could you go and see what is the matter, Cyril?" Flo said. "I hope Joanna hasn't woken up. She's poorly, you know."

While Cyril was upstairs, Hurst whispered to Flo, "Steinhauer didn't tell me about your son. A searchlight unit—and in Dover! Do you think he would work with us? Just think, if he did, we could end up paying you twice as much," he added, eyeing Cyril's empty plate.

Flo did not know what to say. She was more afraid for Cyril even than for herself. But then there was the money … "You must ask him," she replied, non-committal.

Cyril returned. "A bat had got into the attic, and they were frightened. I got it out again; they have quietened down now." He sat down again at the table.

"Cyril—if I may," began Hurst, "I promise to keep the secret you have just told me. But in return I want you to promise to keep a secret that I am about to tell you."

"Well, of course," answered Cyril, puzzled.

"I am here on a special mission from Germany. I think your grandfather will have taught you that Germans are not the monsters that they are said to be by the gutter press and certain propagandists. We are a great and cultured nation, very advanced in science and technology and are becoming a great world power to rival Britain. We have no option but to fight in this war, although we would rather not. Anyone who

helps us is helping peace come sooner, and I am asking you to join in this effort. When it is over, I can assure you that those who have helped us will be hailed as heroes and have a glorious future.

"Your mother is willing to work with us, and we have an important role in mind for her. You will have access to military information—will you join her in helping to ensure that the war is over as quickly and painlessly as possible?"

Cyril stared at the table, saying nothing.

"I can assure you that you both will be handsomely remunerated."

Cyril uncrossed his legs and crossed them again. Slowly, still staring at the table, he began, "I have no problem with working for Germany. I am proud that my mother and I have German blood. But you are asking me to be a spy, aren't you?" he went on. Cyril's hazel eyes met Hurst's cold, grey ones and did not blink.

"Then you must know that as a soldier I could be court-martialled and shot."

Flo gasped. "Then you mustn't, Cyril. Absolutely not."

"Don't worry. It's perfectly safe, no one will ever know," Hurst tried to reassure them. "You must realise that the British authorities think they have destroyed our network by arresting twenty-one members at the outbreak of the war. They have no idea that some of us are still operating and more will join us soon.

"And we have learned from the mistakes which led to that disaster. Our methods have very much improved. Steinhauer told everyone to mail their reports to certain middlemen and then wondered why they got arrested. My people don't do that. Cyril, for a start I would insist that you had no further direct contact with me from now on, but that you give all the information you have verbally to your mother. Never, ever, write anything down. No one can know or suspect what passes in a quiet conversation between a son and his mother."

"But Dover is a good long way from here. How often would I ever get to Littlehampton?" objected Cyril.

"Well, that brings me to my plan for your mother which fits in marvelously with yours. Such an amazing stroke of luck! You see, initially we had intended to ask her to report on ship movements to France from Littlehampton—weapons, ammunition, supplies of all kinds. But my walk around the port this afternoon confirmed my suspicion that, particularly since the port area has been declared a closed military zone, an outsider could hardly gain any information on what is contained in the loads that are transferred straight from the trains to the ships. We would need an insider for that.

"No. What Berlin needs to know most urgently are numbers of troops being shipped across the Channel to fight. And one of the principal ports being used is Folkestone. How far is that from Dover? —it can't be more than ten miles. It should not be difficult for you two to meet up."

"Folkestone!" gasped Flo. "You want me to go to Folkestone? Where would I live? What about the children?"

"I was going to come to that," replied Hurst. "But it's getting late. I suggest that first I brief Cyril here on what to look out for, what we need to know, how to be careful and so on. Then tomorrow you and I talk about what you should do."

While he and Cyril talked, Flo went upstairs to see Joanna. The little girl's forehead was cooler, but she looked so pale, thin, and ill that Flo almost burst into tears.

"Whatever shall we do?" she whispered, stroking the child's arm gently. "How can I save you all?"

When she came down again, Cyril was telling Hurst about his encounter with Jose Weiss and Fred Handley Page.

"Airplanes are going to have an important role in this war," Hurst said. "Let us know everything you can about airfields being built, the numbers of planes there and anything about new types if you see them. And anything you can learn about the Royal Flying Corps and—what's it called? the RNAS—the Navy's air service—and their war plans …"

Flo excused herself and went to bed.

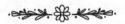

By the next morning Flo had decided she could not go to Folke-stone. What would happen to the children?

"It's just not possible," she told Hurst once Cyril had left and the older children were at school. "I would have to rent somewhere to live; here, at least, we have our own home, the children have their school and their friends, and I have some patients, even though I don't earn enough from them for us all to live on."

Hurst motioned her to calm down. "Don't worry, Mrs. Harris. Now just listen to me." And he outlined his plan.

She was to take a job as a live-in nurse in a household near the harbour in Folkestone. He took a copy of *The Lady* magazine out of his briefcase and gave it her. "This has just come out. There are two advertisements for posts in Folkestone, both of them not far from the harbour. That way you would be able to keep count of the troops embarking for France.

"I suggest you write to them immediately, telling them all the nursing experience you have had to date. And here," diving into his briefcase again, "is a map of Folkestone, which you will find very useful."

"But the children …" Flo began.

"One consequence of the arrests last month was that we now have more to spend on our remaining collaborators. I can offer you ten pounds a week. Of course, if Cyril is able to contribute, we will make additional payments. You can decide between you how much of that you will pass on to him."

Ten pounds! On top of what she would earn nursing! Flo could hardly believe it. That would solve all her problems, and she would probably be able to put some aside for the future.

"So, you are agreed?"

She paused. "Yes."

"In that case, you must take an oath of loyalty to the Kaiser and swear that you will never divulge anything that has passed between us, anything about your activities on behalf of the Fatherland, anything about anyone who might help you in your work. Your son has already taken this oath. Then I will teach you how to operate."

What have I done? thought Flo as she put the Bible back on the shelf. *I've sworn to serve this country's enemy. Papa would have been proud, but I feel terrible. But then, the money …*

Hurst gave her no time to reflect. "Now, in your agreement with your employer you must make sure that you have a certain amount of free time each day during which you will be able to go out. The units being shipped to France normally assemble along a parade called The Leas. You are to note the regiments and make as close an estimate as you can of the numbers. Then—and this may be more difficult—you must try and find out their destination in Belgium or France. It is quite likely they will not have been told.

"You must memorise the details precisely, which I am sure you won't find difficult. On no account must you be seen writing them down, mind. Then you must send this information to us."

"And how am I supposed to do that?" asked Flo.

"We have arranged a totally safe and reliable way for your reports to reach Germany. But first, I will teach you the skills you will need.

"First of all, you must learn to write with," he paused dramatically as if inviting an excited response, "invisible ink."

"Oh, you mean lemon juice?" Flo said. "Frank and his friends learned how to do that from a boys' magazine."

"Lemon juice!" Hurst spat out scornfully. "How primitive! If British spies are using that, they will lose the war in weeks. No, our German scientists have developed much more sophisticated materials which are virtually impossible for the enemy to read unless they know what chemicals are in them. I am going to give you not one, but two, both of which have the advantage of fitting in perfectly with the accoutrements of a nurse."

He took a small phial out of his pocket and passed it to her. The label read "The laxative. Five drops before retiring."

"This contains a substance which, believe it or not, can be used quite safely as a laxative," he said. "Of course you won't use it for that, but should it ever be questioned ... Now if for some reason you are not in a position to use that, I have an alternative for you. For this I will need one of your white collars or a cap. I will treat it with certain chemicals including starch. It will look no different from the others you have but if you need a fallback, all you do is soak it in a small amount of water. You can then use the solution as invisible ink."

"Amazing!" exclaimed Flo. "Do I use a normal pen?"

"Better not," was the reply. "A steel nib could leave scratches on the paper. A slightly blunted toothpick or even a matchstick would be better."

"I have a little ivory toothpick that a guest once left here. Would that do?" asked Flo.

"Just the thing. And try to use a cheaper, rougher type of writing paper so that it absorbs the liquid better.

"Then once you have finished you steam the whole sheet of paper, over a kettle for instance. That makes it more difficult for the enemy to expose the writing."

"Now your number. It is S7F. The S is for South—the south of England—and F is for Folkestone. Don't forget it. Always put it at the beginning of every message."

"Who are the other six? Or eight or whatever it is?" asked Flo.

"Don't concern yourself with that. You are not to know anything about our network and anyone else in it apart from me. Now the important thing is that you do not send these letters through the mail."

"So how do I send them then?"

"Because of the war the civilian communications across the channel are few and highly precarious. But ferries from Folkestone to Vlissingen in Holland are still running fairly regularly."

"Vlissingen?" queried Flo. "I've never heard of it."

"Oh no," Hurst corrected himself. "Here you call it Flushing. I will tell you more about that aspect when you are settled in Folkestone. So that's it," he concluded. "Here are £25 to see you through the first few days. Now you must get to Folkestone as quickly as possible."

"But the children! What shall I do about them?" Flo suddenly remembered. She had been so carried away by the thought of the money that she had forgotten her greatest concern.

Hurst looked exasperated. He had evidently forgotten them too. "Mrs. Harris, you must find a solution for your children as fast as you can. The war will not wait for you. There is no time to lose."

Flo was miserable. Her four darling young ones; she could not bear to part with them. She racked her brains, desperate for a solution. Lizzie, she knew, would not be able to look after them. Impoverished herself after the death of their father, she was shortly to take up a post as housekeeper in a Dorset family.

Klaus and June Frantzen next door were usually able to mind the children for a few hours, but June had a weak heart and would not be able to cope with four lively youngsters day after day, week after week. Even with her new income, boarding school for four would be out of the question. So, of course, were Waifs and Strays and similar institutions—when Cyril finally told her about the reign of terror at the Coopers' she had been horrified and sworn that, no matter what fate befell her, no child of hers would ever end up in a place like that again.

Distraught, she crept up to the attic and quietly opened the door. In the faint moonlight coming through the dormer window, she could just make out the shapes of the three sleeping children. There, spreadeagled under his blankets, was Frank, the son of her heart. Such a sunny, generous nature, so different from Cyril, who seemed increasingly troubled, not to mention Godfrey ... And, curled up on the other side, Prue and Mollie—Prue had taken after her and was going to be the beauty of the family, where Mollie with her dark hair and rounder face looked more like Francis. They were both quiet, obedient girls, good at housework, who gave no trouble. They were all so young, so defenceless. What was to become of them?

Her heart breaking, she padded silently downstairs to look in on Joanna, the youngest, the liveliest, and brightest. She felt her way over to the bed and gently touched the child's forehead. It felt cool now, thank heaven, but that did not solve the problem. She was still very weak, and the doctor had warned that it would take a long time for her to recover.

As she crept back down to the kitchen, Flo remembered the kind Mrs. Snodgrass who had been a good friend to her in Warley and with whom she had kept in contact, exchanging

Christmas cards and odd scraps of news. Mrs. Snodgrass was a member of numerous charitable committees, she remembered, and knew much about the world of philanthropy. She returned to the kitchen, sat down and quickly penned a letter to her, explaining that her "second husband" had died and that she had to resume nursing to be able to support the children. Did she know of any suitable establishment which could look after them for the time being, stressing "with love and kindness"?

A reply came by return of post. Mrs. Snodgrass was so sorry to hear of her husband's death and Flo's plight. She suggested that she might consider a new place she had heard of in the north of England which seemed very promising. It had been founded and was run by an energetic Scottish joiner-philanthropist, James Dixon, and his wife, Jane, who had been appalled at the plight of destitute children in those grim northern industrial towns and took in, not only those who had lost both parents, but also many whose surviving parent was unable to support them. It was very humane, she had heard, not like certain places she could mention. The children were cared for well, they went to the local school, and when they left at the age of fourteen, they were not just put out on the streets again, as so often happened, but found jobs, the boys as apprentices in good firms, the girls usually as maids in reputable households. "It's very modern," she wrote. "I have heard very good reports of the Dixons' work."

But the orphanage was in a place in Lancashire called Blackburn, far, far away. How would she ever be able to go and visit them? She was in an agony of indecision. But if it was really better than the grim orphanages she had heard of on the south coast, would it not be the best solution? She had no time to explore further, as she had to make up her mind. Her hand shaking, she wrote a letter to the Dixons, asking them if they could take Frank and the two older girls, saying that their father had died and that she had to return to full-time nursing in order to support them all.

Mrs. Dixon replied that they would be happy to accommodate her three children and that they could come as soon as was convenient. But how could she get them there? Hurst had written insisting that Flo get to Folkestone immediately, so there was no time to take them to Blackburn. In desperation, Flo set Lizzie a telegram asking if, before she took up her housekeeping post, she would accompany the children to Blackburn. Lizzie, God bless her, was on the doorstep the next day.

The parting at the station was excruciating. "It's only for a short time, my darlings," Flo tried to assure them time and again through her tears. "You will like it there; it's going to be a great adventure." The girls, in particular, were inconsolable. It was all the kindly guard could do to persuade them to get into the train and Flo to stay on the platform, so he could shut the carriage door and blow his whistle.

There remained the even more heart-wrenching problem of Joanna. But Flo had an idea. On her way home from the station she knocked on the door of Anna Marks, a married former nurse she knew who, childless herself, had taken in a couple of foster children to eke out her husband's income. Anna's wet apron, rolled-up sleeves, and sweaty face as she answered the door showed that she was busy doing the washing, but she was glad to invite Flo in for a chat. Over a cup of tea, Flo confessed to Anna that she was in financial difficulties and was forced to take a live-in post in Folkestone. She was desperate to find someone who would care for little Joanna while she convalesced—would Anna be willing to look after her until she was well enough to join the others at the orphanage?

Anna thought for a while. "Yes, of course I will, my dear," she concluded. "But you know," she added craftily, "because she will need nursing for a while, Nick will insist that I am paid double the usual rate. In advance." Double! Flo was taken aback, but after a moment's thought saw she had no choice. Hurst's £25 was dwindling fast, and she had not left Littlehampton yet.

Flo's last memory of Littlehampton was half-carrying the sickly child, both of them weeping bitterly, to Anna's house and another heart-rending farewell.

Can anything be worse than parting with your children? Flo wondered miserably.

Chapter 26

On the London and North Western Railway

T he children lolled on their seats, silent and exhausted, swaying passively with the lurching of the train. The light was fading and Mollie and Prue, in the window seats, stared out in dismay at desolate landscape of dark, barren moors, interrupted only by the odd village of blackened stone houses. Aunt Lizzie dozed under the dim carriage light, her hands clasped over the handbag on her lap, her spectacles sliding down her nose. Frank, pale and unusually sombre, riffled listlessly through a boys' magazine he had read many times before.

It was now thirteen hours since their wrenching separation from their mother at the station in Littlehampton. All had been in tears, including Flo, who was strongly tempted to call everything off and keep them with her. Only the memory of their pitiful breakfast and the knowledge that she had nothing left to give them to eat made her steel herself to say goodbye.

Lizzie and the children had needed to change trains three times, in London, Manchester, and Preston. In London, they had even had to change stations. Each change had taken them further away from Flo, their home, and their friends. And especially from their beloved little sister, Joanna, who was so weak she could hardly sit up to say goodbye.

Mollie and Prue had cried all the way to London, then the cab ride from Victoria station to Euston had distracted them for a while. Now the sight of the bleak, darkening landscape sent Prue into floods of tears again. "Where are we going? It's frightening out there. I want to go back to Mama," she sobbed.

"Don't worry, my dear," Aunt Lizzie said soothingly, "it can't be far now. And you will love it when you get there."

It was another hour before they finally stood, shivering, in front of a large, heavy wooden door while Aunt Lizzie pulled the rope of a loud bell which echoed through the building. They could just make out the outlines of a huge, grey stone house looming over them in the dark.

The door opened and they heard people talking in strange accents they had never heard before.

"Yer late," a woman said. "One lad, two lasses—is this the Harris lot?"

Aunt Lizzie was asked to fill out a number of forms while the children were sat down and given glasses of hot milk, then taken to a storeroom where they were given small piles of clothes—long, dark dresses with equally long, white, sleeveless pinafores for the girls and black knickerbocker pants and jackets with white collars for Frank. After a long and tearful farewell to their aunt, they numbly let themselves be led away, Mollie and Prue to a girls' dormitory, Frank to a boys', where the other children were already sleeping.

They were in Blackburn Orphanage, situated a couple of miles outside the black cotton town in a small village called Wilpshire.

It was cold and spartan and at first Mollie, who had read *Jane Eyre*, feared that they had landed in a place like Lowood

School. She was terrified that they would be subjected to the torments and humiliations inflicted on Jane. She need not have worried. Although extremely austere, it was, as Mrs. Snodgrass had told Flo, considerably more humane than the "Lowoods" of the day. The children had to scrub floors and work in the kitchen, but they got an education at a local school and had sizeable grounds to play in. The Dixons were kind, although when they were not around, some of the other staff were much less so, and the cane still awaited those who misbehaved.

Chapter 27

Folkestone, 1914

A tumultuous scene greeted Flo as she descended from the train at Folkestone. A mass of pale, bewildered-looking people speaking strange languages milled around, some in rags, some well-dressed, some lugging large bundles, others with live chickens and dogs, and mothers with their arms round weeping children. From a large table set up to one side, local ladies were handing out sandwiches and mugs of hot tea and trying, in loud, slow English or broken French, to welcome and organise them. Male voices with Irish, Scottish, and northern accents rose above the noise as groups of young soldiers in khaki uniforms, their kit bags slung over their shoulders, threaded the way through the crowd while travelers tried to make sense of the loud and barely intelligible announcements blaring through the station's loudspeaker. Flo quickly bought two postcards and hurried out of the station to find a quiet spot where she could ask someone the way to The Leas.

She had received replies to both her applications for the post of live-in nurse, asking her to come for an interview. But one, signed by a Matilda Lawson, interested her in particular because the address was on The Leas, where Hurst had said the troops assembled before shipment to the Continent. When she arrived there, she saw that the street was in fact a large and elegant promenade on top of a steep rise over the sea, with a bandstand, gardens, and big hotels. The house, large, white, and very handsome, had a superb view of the sea and the harbour down below. And along the street a long line of soldiers was marching, singing, in the direction of the harbour. *There they are!* she thought in amazement. She could hardly believe her luck. *Oh, I how I do hope these people take me on!*

Her fingers tightly crossed, she rang the bell.

"Nurse Harris? I'm Matilda Lawson." A tall, middle-aged woman strode purposefully into the parlour where Flo had been told to wait. She was wearing a nurse's uniform. Flo must have looked puzzled as she shook the outstretched hand.

"I'm in the VADs," Matilda Lawson explained. "In fact, I'm in charge of our local group and this is partly why we need someone to look after our mother. We have our hands full, as you can imagine, helping the poor Belgian refugees."

"Ah, that is who they are!" Flo exclaimed. "I saw a whole crowd of them at the station."

"Yes, poor things. There are even more at the harbour—thousands and thousands of them. They need everything, food, clothes, a roof over their heads. We feel so sorry for them, as they have been through such terrible things; I can't even bear to think about it. We have just brought a family to live here on the top floor, acquaintances, actually, so James and Dora and the maids have had to rearrange the rooms. But I may not be here for much longer, our group may well be sent over to care for the wounded soldiers somewhere in Belgium. My brother and his regiment are already over there.

"The problem is that my mother is becoming frailer and needs someone constantly around her, not least for moral support—she is so dreadfully worried about my brother and probably would be about me too, if I am sent out there. She suffers very badly from rheumatism. I see from your letter you have quite a lot of experience."

Flo opened her handbag and took out her letters of recommendation, from Francis himself, Dr. Willoughby, and Dr. Richards all praising her skills as a nurse, as well as the certificate qualifying her to run a nursing home.

"That is very encouraging," Mrs. Lawson said after glancing through them. "We have had a couple of applicants who had no experience whatever. I could not let them near my mother."

She looked at Flo's uniform. "Did you never think of joining the VADs?"

"I would have liked to," replied Flo, "but I can't afford to volunteer. My husband died in April and left me with our four young children and nothing to live on."

"I'm so sorry," Matilda said, her voice softening. "Where are the children now?"

Tears welled up in Flo's eyes. "I had to put them in a home, an orphanage," she said, choking and fishing for a handkerchief.

"Oh, my dear," said Matilda soothingly, reaching out to stroke her hand. "Poor you, I'm so very sorry. You must be heartbroken. Your poor children!"

Matilda seemed happy with Flo's recommendations and declared that she was prepared to engage her as a nurse-companion for her mother on a month's trial basis— "on condition, of course, that my mother agrees. Let's go and see her now."

Mrs. Clementine Appleby, ensconced in a wicker armchair on the veranda overlooking the beautifully kept garden, was as charming as Laura Darnley had been odious. She was thin, bent, and very deaf, but she had bright, lively eyes and a sweet smile.

"Nurse Harris has a lot of experience looking after people. Her husband has just died so she has to go back to work. If you like, she could come for a month's trial to see how you get on!" her daughter shouted into her ear.

"Welcome, my dear," the old lady said to Flo, smiling. "If my daughter likes you, I'm sure I will too."

The three of them quickly agreed on her pay and free time—Sundays and the usual hours between two and four o'clock in the afternoon. She was introduced to Dora, the buxom, competent-looking housekeeper and James, the elderly manservant, who showed her to her room which, since the attic rooms in the top of the house were now the preserve of the refugees, was a converted storeroom in the basement. Flo smiled to herself, remembering her room, also a former storeroom, in the Darnley household.

Mrs. Appleby's needs were not burdensome. She required help in dressing and bathing, moving around the house, and having things fetched and carried. Flo had to see she took her few medicines punctually and correctly, but it seemed that her main task was to keep the older lady company. She was pleased to hear that she loved being taken for walks in her somewhat cumbersome leather bath chair—a good way, she hoped, of seeing what was going on in the town.

"I hope you will have dinner with us tonight," Mrs. Appleby said to Flo's great surprise. "If we are lucky, my son Richard will be able to join us. He leaves with his regiment for the front tomorrow. And the Janssens will be with us. We want to make them feel as much at home as possible. We are on a war footing now, you know, my dear, and we must to adjust our lives accordingly."

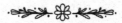

The atmosphere as they began dinner that evening was sombre. The Belgian guests were a well-to-do family from Antwerp who had fled when the German army swarmed into Belgium.

"Mrs. Janssens' husband," Matilda told Flo quietly, indicating the elderly lady sitting at Mrs. Appleby's right, "was a shipowner, like my late father." She nodded in the direction of the large portrait in oils of a distinguished-looking man with a bald head and a bushy beard hanging over the fireplace. "They had been business acquaintances, so it was natural that Mrs. Janssens should contact us as soon as they arrived in Folkestone.

"The lady next to you, also Mrs. Janssen, is her daughter-in-law and those are her

children." "Those" were a girl of about sixteen, pale and with what looked like dark bruises on her face, who seemed to have no interest in eating, and a young man of about nineteen wearing an unfamiliar uniform.

"Gerrit is an officer in the Belgian army and escaped with some men from his unit when Antwerp fell. He had no idea where his family was until he bumped into them quite by chance here at the harbour. Isn't that amazing?" Matilde added, louder this time so that her Belgian guests could hear.

"And he is returning as soon as he can to fight the Germans," Gerrit rejoined in excellent English.

"No, Gerrit, no!" pleaded his mother and continued to remonstrate in Flemish.

The Belgians had obviously already recounted their experiences to their hosts, and no one seemed inclined to repeat them for Flo's benefit. The conversation was limited to discussion of the organisations being formed to help the refugees and how those around the table could take part.

Suddenly James, with a broad smile, held the door open and, with a breezy "Good evening, all," in walked Richard Appleby. With a cheerful collective wave to all present, a comradely slap on the back for Gerrit, and an affectionate kiss for his delighted mother, he sat down in the empty chair that had been kept for him. He was chubby faced, of medium height but slightly plump, and a natural comedian with a sly, infectious smile that made anything he said seem amusing. Richard was much younger than Matilda, born long after his parents had given up hope of a male heir, and the apple of his mother's eye. He was a lieutenant in the Buffs, the East Kent Regiment, but despite his uniform, he seemed for all the world simply a merry, carefree, young son of the house. Before long he had everyone, even Antje, laughing. Flo liked him immensely.

Later, after she had helped Mrs. Appleby change and put her to bed, Flo retired to her room and took out the postcards she had bought at the station. They were views of Folkestone harbour. One she addressed to Cyril at his unit in Dover, giving her new address. On the other she wrote "Lovely weather. Wish you were here." Underneath, with her ivory toothpick, she wrote out carefully the address of the Appleby house in invisible ink. She would post them in her free time tomorrow.

"You will be having an affair with the first mate of the Flushing ferry," Hurst said in a low voice and paused, smiling, to see the effect of his announcement on Flo. She was floored.

"What do you mean? What do you think I am? I'm a respectable woman!" she exclaimed indignantly.

"Keep your voice down, even here." He looked round to see if there was anyone on nearby boats who might have been able to hear.

They were sitting in the tiny cabin of a small fishing boat moored in the harbour. It smelled of tar and pipe smoke but not, Flo noticed, of fish, although there were nets piled up everywhere. It looked like so many other fishing vessels that she had seen in and around the harbour. There was a neat bunk bed in the stern, a clean mug on a shelf, but no personal objects or any sign of who it might belong to. Yet Hurst was dressed in a rough navy jersey and shabby navy trousers stuffed into rubber boots and looked for all the world like just another fisherman.

"Is this your boat?" she asked.

"Let's say I use it sometimes," answered Hurst and, cutting off any further questions on the subject, returned to the business at hand.

"Now you are not to be alarmed," he went on quietly "You only have to pretend. Dan Schuil is a respectable married man—I believe, happily married—with children in Holland. But he is working for us, and he is prepared to pretend to be having an affair with a woman here: you.

"You will meet up with him when he is here, have drinks, go for walks, whatever, and from time to time go to a little hotel with him. You don't need to do anything there, of course, but if anyone is watching you or him, it will make it all the more convincing.

Now, how to pass messages to us. This is not easy because British agents are swarming all over these ferries and they search the ship, the crew, and the passengers very, very thoroughly."

He felt in his pocket and pulled out two half-crown coins. He put one on the little table and very gently pulled at the other with the fingers of both hands until it opened like a little tin box. Inside it was hollow, with a couple of tiny dots of dark metal stuck to the inner surface.

"These are bits of lead to give it its proper weight," he explained.

"You will write your messages on small pieces of tissue paper—do you have tissue paper?"

Flo nodded. There was plenty in the Appleby house.

"Then when the ink is dry you fold it up as small as you can, without damaging it, place it inside the coin and close it, like this.

"Now Dan will bring over your pay in instalments, in pounds, shillings, and pence—not Dutch guilders, don't worry. You will pass him one of these half-crowns with your message inside it. That, of course, is in case anyone should see this transaction, though you should take care that they don't. It would never be noticed if Dan were searched on the ship.

"The ship, the *Mecklenburg,* comes to Folkestone overnight twice a week, arriving on Tuesdays and Fridays. For now, at least, though, the war is complicating matters greatly. If you don't see it in the harbour those mornings, pass by the company's office on the quay. They will be bound to have the arrival time posted on a board.

"Your first meeting will be at 2:30 p.m. at the Mole Café over there. Then he will take you to a small hotel he knows, you will give him the coin with your message and, in future, he will give you back the first coin while you give him the second. And you can arrange your meeting place for the next time. It would be advisable to meet always in different places. Also, very importantly, he will convey to you any messages from us.

"If anything goes wrong, you are to contact me immediately by mail. But not at the previous address. Use this one," he said, taking out a small, folded piece of tissue paper, putting it in one of the coins and handing it to her. "Memorise it and burn the paper as soon as you get home.

"And finally, if you should get caught—which is very unlikely as you have an excellent cover—you must deny everything. No matter what proof they may have against you, deny, deny, deny."

Chapter 28

It was not easy for Flo to adjust to being an employee again after several years as head of a small nursing home, owner of her own house, employer of at least one maid, and mother of a sizeable family. She often had to bite her tongue and accept the ways of her employers and the household in general without trying to change them. She had to remind herself to be thankful that Mrs. Appleby had such a sweet nature and that James, Dora, and the maids were decent, reasonable people. Her main worry at the moment was how on earth she was going to be able to do the tasks Hurst was requiring of her.

It turned out to be easier than she had feared.

She was getting on well with Matilda Lawson who clearly respected her and had immediately suggested that she might spend her free afternoons helping out down at the harbour where she and her unit were looking after the crowds of Belgian refugees who were arriving in boats. Flo jumped at the idea, as it would enable her to have a good look at the harbour where at the same time thousands of troops were embarking ships taking them to the Continent. As soon as she could, she walked down to the port and was pleased by her first discovery: the police and others took one look at her uniform and immediately let her through. *This is going to be very useful*, she thought.

The scene at the station had been quiet compared with what seemed at first like chaos on the quays where swarms of people were arriving, crammed into fishing smacks, private sailing boats, tugs towing barges, perilously overloaded steamers—anything that floated. They were pitiful, many were weeping for loved ones left behind, others were injured and in rags, escaping from who-knew-what violence, and lost and traumatised children. Some had brought their animals with them, bedding, household items. And there were many soldiers, many of them wounded.

Townsfolk—like everyone else in the country—had been appalled at the German invasion of plucky little Belgium, and despite requests to stay away, many had flocked to the harbour to give them food and drink, toys, flowers, and above all, to invite them to stay in their homes. The volunteers were still struggling to set up a system by which the arrivals could be fed and looked after while their needs were ascertained and accommodation found. The efforts were hampered somewhat by the fact that few of the volunteers spoke any French and even fewer Flemish.

Close by was a group that were tending to the sick and injured. Bad cases were being dispatched to the many hospitals that were being set up in hotels, nursing homes and large country houses in the area, while lesser injuries were being tended to on the spot. Flo immediately joined this group and busied herself washing and bandaging injured limbs and comforting hurt and crying children while trying to keep an eye on the troop departures from the long arm of the harbour which carried a railway and a road out into the sea, far beyond the parts where smaller vessels moored, and where trains brought passengers directly to the ships. She could see the soldiers, many new and hastily trained recruits with their rifles and heavy kit bags, lining up on the long quay, sometimes grabbing some tea and cake at the Mole Café there, then piling into repurposed cross-channel steamers still manned by the crews that had taken travellers to and from the Continent before the war. She saw how the horses were led into the ships by a different route, and how some of the people boarding were nurses or civilian volunteers, many of them women, who would act as drivers or other support staff to free the troops to fight. Occasionally, a steamer would arrive with wounded soldiers who were taken off to designated hospitals, and sometimes with heavily-guarded groups of men in foreign uniforms—German prisoners of war.

Flo decided that she would come and help at the harbour every afternoon that she was not meeting Dan, it would give her a close-up view of the troop departures. At first, it all seemed extremely bewildering, but slowly, putting together her observations of marching troops on The Leas and the departures of laden ships from the harbour, she managed to calculate roughly the numbers of men who left each day, escorted across the Channel by Navy warships. She had told Hurst she would never be able to provide exact figures, and he had understood.

Everyone in the Appleby house was becoming worried about Mrs. Janssen's daughter, Antje. She was thin and looked ill, said scarcely a word, and only picked at her food during their, by now, routine collective dinners. Her mother and grandmother tried to induce her to eat, but she was scarcely able to force down a mouthful. Flo tried to give advice but in vain.

"Why don't we call Dr. Evans?" suggested Matilda. "There must be something wrong with the poor girl." But Antje would not have it.

One evening after supper, the younger Mrs. Janssen asked Flo if she would come up to their rooms for a moment.

"Nurse, please, please can you help us?" Mrs. Janssen said in a near-whisper as she closed the door of their little makeshift living room behind them. "You should know … something terrible happened. We were in our summer house, in the country … the soldiers come. They are drunk, they come into our house, they take things, they break furniture. They find Antje and …" She stopped, unable to speak.

For a moment Flo was puzzled, then she realised the horror of what Mrs. Janssens was trying to say. Instinctively, she put her arm round the sobbing woman. "Oh, no! How terrible!"

"I … I … could not help her. They had guns …" She made the gesture of pointing a pistol at herself. "Then they set fire to the house, and we run … and run."

Flo was shattered. Silently, she held the woman to her until the sobbing had subsided.

"And now, Antje …" Mrs. Janssens put her hands on her belly. "German baby."

"German?" Flo stared at her in a moment of incomprehension.

"Of course, it was German soldiers!" Mrs. Janssens was astonished that Flo did not seem to understand. "They invade, they destroy Belgum! Now Antje … she is desperate. She want to kill herself. We are Catholic, but this, this is different. God will forgive! Nurse, please help!"

Flo had no time to ponder. She was being confronted with a situation that was all too familiar. Time and again, girls and women, afraid, ashamed, or simply too poor to go to a doctor, had begged her to help them have an abortion. It was illegal, of course, but it was far more common than anyone would ever admit. There were various pills on the market, typically advertised as being beneficial for women's health, but which many knew were designed to bring on miscarriages. If the pills failed, as they often did, she would advise them to go to one of the better back-street abortionists but had always flatly refused to perform an abortion herself, painfully aware of the dangers both for the patient and for her own reputation.

"Don't worry, Mrs. Janssens. I will do whatever I can. Can I speak to Antje?"

Antje was lying listlessly on her bed, staring at the ceiling, her face swollen from crying. The bruises on her face had faded, but she still was a pitiful sight. Flo wanted to cry but forced herself to act the reliable, reassuring nurse who Antje could trust absolutely. She sat on the bed and took the girl's hand. "Don't worry, my dear, you will be fine. I'll bring you some medicine tomorrow. It will make you a bit poorly, but then it will be gone, and you will have your life back again."

She was not certain how much Antje understood but the girl smiled wanly and gave her hand a feeble squeeze.

"Try and persuade her to eat," she told her mother. "Tell her she needs to get her strength back as quickly as she can."

The pills made Antje very ill. She was running a high fever, vomiting, and moaning that her head hurt terribly. Flo was rushing up and down the stairs, tending to Mrs. Appleby and trying whatever she could to relieve Antje's suffering. Once she had put the older lady to bed, she went upstairs again and joined the girl's mother and grandmother at her bedside. She stayed there all night, bathing her forehead, holding her hand, and whispering encouragement. In the early hours of the morning, the pains and the bleeding began. The next hours were almost as traumatic for the three women as for the girl. She was white and so feeble she had to be lifted from her bed. They began to fear she was dying and asked themselves if they should call a doctor—knowing they could face the direst consequences. But finally, the worst was over. Antje lay comatose on her bed. Flo took her pulse and found it reassuring.

"Let her rest. She will be bleeding for some time, but she is safe now," she told the other two. "As soon as she is able to drink, give her some Liebig meat broth, and ask cook to make her some gruel. I will keep coming up to see how she is."

There was only an hour left before she was due to wake Mrs. Appleby. She threw herself on her bed, exhausted, but was too shaken by the night's events to think of taking a nap. Until now, it had never occurred to her to think what war was really like. But now, here in this house alone, was a young girl who had been raped, a family that had been forced to flee, and down in the harbour, she had seen countless others escaping who-knew-what other horrors that were taking place not so far away. She began to feel uneasy.

Almost every day, the residents along The Leas were treated to loud renderings of "It's a Long Way to Tipperary," or "Men of Harlech," and the sound of marching feet as columns of young soldiers with their packs headed along The Leas and then, shortening their stride, down the The Slope, the steep descent towards the harbour. They were merry, these young recruits, eager for the adventure ahead, fueled by urgings to "do their bit" for the war effort, to "give the Hun a bloody nose" and be back in time for Christmas.

Mrs. Appleby would wave and call, "Good luck, boys!" as Flo pushed her bath chair along The Leas. If they came to a unit which had not yet been drawn up in formation, Mrs. Appleby would hand out chocolates and sometimes woolen socks that she had knitted and would chat with them, which gave the recruits an opportunity to flirt with Flo, and Flo a chance to find out more about them.

"Off to gay Paree, you lucky fellows!" she would tease them.

"No such luck," would be the reply and then sometimes the name of their Belgian or French destination.

The evening before the arrival of the ferry from Flushing she would cut out a square of tissue paper and write out the approximate number of troops, the name of their units, and, where possible, their destination. She marvelled at the numbers. Tens of thousands of young men, cheerful as if setting out for a great adventure, were heading off to the Low Countries. She did not ask herself what would happen to them when they got there.

Christmas was approaching, and it would be the children's first away from home. Oh, if only they could be together! Flo had always tried to make it a special time, full of treats and surprises, with a tree laden with decorations, paper streamers across the rooms, sprigs of holly over the pictures on the wall, and plenty of good things to eat. The children were always enchanted, Cyril was always there, and last year, after their father had died, Lizzie had been there too.

She wondered what Christmas would be like at the orphanage. She had written often but had not yet been able to go to see them. It was hard to tell from their brief, childish letters whether they were really happy—or at least not unhappy—in their unaccustomed surroundings. At least they did not report any ill-treatment. She could only rely on Mrs. Snodgrass's recommendation and tried not to worry. She knitted them warm scarves and gloves and while she was packing them, in the fond hope that it would remind them of Christmas at home, she popped several mince pies into the parcel.

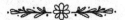

As it happened, the three older children had adapted reasonably well to life in the institution. Their files recorded them as intelligent, well-brought-up children, willing and good at the housework required of them—Flo had trained them to clean house and help prepare their frugal meals after Margie was dismissed. Frank, with his sunny, outgoing nature, was loved by the staff, devoted to his sisters, and took particular care of little Joanna, who, having supposedly recovered from her illness, had joined them a couple of weeks earlier. Joanna was desperately unhappy. Contrary to Flo's expectations, Anna and her husband had been cold and uncaring and made little effort to help her recover. June Frantzen, who had visited her one day, had been alarmed to find her still so pale and visibly miserable and had reported to Flo that, if there were no better alternative, her youngest should at least be close to her brother and sisters. Thin and still weak, she had arrived a couple of weeks earlier, and although relieved to be close to Frank and her sisters, she was no happier. She deeply resented being abandoned—as she saw it—by Flo; she had hated Anna and her husband, and now she hated the orphanage. Her one escape, she soon saw, was in school—in study and reading. Any book she could lay her hands on—and there were far too few—she would devour in the evenings, standing directly under one of the dim electric light bulbs which was the only spot where there was enough light to read.

The Harris children were overjoyed when, a couple of days before Christmas, the parcel arrived from their mother, and they set about excitedly unpacking it. Alas, what met their eyes found was a sticky, crumbly, woolly mess: Flo had not thought to pack the mince pies properly. While the three older children discussed how to get mincemeat off the scarves, little Joanna burst into tears. For her, the contents of the parcel said everything about the bitter loss of her mother, her home, and her happy childhood. She howled and turned instinctively to the matron for a cuddle but was shaken off.

"Cry more, pee less," was all the comfort she received.

Chapter 29

FOLKESTONE

F lo's first meeting with Dan Schuil was a little awkward at first. She was sitting in the café reading, at Hurst's suggestion, the *Daily Mail* so Dan could identify her—when a voice behind her said, "Darling, at last!" She turned and was taken aback to see a man in his late forties with ruddy face and a short, greying beard, wearing civilian clothes. She had somehow expected someone younger, wearing a seaman's uniform.

He put his arm round her shoulders and kissed her. "Try to look pleased to see me," he whispered in her ear. "We're supposed to be lovers."

Flo laughed and took the cue. She flirted and chatted animatedly, reaching out to hold his hand, looking longingly into his eyes. After they had finished their tea, he said in a low voice, "Let's go to the hotel. Don't be afraid—business purposes only."

The receptionist at the little hotel in a back street was clearly accustomed to unmarried couples, although he looked a little puzzled to see a guest in a nurse's uniform. Once in their room, Schuil locked the door and immediately became cool and businesslike.

"You have something for me?" he asked.

Flo reached into her purse and gave him the half-crown with her first message inside.

"Good," he said, pocketing it and giving her a five-pound note, the first installment of her pay.

"Our friends want to know something. They have received reports that thousands of Russian troops have arrived in Scotland from Archangelsk and are making their way through Britain on their way to Antwerp. Have you heard anything about it?"

"Nothing at all," said Flo, who in the evenings usually read the newspapers that had arrived in the Appleby household.

"Sounds highly unlikely to me, but could you keep your eyes and ears open? They are quite worried about it."

"Of course. Tell me, what will you do with my reports when you get back to Flushing?"

"The less you know about that the better," said Schuil. "All I can say is that before long there will be *beep bip bip beep bip bip* on the wires to Antwerp and probably Berlin," imitating the Morse code.

They chatted on for some time in low voices. Schuil told her he had agreed to work for the Germans because his father's import-export firm had gone bankrupt. All his assets had been seized and they were about to lose their family home. "The shock has completely broken my father. It is up to me and my brother to find enough money to save it."

They made an appointment to meet again at another café the following Tuesday and left the hotel separately.

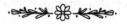

Soon after, she received a postcard from Cyril. It was a photograph of his company, well over 100 men in uniform, each face so small as to be almost unrecognizable. There was a cross under the fifth from the right in the first row—himself.

My dear Mater,
We've got lots of work down here and plenty of fun but unfortunately very seldom get any leave out of town. Love and kisses.

That meant, Flo deduced, that he would not easily be able to come to Folkestone; she would have to try and get to Dover if he had information for her. That afternoon, she went to the station and inquired about the times of trains to Dover and back.

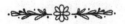

Flo was returning Mrs. Appleby to the house after their usual walk when they were met by Dora. "There's a telegram for you, Nurse" she announced. "I hope it's not bad news."

Flo opened it and read it.

3PM CAFE PRIORY STATION TOMORROW. CYRIL.

"It's my son, he wants to meet me in Dover. He must have a little free time, which is nice. He said his unit is very busy there."

"Oh, my dear, you must go," said Mrs. Appleby. "It will be lovely for you to see him. Don't worry if you are back a little late."

How lovely! thought Flo. *If this is spying, it is all very pleasant.*

She arrived in Dover a few minutes before three, found a table in the station café, and ordered herself a cup of tea. As on her arrival in Folkestone, the station was swarming with people of all descriptions but particularly young men in uniform. Soon, Cyril emerged from the crowd, hugged her, and sat down at the table, ordering a sausage roll and a large piece of cake.

"I'm so hungry," he said. "You could starve on the rations they give us. Listen, Mater," he went on. "I have only a few minutes, I've got to get back quickly. But I have something for you to pass on to you-know-who."

He dropped his voice and moved closer to Flo so she could hear.

"We have heard that the Germans are planning to send over airships—Zeppelins—to drop bombs."

"Oh, my God," exclaimed Flo in a whisper. "Do you think they might drop them on us? You mean they are going to bring the war over here?"

"They will try," said Cyril, "but we have got to stop them. So, we have had orders to train our searchlights not only on the sea but also up in the air to spot them before they reach us. Then we have to alert the fellows in the Flying Corps and the Naval Air service to shoot them down. And the artillery. They now have armoured cars with machine guns to chase them. That's what you can tell them."

"Searchlights in the sky," Flo repeated. "Zeppelins. That's easy to remember."

"And mobile machine guns," insisted Cyril. "You should see our emplacement," he went on eagerly, starting on the sausage roll. "We have these huge searchlights, like great drums, some-thing like a yard across, with parabolic mirrors inside and enormous carbon arc lights. You can't imagine how powerful they are. On a good night, they can pick out a ship eight or nine miles away. They are really dazzling, even from behind, and you have to be careful because you can bump into things and fall over things in the dark—generators, cables, telephone lines. It's not easy to maneuver them, and it will be a damn sight more difficult to look for airships with them. But it's exciting! Even though we are up much of the night, either on the early shift or the late shift," he added with a little less enthusiasm.

"I've heard they are setting up airfields around here too. When I know more about them, we can meet again. What do you say, Mater?"

He polished off the sausage roll and the cake and, with a couple of chocolate bars that Flo had brought him stuffed into in his pocket, he disappeared into the crowd again.

That evening, before going to bed, Flo got out her ivory toothpick and her little phial of "laxative" and began writing.

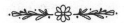

She had met up with Dan Schuil several times, in cafés or parks. They were getting practiced at pretending to be lovers and, when alone, exchanging messages and money behind a locked door, became good friends. Dan even hinted that they might even have a real affair. But Flo, although tempted, refused. "No more babies! It would be the end of me!"

One afternoon, Dan did not turn up at the appointed meeting place. Flo waited, growing increasingly anxious, then after an hour walked down to the offices of the Flushing ferry. Outside was a large sign "FLUSHING/FOLKESTONE SERVICE SUS-PENDED OWING TO ENEMY ACTION. FERRIES WILL ARRIVE/DEPART AT TILBURY."

Tilbury! The other side of London! How ever would they be able to meet up there? She would never be able to get there in the brief free hours she had. What ever should she do now? She wandered round the town in a state of agitation until all at once the penny dropped. Of course. Tell Peter Hurst.

She returned quickly to the house and wrote a quick note in invisible ink on the usual holiday postcard.

For several days she waited anxiously. Would the heart-warming flow of money—which she was squirrelling away as a bulwark against further disasters—dry up now? Her work was not onerous, in fact, it was sometimes quite interesting, and she felt reasonably safe. Would Hurst find a solution?

Finally, a letter arrived. It was typewritten and impersonal. She had an appointment at a certain doctor's surgery at 3 p.m.
Please bring documentation. PH.

The address was a large house containing doctors' and lawyers' offices. She arrived punctually and stood outside, uncertain what she should do.

"Nurse Harris, do you remember me?"

She turned and saw a white-haired man in a clergyman's dog-collar and dark coat standing behind her.

"Mr. Hurst, of course! How are you? How is your wife?" she improvised.

"Very well, thanks. She often talks about you and the wonderful care you took of her when she was so ill. And I have news—I now have a new parish, in Hampshire … Do you have time for a quick cup of tea?"

They strolled to a tea-room just up the street and Hurst led her to a far table where they could not be overheard. They ordered a pot of tea and some seed cake.

Sitting with his back to the rest of the tearoom, Hurst said in a low voice, "The news about the ferry was a big blow. We are still trying to find a good solution. In the meanwhile, you should do this: you should write to him at the poste restante at Tilbury—passionate love letters, please—with your reports in invisible ink on the back. He will send your money to you at the poste restante in Folkestone.

"It is not ideal. I have always tried to avoid the mail, knowing how His Majesty's secret service likes to keep a close eye on it, but it is the best we can do for the moment, while we try to set up a more secure route."

"I'm not sure I like that. It sounds dangerous!" Flo was alarmed.

"Don't worry. It would only be discovered if someone tipped off the security services. But since only you, I, and Dan Schuil know about it, that is extremely unlikely. Your reports are important, and Antwerp is very anxious to go on getting them. They are very pleased with what you have done so far."

"The message about the searchlights was thanks to my son, as you may have realized," said Flo, hoping to jog his memory that Cyril should be paid too.

"I am told the top brass were very interested in that dispatch and they are asking for even more information about airfields and the build-up of air defenses along the south coast. In view of this, I feel that Cyril needs to be more mobile, and I propose to give him some money so he can buy himself a motorcycle."

"I'm sure Cyril will be thrilled." Flo laughed. "He always wanted a motorbike."

"A second-hand one, I must hasten to add. Here ..." He reached for the menu, surreptitiously slid an envelope underneath, then nonchalantly pushed the menu over to Flo. "This should cover the cost of a good second-hand machine and it will bring you and Cyril up to date financially too. I believe you have something for me as well."

An envelope with the two coins and their contents inside crossed the table by the same route. Hurst excused himself and went to the toilet. When he returned, he dropped the empty coins into Flo's pocket. "You must keep these, you never know."

"I must be going," he said when they finished the tea.

"It was so nice to see you again," Flo said loudly, rising too. "Please remember me to your wife and your lovely children. And thank you for the tea." At the door they

shook hands again and parted, each going in a different direction.

Cyril was in heaven, roaring over the frosty Downs on his black Triumph motorbike, bought with Hurst's money from the brother of a pal in his unit. It was freezing cold, but he hardly noticed it, thrilled as he was by the racket it made and the speed at which he could tear along the country lanes, sending dogs and chickens flying. He had spent every moment of his scarce free time on it, roaming the countryside and pursuing his other passion: aircraft.

Airfields were popping up all over Kent from which the Royal Naval Air Service and the army's Royal Flying Corps would take off, the former to patrol the Channel, watching for enemy ships and submarines and the latter to conduct reconnaissance, fight enemy planes, and bomb enemy installations. Cyril particularly loved Swingate Down with its assembled aircraft and wooden huts and hangars close to Dover Castle. From here, in the first days of the war, sixty-four fragile biplanes had set out bravely across daunting expanse of the Channel to support the British Expeditionary Force in France. Because of his new-found mobility and his enthusiasm for flying, Cyril was able to persuade his superiors to let him act as informal liaison officer for non-urgent business—for air raid alarms they had telephone lines—with the squadron leaders. He was allowed to sit in the planes and occasionally, if he was lucky, be taken up in one. Thus he learned that a new airfield, or aerodrome as some called it, was being created at Walmer, to the east, where crack pilots were to protect shipping, that new and improved seaplanes were arriving in Dover where a skating rink had been converted into a slipway, that airships were being assembled and stationed at Capel-le-Ferne, half-way to Folkestone, that aircraft at Lympne were to defend London against German Zeppelins and Gotha bombers and so on. It amused him to appear unexpectedly at the Appleby house to pass on his latest gleanings and Mrs. Appleby, far from being annoyed, had taken quite a liking to him. On his way back, he would dream of becoming a pilot and wished he had joined Fred Handley Page's venture. Darnley had been wrong, there was quite clearly a great future in aviation. *Damn Darnley!* he thought, though he had to admit that flying was still very much a rich man's preserve, and an extremely dangerous one at that. So many pilots died in accidents and crashes. *Maybe*, he fantasised, *when the war is over ...*

As he returned to the camp, he saw a group of his companions standing staring out to sea. He went over to them. "What's going on?" he asked.

As long as he had been in Dover there had been plenty of going on in the Strait, both by night and day: ships laying mines, naval vessels patrolling on the watch for the enemy, protecting troopships and merchant vessels, and engaged in other war missions. But now there was even more activity, small fishing trawlers tugging something heavy, others stationary with the crews working at something Cyril could not make out.

"They are laying great steel nets under the water to stop German submarines," one of them said. "There is going to be a barrage of them all the way from here to France. That should make the Hun think twice about trying to get through the Channel."

I'll have to pay another visit to Mama tomorrow, thought Cyril.

Antje was recovering slowly but steadily. By now, Flo had become almost one of the Janssen family and spent many of her free moments up in their attic, chatting, her dimly remembered German helping her understand some words in Flemish. The two women were embarrassingly grateful for her help, and the older one tried to give her a diamond brooch that she had managed to save when they fled. But Flo refused to take it, knowing that they had left with so little and that it would doubtless one day become a family heirloom, a reminder of their life before the war.

Gerrit, too, was grateful. He spent most of his time out of the house, and Flo imagined he was training with his Belgian army comrades and preparing for their return to the war. Although he adored his younger sister, both he and his womenfolk were thankful that he was around very little during those difficult days. Flo liked Gerrit, as he was full of fun and enthusiasm, and his excellent English made it easy to talk.

One evening he was back relatively early and, as she and his family sat chatting in the little attic living room, Flo asked him when he expected to be sent back to Belgium to fight.

"Not for the moment," he said. "The others will go soon but some of us are working now with Captain Cameron down on Marine Parade, gathering all the intelligence we can from Belgium and France about what is going on in the war. There are some French comrades there too."

Flo pricked up her ears.

"How do you find out what is happening?"

"Oh, people escaping here in boats, secret communications. I'm not really allowed to say."

After she had said goodnight to the Janssens, Flo sat in her nightdress, her ivory toothpick and her little bottle of invisible ink at the ready, and pondered what she should put in her next message. Steinhauer's people would certainly be interested. After several minutes, she put them away again and slipped into bed. Somehow, she did not like the idea of telling the Germans what her friend Gerrit and his pals were up to.

Chapter 30

ANTWERP, BELGIUM

"Ah, thank goodness you've come," Commander von Schiller said as his deputy appeared at the door of his new office. Captain Boehnke had to weave his way past piles of boxes to get near his boss's desk. The commander made a sweeping gesture to encompass the whole room. "I'm supposed to be getting this outfit up and running and they haven't even got me shelves and cupboards to put all this stuff. My secretary is in despair. First, they send us from Berlin to Brussels, now from Brussels to here in Antwerp in the space of a year. They want us to be the biggest and most important of our intelligence centres, but how they imagine we can function while moving everything lock stock and barrel across the Continent at a moment's notice I really do not know. But orders are orders and here we are—in total confusion."

"Frankly, sir, you seem to be managing very well. I saw that the radio people are all set up and working hard downstairs."

"Well, yes, at least the dispatches have started coming in properly now. Have they found you somewhere to live?"

"Yes, a lovely big house in the centre. The people have obviously fled. They must have been pretty rich. Everything is just as they left it. I would like to bring my family here when the fighting stops."

"Don't make plans yet. By the look of it, the fighting is going to go on for several more months."

The commander looked at a clock which was still on the floor, propped up against the wall. "Look, I have to go and brief 111b, our army counterparts, on our latest dispatches from Britain. They still are very dependent on what we in the Navy have to tell them. Would you like to join us? That way you will soon be up to date."

The two men descended the stone stairs, crossed the small courtyard and smartly saluted two army officers, Lieutenant Colonel Braunmuehl and Major Berger who were arriving simultaneously at the door of the 111b offices.

"Do sit down," said the Lieutenant Colonel after introductions had been made. "What have you got for us today, Commander? There must be quite a lot to catch up on after the move from Brussels."

"There is indeed," answered von Schiller. "I'll not bore you with naval movements, that's our business. But you will be interested to know that the British have figured out that we are planning to send over Zeppelins with bombs and are boosting their defences accordingly."

"In what way?" asked the major. The captain handed him the dispatch.

"As you will see, they have instructed their coastal searchlight units to sweep the sky in search of airships and aircraft as well as watching out for ships on the sea. They have aircraft at the ready in an increasing number of airfields and many more aircraft. They have also put machine guns aboard vehicles so they can chase the Zeppelins overland. What the range of these machine guns is, though, we do not know.

"On the basis of this information we have sent in a couple of special agents, women actually, to investigate in greater detail."

"Women!" snorted the major. "What will women be able to tell us about air defences?"

"A good deal," retorted the commander. "They have been trained at our new spy school here which has just been set up and is being run, believe it or not, Major, by a woman, Fraeulein Doctor Schragmüller, who is very, very good. So good that she has also been put in charge of intelligence gathering in France, while we are looking after Britain.

"You may sneer, but it also happens that some of our most reliable spies on the south coast of England are women. Like this one."

He read out another dispatch. "'Fifteen thousand volunteers left Folkestone November 10 for Calais.'" He showed it to the lieutenant colonel.

"And then this: 'Fresh troops left Folkestone for Nieuwport to relieve the Belgians.'"

"And this: 'English soldier told me that he will sail with 25,000 men from Portsmouth to Le Havre on November 20. Eighteen transport ships said to be lying ready in Dover and Folkestone, destination Calais.'"

He passed the papers over for the army officers to see. "You will be sent formal notice of all this as soon as my secretary has a typewriter and somewhere to type."

"Who is this woman in Folkestone, if I may ask?" queried the lieutenant colonel.

"I don't know her actual identity myself. As you can imagine, for safety's sake, we do not keep records of our peoples' real identities anywhere. She was apparently recruited by Steinhauer but is being run by our man who calls himself Peter Herz when in Germany and Hurst when in England. I'm not too sure that that is even his real name. Very charming when he wants, but a cold fish underneath. The killer type, if you ask me. But he is very clever at finding ways to get the dispatches out. Has been avoiding the stupid mistakes Steinhauer made. Long may they both of them last.

"And anyway, Major," he added, changing the subject, "don't tell me you don't have women passing you information on the Continent; I've heard rumours of a particularly glamourous one. Some exotic dancer."

"More glamorous than effective, actually." The Major sniffed. "I prefer unobtrusive men who know their job and work quietly."

Chapter 31

FOLKESTONE

A s the Commander was speaking, the object of his praise was in a state of intense alarm. Flo had received a letter addressed to her directly at the house. It was in Hurst's handwriting but purported to come from Schuil.

My love,

A. has discovered our beautiful secret. We must break off all contact for the moment. Don't despair, I will find another solution. Oh, to be able to hold you in my arms again! Your adoring, and suffering, D.

Flo panicked. She knew exactly what that meant. The secret service could be after her. She had of course used a false name on her letters but the clerks at the Folkestone poste restante would have no trouble remembering the woman who came regularly, often in her nurse's uniform, to collect her letters. What should she do? The police might come and search the house! She must quickly get rid of the incriminating evidence—the invisible ink, the toothpick, the writing paper!

That evening, after the staff and everyone had gone to bed, she crept into the kitchen and stoked up the dying fire. She tore

Hurst's letter and her own envelopes and sheets of writing paper into small pieces and fed them into the flames, a handful at a time,

crushing the charred remains with the poker into the smallest flakes possible and stirring them among the ashes. She threw in the toothpick, but it did not seem to burn too well, so she scraped it to one side and when it had cooled, broke it into tiny pieces and mixed them, too, with the ashes.

And the invisible ink? The phial looked totally innocuous but nevertheless she tipped the content down the plughole of the sink, washed the bottle out and soaked off the handwritten label. It looked just like any other medicine bottle, so she threw it in the rubbish bin. It had all been much easier than she thought. And in an emergency, she still had the white collar that Hurst had soaked in some solution and which he said she could use as invisible ink. No-one could possibly suspect that. But she could still have been found out, somehow. She lay awake all night. What had happened? Had Dan been caught?

From then on Flo changed her movements as far as she could. Declaring that The Leas in winter was far too cold and windy, she cast an eye quickly on the assembling troops then steered Mrs. Appleby's bath chair round more sheltered streets. She avoided the post office, buying stamps at the station instead. She knew that Hurst would appear or somehow contact her sooner or later but was happy and somewhat relieved not to have to report for the moment. She was dismayed that the flow of money had stopped but consoled herself with the thought that she already had a comfortable sum stashed away in the lining of her hold-all in her cupboard and needed to worry less that she might suddenly be reduced to indigence again.

A distant booming sound swept over the cliffs and the white Appleby house. When she first heard it, she had thought it was thunder, but James told her it was the sound of great guns from the battles raging in France and Belgium. Flo was heartily thankful that twenty miles of water lay between them and the war.

Three weeks passed before she heard from Hurst again. It was another letter, saying simply,

3pm Wednesday Holy Trinity Church, Sandgate Street.

It was the nearby church where Mrs. Appleby and Matilda had worshipped for years, always in the same pew, and where Flo went too every Sunday, pushing the older lady's bath chair. Flo wondered whether he knew that.

She arrived at the church a couple of minutes late. There was no sign of Hurst outside or in the entrance, so she went in and saw him in the pew she always sat in, immediately behind the Appleby family pew. He was kneeling, apparently in prayer. After a moment's hesitation she went and knelt beside him.

"What happened?" she whispered.

A verger appeared. Hurst lowered his head as if still praying and said nothing. They waited until the verger vanished into the sacristy again.

"Dan Schuil found that the envelope of your latest letter looked as if it had been opened and badly stuck together again," he murmured. "Don't be too alarmed, the letter itself did not appear to have been read—the invisible ink was still invisible. The money was still inside."

"Who do you think it could have been?"

"I don't know. It is a mystery. But obviously we daren't use that route again."

"I'm frightened," whispered Flo. "I don't want to go on."

"Don't be silly," Hurst snapped. "There is no evidence they are able to read our invisible ink, and your cover is entirely credible. We must just make sure that if the worst comes to the worst, you both have the same version of how you met. I suggest that you met in a café when a waitress tripped and dropped a teapot of scalding hot tea over Dan. Being a nurse, you stepped in and applied first aid, and he invited you to join him at his table."

"That sounds plausible," whispered Flo. "Will you make sure Dan knows it too?"

"Of course," said Hurst, "and if you should be questioned, just stick to the story and only the story.

"Now I have at last been able to arrange a different route for your dispatches," he

went on, getting up and sitting on the pew seat. "It will be much easier for you and even safer. Here ..." He took four pennies out of his pocket. "These are the poor relatives of our half-crowns. I can never understand why the British insist on having such large coins when they are worth so little, but at least they are useful for our purposes. See, you can open them like the others and put your message on tissue paper inside. Now come with me …" He led her to a pew in a side aisle towards the back of the church.

"Then, whenever you have a message to deliver you slip one in here …" He bent down and lifted a heavy, battered old hassock from the floor in front of him. There was an opening in the seam between the side of the hassock, which was made of old tapestry-type material, and the bottom, which was of worn leather. It looked as if it had come apart with age.

"… and you leave it like this." He put it under the pew seat instead of in front. "This is also where the pennies will be returned to you empty, and where you will find your remuneration.

"Of course, I don't need to tell you to not go anywhere near it at the service on a Sunday when there are people around. Instead, I would ask you to become very devout and to visit the church in your free time when there is likely to be no one there; you could say you go to pray for your son who is away fighting. The best time would be in the early afternoon when the verger is off duty."

"Would it not be simpler to put it where I always sit?" asked Flo innocently.

"That would be extremely foolish, Nurse," Hurst snapped. "If the hiding place were ever discovered it could immediately be linked to you."

Flo blushed with embarrassment.

"Here, by the way, is some more of that 'laxative' which you are going to need," Hurst said, giving her another small phial.

And once again, he was gone.

Strange man, thought Flo. Quite sinister. He never engaged in small talk, never revealed anything about himself. Was he married, did he have children, as one might expect in a man of his age? She found his coldness disconcerting, even intimidating. She was so used to being able to charm people, especially men, to be able to chat with them and quickly strike up a friendly relationship, but Hurst seemed so cold-blooded, impervious to any kind of charm and uninterested in any kind of rapport.

She wondered, too, where he lived and how he moved around. What was the role of that fishing boat they had met on some months earlier? Could that be how he travelled from one port to another? Is that why the constantly changing addresses he gave her in case of emergency were no longer around Epping but in fishing villages? As a fisherman, certainly he would scarcely be noticed, and if there was trouble, he could simply sneak across the Channel to occupied France.

One thing was certain, he would never tell her.

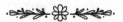

That evening, Mrs. Appleby, Flo, and the Janssens were just about to sit down to supper when they became aware of a disturbance out in the street. James opened the front door, and they heard a neighbour's voice saying, "Germans" and "Here, here." Before he could shut it again, two men appeared on the steps, a policeman and a distinguished-looking man in civilian clothes who seemed vaguely familiar to Flo. Two more policemen were standing in the street.

"Good evening. There have been reports that someone has been signalling from one of your windows, possibly to some enemy ship in the Channel," the policeman said, looking slightly embarrassed. "I'm afraid we have to search your house."

Flo froze with terror.

"It was the top window; I saw it!" came the woman's voice from behind them.

"I'm so sorry. Could you show us up to the top room?" the other man said.

It was the room where the Janssen ladies slept.

"It's impossible!" Mrs. Janssen protested when she understood what they wanted. "We are not spies!" But she finally agreed to go with them and James up to the room.

As they went up, Flo, trying to stop herself shaking with fear, explaining in a loud voice to a bewildered Mrs. Appleby what was going on.

There was an agonising wait. Then, to her astonishment, she heard the two men, Mrs. Janssen and James coming down the stairs again, laughing. James had a light bulb in his hand.

"It was just a defective bulb, the one over the dressing table by the window," explained James. "It kept going on and off. Mrs. Janssen says it has been doing that for some time. I must put a new one in. It sounds as if it was that Mrs. Seymour making trouble again."

Flo relayed his comments loudly to Mrs. Appleby who rolled her eyes and murmured, "Nasty woman. She should mind her own business."

At that moment, Gerrit let himself in the front door and immediately exclaimed, "Captain Miller, what are you doing here?"

"Janssen, old boy, do you live here?" exclaimed the man in civilian clothes. The two slapped each other jovially on the back. "Captain Miller is in, er, security. We work together," explained Gerrit. Flo, terrified anew, explained to Mrs. Appleby.

The captain and the policeman agreed that there was obviously no need now to search the whole house, and the policeman left. Captain Miller was invited to join the others for their interrupted supper. He looked at his watch. "Well, I'm off duty now, so yes, I'd be happy to. Thank you very much."

Over their hastily warmed-up soup, he tried to reassure his hosts. "Don't worry, this is happening all the time. People are convinced there are German spies everywhere, on the roofs, under the beds. Of course, we have to follow up all these reports, but it is all such nonsense, an awful waste of our time. There *are* German spies in Folkestone, possibly several of them, but they are cleverer than people think."

Flo's heart began pounding. "What do they do here?" she asked as innocently as she could.

"Oh, probably report on the numbers of troops leaving for the Continent, ship movements, anything they can find out about our defences, what Gerrit here and his colleagues are doing, anything which would be useful to the other side."

"But how do they get this information to Germany?"

"Well, not by flashing Morse messages to imaginary ships out at sea! If we knew, of course, it would be easier to catch them. But we think that many messages, and of course spies themselves, often come and go on the ferries. That's why we have so many people searching the ships and the passengers, even the crew.

"I thought I had caught one the other day. A Dutch lady, very attractive, very expensively dressed, furs, jewels, perfume, and all that, arrived on the boat from Dieppe. Our boys in France had had their eye on her for some time. Her luggage was searched, and I questioned her for quite a time, but I could find no reason to have her arrested so I had to let her go. She was not planning to stay in England anyway, as she was on her way to Holland to see her beau, she said, a certain Dutch colonel. One of many lovers, I suspect. She was, or is, for that matter, an exotic dancer, quite famous, at least she thinks she is." He imitated a haughty woman with her nose in the air and a cigarette in her hand. "'Don't you know who I am, officer?' Goes by the stage name of Mata Hari."

As he went on talking, Flo noticed that he had a small, dark red, birth mark, like a squiggle, on one side of his face. She was sure she had seen him somewhere before, but where?

The conversation moved on to other matters, but a little later Captain Miller turned to her and said, "You know, Nurse, I have this odd feeling that we have met before, but I can't for the life of me say when or where."

Flo, laughing, confessed she had the same impression.

He suggested few possibilities but there seemed to have been no point at which their paths could ever have crossed.

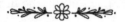

Curiously, in the next few days Flo and the captain met twice by pure chance, both times on the Sandgate Road, not far from the church. The captain explained that his lodgings were just up the road. Flo, slightly unnerved, claimed that she often went to the church alone to pray for her son who was away at the war. If they met another time, she would tell Hurst she had to stop using that route for her messages.

The second time they, met the captain, who had evidently taken a liking to the vivacious redheaded nurse, had said, "Nurse, Fate seems determined that we should get to know each other.

May I suggest we meet up on Sunday and go for a walk while we try to establish where and how we first met?" Flo, by no means averse to the charming captain, had agreed.

Chapter 32

O nce again, Christmas was approaching. Flo had asked for, and been granted, a week's leave after the New Year so that at last she could visit the children in the orphanage. She had sent off two dispatches before the festivities started, one was a report from Cyril about the airfields that had been set up in the Dover-Folkestone area. The other was news about a contingent of troops who were being shipped back from the front for two weeks' leave before being sent out again in January. They were to include Richard's regiment.

His family was overjoyed. Mrs. Appleby and Matilda had been planning a simple, low-key Christmas in keeping with the times and the food rationing, but as soon as the news arrived, James and Dora were sent out to buy the biggest Christmas tree he could find and scour the shops and activate their contacts in the hopes of getting an extra-large turkey, champagne, and whatever luxuries they could lay their hands on.

"We want to have a wonderful celebration!" Matilda announced.

Dora and James had just left to go shopping when the postman arrived with a letter for Mrs. Appleby. At the old lady's request,

Flo opened it and was about to read it to her when she gasped and stopped.

"What is it?" Mrs. Appleby asked, alarmed.

Flo had no choice but to tell her. "Mrs. Appleby, your son has been wounded and will be arriving in Dover on the HMS *Glenart Castle* this evening."

The old lady went white.

"Then we will go to Dover and bring him back here," decreed Matilda who had just come into the room.

"Don't worry, Mama, we will look after him," Flo assented heartily.

❧·❀·☙

That evening, Flo and Matilda, with James driving the family car, arrived with some difficulty, owing to restrictions on civilian access, at the port in Dover. Flo was appalled. The *Glenart Castle*, large red crosses painted on its sides, turned out to be a hospital ship. Wounded men, many supported by comrades or nurses, were staggering down the gangways, others, heavily bandaged, groaning or gasping, were being carried on stretchers to the ambulance train waiting nearby.

What a good thing those boys marching along The Leas can't see all this, Flo thought. Matilda, who was wearing her VADs uniform, briskly found her way to the matron who was directing the operation on the deck and asked for Lieutenant Appleby. Flo saw the matron's face grow serious. She was explaining something to Matilda.

Matilda returned, her face pale. "We can't take him. He is very badly wounded, and he and other critical cases have been taken straight to hospital here in Dover." She began to cry. "How am I going to tell Mama?"

Even though Matilda kept the full details of his condition from her, her mother was devastated. Flo put her, weeping uncontrollably, to bed and held her hand, trying to comfort her, until the older lady finally fell asleep. The next morning, Mrs. Appleby demanded to be taken to see Richard.

"No, Mama, not yet. Let him rest and recover for a while," pleaded Matilda.

But Mrs. Appleby was so insistent that Flo finally whispered to Matilda, "Let's take her. If it was one of my sons, I would want to see him. And from what you say it could be the last time."

It was the last time. The nurses tried to prevent them entering the ward but the frail Mrs. Appleby, in a borrowed wheelchair, showed a will of iron and demanded in no uncertain terms to be taken to Robert.

Or what was left of him. A ball of bloodstained bandages covered what was left of his head, and more were wrapped around the stumps of both arms. The rest was hidden under the bedclothes. Only his nose and mouth were visible. He was scarcely breathing. A doctor came over and took Mrs. Appleby's hand.

"I'm so very sorry, ma'am," he said gently. "We can do nothing more for him. If it is any consolation, at least he is unconscious. I'm afraid it will not be long now."

Her hand shaking, the older lady reached out and stroked the remains of her son, weeping and speaking to him gently. Flo was devastated. She and Matilda watched helplessly, tears streaming down their own faces. Robert, so lively, so full of fun, such a lovable young man with all his life in front of him, now lay here horribly mutilated, dying. As were so many others here in the ward. It was unbearable. She and Matilda pleaded with Mrs. Appleby to go, but she insisted on staying at his bedside. She and the others were still there at eleven o'clock at night when, never having regained consciousness, Richard breathed his last.

Richard's death cast a black pall over the Appleby household. Mrs. Appleby had become an invalid, lying immobile in her bed, staring unseeingly into space, her face waxen. She rarely spoke, would hardly eat or drink, and wanted only to die. People tiptoed around the house, speaking in whispers. They ate dinner in silence. Flo realised with a heavy heart that her visit to the orphanage would have to be postponed. Who knew when she would see her little ones again?

Outside, town seemed to be given over entirely to the war effort. Thousands of Canadian troops had arrived at the red-brick barracks up at Shorncliffe, on a rise outside Folkestone—so many that the base, although huge, could not hold them all, and tent cities had sprung up around it and hundreds of huts were being built and concerts, tea parties, sports and film shows were being arranged to keep them entertained. Some were billeted on families in the town. Many were training in trenches and fortifications thrown up outside the town. Thousands of British troops were also flooding in on their way to the war and rest camps had been flung all over town—including on part of The Leas—to house them as they waited to embark. Posters appeared by their camps and along their routes warning them against "loose talk"; spies were everywhere. The units marching along The Leas to the harbour no longer sang. The fighting was dragging on and on, the papers were full of lists of the dead, wounded, and missing, and no one thought it a romantic adventure anymore. The thunder of distant guns across the Channel seemed louder than ever.

In the spring, however, new life, unasked, invaded the house. Three young Canadian recruits had been billeted on them, and while Mrs. Appleby appeared indifferent, the others welcomed them and were glad to hear their cheery voices on the stairs as they came and went. James and Dora quickly rearranged Richard's old room for them—"I'm sure Richard would have wanted it," Matilda said, and she invited them to dinner each evening with themselves and the Janssens where they chatted merrily and brightened up everyone's mood considerably. Soon, one of them, by the name of Parsons, took a liking to Antje and tried to flirt with her, seemingly interpreting her fearful rejection of his advances as girlish shyness. One Sunday, after the others had failed to discourage him, Gerrit went into the Canadians' room for a chat. What he said Flo never knew, but from then on Antje was left alone.

Chapter 33

Pozieres France, 1916

The world exploded. Then blackness fell.

Slowly Godfrey came to, his head spinning, a shrieking piercing his ears. He

could scarcely breathe, and soil clogged his nose and mouth. He tried to lift his head and arm to clear them, but he could not move. Tons of earth, it seemed, was pressing on his body, crushing him. He was buried, buried alive.

Silence.

So, this is it, he thought. *Now it's my turn*. His twice-gassed lungs were struggling unbearably, he choked, and then, reflexively, coughed. It drove some of the soil out of his mouth and perhaps loosened a little earth around it, for it became slightly easier to breathe. He coughed again.

Was he conscious or not? "Mama!" he cried, trying to reach out. "Mama!" But she was walking away, holding Cyril's hand. Then he vaguely became aware of thuds, and—could it be? —muffled voices? He tried to shout but out came only a useless croak. He shouted again, this time it came out louder. More voices, closer now, and the sound of digging. Blackness again, then, gasping for breath, he was being dragged out into the light.

"Was Davies near you?" he heard someone ask. The filthy faces of his rescuers swam around him. He coughed and choked, then grunted, "Fielding."

"We've found Fielding." The tone of voice told him Fielding was dead.

More faces. They were trying to heave him on to a stretcher.

"No! No!" He pulled himself away and sat down on a pile of earth, breathing heavily and coughing to clear his lungs. *No,* he thought confusedly, *I must have been hallucinating, my mother is far away, and that's where she should stay.* Someone passed him a hip flask of whisky. He drank gratefully. "I shall be fine, just give me time."

"So, you are enjoying your stint at the front line!" One of the stretcher-bearers thought he was being funny. He had happened to see Godfrey pleading with his commanding officer that morning to let him take part in the attack.

"But why, Harris? You are supposed to be looking after the guns." The major had frowned at the neat-looking armourer sergeant, the state of whose uniform clearly indicated a non-combatant. "We can't afford to run out of weapons in the middle of everything. Get back there now."

"Sir, Smith and Mather are both there; they're very good, and I brought along a whole consignment of new rifles and ammo from HQ. If you'll permit me, sir, there's no danger of that. Please, sir, please."

The major had paused. He'd understood the armourer sergeant only too well. A frustrated young soldier, almost embarrassed to be working in the relative safety of a support job behind the lines while his mates were risking their lives, was raring to join in the action, come what may. He was surprised, though. Harris was so quiet, reserved. He was definitely not the daredevil type.

"You sure?" he'd asked. Godfrey had been sure.

"Very well. Get yourself a helmet," the major had said and turned away.

Godfrey sat among the dirt, trying to clean his face and hands. A huge crater gaped a few yards away where none had been before. Their trench had vanished. Godfrey's head cleared. "The ammo!" he suddenly shouted. It was all coming back to him.

At some point, it the midst of the attack, Godfrey had seen that the officer commanding the battalion's forward ammunition dump had been killed. Instinctively, Godfrey moved the body aside, took over the dump, and being skilled now with supplies, quickly restarted the distribution of crates of bullets and shells to the front lines and sent back to the rear for more. Now he saw that the dump had been buried in the explosion. It was a miracle it had not blown up and killed them all. The fighting was still raging, the ammunition would be urgently needed, they must dig it out fast.

"Briggs, McConnell, quickly!" Godfrey shouted and organised a digging party. In less than an hour, he had the dump functioning again and had just accepted a mug of tea when there was a deafening roar and a blast that threw them into the air.

They lay immobile, as if dead.

Godfrey was the first to move slightly. His head was splitting, his whole body was shaking. It was strangely silent, had the fighting suddenly stopped? Slowly he raised

himself on one elbow and looked at the others. Were they dead? Like him, they did not seem injured. A high explosive shell had evidently landed a couple of hundred yards away; it was the blast that had knocked them out.

He called out to the man lying nearby, "Briggs!" He could not hear his own voice. *So that's why it's all quiet. I have gone deaf!* he thought.

Back at the dump, as he was shakily shifting crates of ammunition, the major appeared and was saying something to him. Godfrey gestured that he could not hear. The major gestured back: he must stand down and go and get some rest. Godfrey obeyed.

<hr/>

When he awoke, on a blanket in a dugout, it was dark. His ears were ringing but he could hear, more or less.

"Harris! Stew!" Someone thrusted a tin at him. It was a junior officer. "We've captured the ridge!"

Godfrey ate hungrily.

"They need supplies. The major wants the ammunition brought out to them."

Godfrey pocketed some bread and biscuits and went outside. It was a clear summer night. The half-moon and the stars shed a little light, and he could see the contours of what, until that afternoon, had been the No Man's Land. It was a moon landscape.

"First, I'll have to find a route to get there safely," he said. "Then we must organise carrying parties."

He climbed out of the trench and, fearing the enemy's flares which could light up the whole scene in an instant, he kept low, crawling forward on hands and knees, seeking a clear way though the craters, tangles of barbed wire and wreckage, and clambering over blackened, rotting corpses. They would have to cover at least 300 yards in the open, he realized, and the men, with their heavy loads on their backs, would have to walk, not crawl. They could easily be seen, though it would have been better if there was no moon. He worked out a route through the deepest shell craters, a clump of shattered trees, a ditch, and the remains of a stone wall which could afford some small degree of protection from enemy snipers. When he was sure of the route, he crawled back.

The officer had lined up half a dozen men and, warning them to keep down and follow him closely, Godfrey led them silently across the desolate landscape, lugging their heavy loads. Sporadically, bullets whistled past, but they seemed haphazard, as there was no sign the party had been detected. Six times he guided them to-and-fro before the dawn began to break. They had not suffered a single loss.

After fifty hours in the trenches, the battalion was relieved. The survivors staggered out, haggard, filthy, exhausted, their eyes dull from lack of sleep, their uniforms in rags, barely able to greet the fresh troops who were about to take their places.

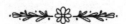

The next morning, Godfrey was roused from his sleep in the cellar of a ruined farmhouse with an order to present himself immediately at the battalion's makeshift headquarters. The major, his head bandaged and his arm in a sling, looked up from his table.

"Harris, my compliments, you've done very well," he began, shuffling the papers on his makeshift desk.

Godfrey blushed with embarrassment and pleasure.

"I'm going to recommend you for the Military Medal. Exceptional bravery, you know."

Godfrey was overwhelmed. "Thank you, sir. Thank you." Not knowing what else to say he saluted and turned on his heel.

"I've not finished, Harris."

Godfrey turned back.

"I want to get you a commission. I am recommending you for promotion to Second Lieutenant. I'm almost certain it will be approved."

Godfrey was speechless. He had always thought of himself as a small cog in the great machinery of the army; it had never occurred to him he might become an officer.

"Th-th-thank you, Sir," he stammered. "I h-hope I will be up to it."

"You are up to it, Harris." The major turned back to his papers.

Funny fellow, the major mused. Seems so quiet and reserved, not pushy at all, but there is obviously more to him than I thought.

Chapter 34

Ypres, Belgium, 1916

G odfrey tried not to think of anything as he was being driven along the straight, flat road southward from Ypres. Long rows of splintered, blackened tree trunks lined each side of the road—*they must be the remains of those tall poplars in Flemish old master paintings*, he realised—then quickly shut down his mind again. The battered military vehicle inched ahead, stuck in an endless procession of carts and limbers, bearing food and water, duckboards, ammunition, big guns, and cannon. From the other direction came carts and ambulances carrying bodies, some moving, some not ... hundreds of them. The familiar roar of guns and shellfire was growing ever louder, and ruined buildings, dead horses, overturned carts, and assorted wreckage lay on each side. And mud. This was high summer, but it had rained for weeks, and mud stretched as far as the eye could see. Shell holes were full of filthy water, spiked with broken stumps, barbed wire, and debris alongside rounder, softer objects, severed limbs, and the corpses of dead men. All around lay hills, and on those to the east were the Germans, well entrenched, with a good view over the valley and the road. Two long, bitter battles for those hills had felled thousands of his fellow Australians, and now they had started a third.

He could hardly believe that only three days ago, he had been sitting in a punt on the Cambridge backs, kissing a beautiful girl. Promoted a second time, now a lieutenant, he had been sent on a three-month officers' training course in Cambridge. It was heaven to be away from the fighting, in such beautiful surroundings, with a soft bed, clean clothes, enough water for baths, and decent food to eat. Much of the instruction had been about boring paperwork, but the theory was fascinating and the subsequent intelligence training even more so, for he was no longer to concern himself with guns and ordnance, nor, to his slight regret, was he to be a sniper, which had been his last assignment and at which, being a crack shot, he had excelled. Instead, impressed by his skill at scouting and guiding the carrying parties at Pozieres, they had made him a brigade intelligence officer.

But more important than anything, as far as Godfrey was concerned, he had fallen in love. Sarah was the cousin of an English fellow officer who lived in Cambridge, and she was intelligent and vivacious—and she seemed keen on him, he reflected, although her widowed mother strongly disapproved of him. She did not want Sarah disappearing off to a farm on the other side of the world. What should they do? He hoped to win them both round, but Sarah and he had known each other such a short time, and now he had to go back to the front again. The first thing he would do when he reached his unit would be to write to her.

"Briggs still there?" he asked one of the others in the battered car, the only man he recognised.

"Gone."

"Barton? Fields? Thomas?"

"Better not ask. You won't know hardly anyone there now."

He would not think of that either. He must focus on the missions ahead. Godfrey had changed. He had gained self-confidence and had even become ambitious. Helped by aerial photographs and intelligence gathered by the British whose resources were far greater than the Australians' and who had been in the area much longer, he and his comrades in the intelligence unit were to find out as much as possible about the enemy's strength and positions in their designated area, grilling prisoners of war and keeping close track of the ever-shifting topography of the battlefield.

The attack, he learned when he arrived at brigade headquarters, had gone well; their front had advanced just under a mile, the troops were digging in and thousands more were assembling for the next one, scheduled for the following day.

Unexpectedly, the Germans had opened a massive barrage and launched a counterattack, aiming to recover the lost ground. By the time they were beaten back, thousands more bodies lay motionless in the mud.

***

"So much for tomorrow's attack," someone remarked as Godfrey and his colleagues gathered at the brigade's makeshift headquarters to review the situation.

"On the contrary," said the colonel who had just returned from consultation with the general, "it's got to go ahead."

"But ... but ..." Several officers pointed out that their flank was now much weakened, and they were extremely vulnerable.

"That's just the whole point," retorted the colonel. "Surprise. The Fritzes will never expect us to hit back so soon. The attack will begin at 5:30 and we are bringing up fresh troops, but first we need to know where we are going."

Hell, thought Godfrey. The attack that day had been devastating. Few of the front- line troops had survived and would be able to tell them what weapons the enemy had used, who they were, and what the area looked like now—all vital information he needed before morning.

Godfrey took two men, making sure that they, like him, were armed to the teeth with pistols, rifles, hand grenades, flares, and knives. They blackened their faces, grabbed their gas masks, and silently headed towards the front. Makeshift roads of duckboards and planks, laid across the mud to help heave the artillery forward, led to what was once a small forest and was now a wasteland of splintered stumps after the battle. Stretcher-bearers were still carrying off the dead and wounded. There was little cover, so they wormed their way to the far edge of the wood and tried to make out what was going on in the German lines.

"Not much," muttered Evans, one of Godfrey's companions. It was strangely quiet, and as far as they could make out, the Germans—only three or four hundred yards in front of them—were resting, perhaps eating. Even the No Man's Land, where patrols and spies often moved around at night, seemed deserted.

Probably waiting for reinforcements, thought Godfrey. The counterattack had probably been a delaying tactic.

The Germans had built artillery emplacements and a series of concrete pillboxes within range of each other which formed a formidable barrier to an attack. They had to find out which, if any, had been destroyed and which could still be crewed.

They slithered forward through shell holes and debris, until they reached the first one which they found wrecked and empty. Godfrey bumped into the body of a dead German. Moving quickly, he stripped off his tunic and put on the German's helmet and jacket. Standing up, he saw that the man, probably a sapper, had been carrying coils of telephone wire and seized that too. He whispered to his companions to keep him covered from about fifty yards and moved quickly leftwards along the lines, pretending to be a German telephone engineer and making a mental map of the enemy's defences. He was astonished to find they were remarkably thin, there was little activity in the trenches and few barbed wire and pillboxes had been wrecked—it was clearly a weak point in their front.

He was moving back towards the others when he heard shouts and firing. A German patrol had spotted Evans and Grieves, his companions, who instantly threw grenades at them and ran for their lives. Within moments, flares were lighting up the scene and heavy shell fire was raining down. Tearing off his German cap and jacket, Godfrey ran too, screaming as shrapnel tore into his left side. He stumbled on, calling for the others, until the light of a flare showed he was on the brink of a ravine.

Sliding and falling, he saw there was a whole network of ravines which was protecting him somewhat from the shelling. Bleeding heavily and shouting for help, he stumbled into the Anzac front lines, demanding to be taken instantly to brigade HQ. There, writhing with pain and giddy from loss of blood, he reported his findings. It was 3:30 in the morning.

Godfrey was shakily counting the shrapnel pieces which had been cut out of his body in the field hospital the next day when his commanding officer was shown in.

"Congratulations, Harris," he said, slapping him on the shoulder.

Godfrey winced and looked at him enquiringly.

"I'm proud to say, they're giving you the Military Cross, Lieutenant. 'Courage, devotion to duty and plucky and clever reconnaissance,'" the officer said, reading from a document in his hand.

"Thank you, sir," replied Godfrey. "How did it go?"

"Thanks to your information, there was not a single casualty while we were assembling for the attack," said the officer. "As you said, their defences on that stretch were surprisingly weak. We have gained at least another mile."

Godfrey lay back happily. "I should be out of here pretty soon," he said. "Only flesh wounds, nothing serious."

"Good lad. See you soon, and congratulations again," said the officer, and slapping him painfully on the shoulder once more, departed.

❀

Westhoek, Broodseinde, Framerville, Mont St. Quentin: names of battles that would go down in the history books, but which for Lieutenant Harris later merged into an endless barrage of shells, a boundless landscape of mud and wreckage, never-ending slaughter and mutilation of his comrades, and the constant knowledge that any minute he could be next. Nevertheless, he was thankful that he had no time to ponder, as he was working night and day, collecting intelligence from the front, interrogating prisoners, passing the information on, and going on perilous reconnaissance missions rather than waiting for action or death in the trenches. By the time the Germans sought an armistice, he had been wounded three times on such missions and been awarded a Bar to his Military Cross. He had been promoted to temporary captain but was so successful at his brigade intelligence work that he was kept at it on secondment until the end of the war.

Chapter 35

Folkestone, 1917

Flo, you won't believe it! Godfrey is going to be given his medals by the king at Buckingham Palace on the twenty-fifth! I am so proud of him, and you must be too. I begged and begged him to let you and me come, too, as apparently close relatives are allowed to watch, but he flatly refused. He wants to be alone. Well, you know what he is like; he never changes, but I did get him to promise me something which is even more exciting—I am to join him in Australia to keep house for him when he goes back! Can you imagine? Of course, I will be sad to be so far away from you, Emily, Martha, and everyone, but at least I can be of use to our dear Godfrey. And the climate will be good for my rheumatism! No dates for our departure yet, but I will let you know. I do hope we can meet again before I go. Your loving sister, Lizzie.

Australia. Now that's an idea … Flo mused. *Maybe* … Then she pushed the thought away. Godfrey was going to be given his medals by the king! Godfrey didn't know—in fact he had forbidden it—that Lizzie had long been passing on to her all his news, photographs, and most recently, the citations for his medals. She was horrified to hear that he had been buried alive, that he had nearly died, that he had been wounded. She was immensely proud of him, but it was a bittersweet pride, knowing how firmly he had rejected her.

But Godfrey was going to be in London on the twenty-fifth. She must try and see him on his special day, see him for the first time in so many years, congratulate him, kiss him one last time before he set off again for the other side of the world. Perhaps she could at last tell him in person how bitterly she had regretted having to leave him all those years ago, how intensely she had missed him. Surely, he would not object to that.

Flo remembered at last where she had seen Captain Miller before. It was in the train which had taken her and Cyril to London the day Josiah threw her out. Cyril had even embarrassed her by asking why Josiah had called him "bastard." Flo winced at the memory. She was certainly not going to remind the good captain of that. But she was looking forward to their planned meeting the following Sunday—weather permitting.

Flo liked the captain. He seemed open, relaxed, straightforward, and not at all like Hurst. She felt she could trust him. At first, she regretted having agreed to go and was about to ask Gerrit to make excuses for her. After all, he had said himself that his work involved hunting for spies! But then, as Hurst and Steinhauer had said, who would suspect a monthly nurse caring for an older lady in a highly respectable family? On the contrary, becoming friends with him could be the best possible way of averting suspicion. She would just have to be careful.

The following Sunday dawned fine and sunny, and on the dot of two o'clock, he was at the door of the Appleby house. At his suggestion, they took the old lift down from The Leas to the beach level.

"We really must solve this riddle of where we have met," began the captain as they strolled westwards along an enchanting coastal path through pine trees and holm oaks. "It must have been some years ago. I seem to remember that you were with a little boy. I vaguely see you sitting opposite him—could it have been on a train?"

"Well, I suppose it could," conceded Flo vaguely.

"Oh, yes, it's coming back to me now. Could you have been going to visit your sister and I was suggesting that you see the sights of London from the cab when you change trains?"

"Ah, now it is coming back to me too!" exclaimed Flo. There seemed no point in pretending any further, but to deflect further recollections she launched into the story of how, following his suggestion, they had spent so much time sightseeing that they missed the last train to Brentwood and had to spend the night in the station hotel.

The captain laughed heartily. "I think I was investigating a murder in Gloucester at the time," he said.

"A murder? So, you are a policeman too," Flo said, thinking of the uniformed officer who had accompanied him to the Appleby house to investigate the flashing light. "Why don't you wear a uniform?"

"I used to when I was junior member of the force, but then I became a detective and no longer needed to."

"A detective! How exciting! Have you solved many murders?"

They were on the beach now, picking their way gingerly across the pebbles. The captain stooped and gathered some flat stones which he sent skimming across the surface of the water.

"Some," he replied. "But then I moved to, er, security, keeping an eye on troublemakers who might try to subvert or overthrow the state, either here or elsewhere."

"Who would want to do such a thing?" Flo asked, pretending naiveté.

"Oh, wild-eyed Irishmen, left-wing revolutionaries, maybe the crazier suffragettes, anarchists, as well as spies, of course. I spent much time working in East London where there are all sorts of Russian and Eastern European anarchists among the thousands of émigrés living there."

"Russian anarchists?" That rang a bell. "Like the ones who plotted to kill the Kaiser at Queen Victoria's funeral?" Flo asked.

The captain stopped in mid-throw and looked at her searchingly. "Where did you hear about that?" As far as he knew the incident had never been made public and only the staff in the bureau knew about it.

Flo's heart stopped. Of course, it was Steinhauer who had told her! How could she have been so stupid!

"I—I can't remember. I must have read it in a newspaper." She pretended to stumble and twist her ankle, hoping to distract him. "Ouch!" she cried as he helped her to her

feet. She pretended to limp painfully as he steered her towards a small tea pavilion so she could sit down.

The moment seemed to have passed without consequence, and they began chatting about themselves. The captain turned out to be a widower with two grown children, a girl who was married and a boy who was away fighting in France. Flo told him about Cyril in the searchlight unit and Godfrey and his medals, hoping they might reinforce her patriotic credentials.

Time was flying and, declaring her ankle to be much better, she said they must be walking back to The Leas. They agreed to meet again for a walk the following Sunday. After they had parted, Flo thought, *What a wonderful man. If only I had married someone like that, my life would have been quite different. If only ...* She sighed.

The captain went away puzzled. *Another riddle*, he thought. How could Florence possibly have known about the plot against the Kaiser? The next time he saw Melville, his boss, he must ask him if he had any clue.

A large crowd had gathered outside the Buckingham Palace railings, keen to see the heroes of the terrible battles that they had read and heard about. Flo was unable to get near the railings as she had hoped but found a spot on one side of the great wrought-iron gate where she thought Godfrey was likely to come out. She had put on her smartest outfit for the occasion, a slim calf-length lavender skirt and jacket topped by a chic little black hat—she wanted to look her best for the occasion. She had a long wait, for the heroes were many, but finally they emerged: young soldiers with their proud parents, older ones with their wives, generals, and assorted dignitaries. Flo began to despair of spotting Godfrey. Thanks to the photographs Lizzie had sent her, she was sure she would recognise him.

Then she saw him. That was her son! A slim, mustachioed officer in his spotless, greenish-khaki Australian uniform with knee-breeches and leather gaiters, peaked cap, and baton. And, to her surprise, he was not alone. At his side was a beautiful, young woman in a wide-brimmed hat and an elegant fur-trimmed coat, laughing and talking animatedly. He was looking down, listening attentively. Who was she? Lizzie had never mentioned any lady friends.

Flo pushed forward through the crowd to meet them, calling, "Godfrey! Godfrey!"

He looked up, saw her—and it was as if a shutter came down over his face. He took his companion by the arm and, staring straight ahead, walked resolutely past her, ignoring her.

"Godfrey, Godfrey, don't you recognize me? It's me, your mother! Your mother, Godfrey!" she cried, trying to grasp his free arm.

Without looking at her, he raised it and, with the side of his baton, firmly pushed her away, saying coldly, "Madam, I don't know you. Please leave me alone."

"But Godfrey …!" She gasped, running after him. She saw his lady friend, looking greatly perturbed, whisper a question. "Some mad woman, probably," she thought she heard him say as they walked away towards the Mall. She remained standing there, paralysed with shock.

A group of people who had been at the investiture were gathered in Flo's compartment on the train back to Folkestone, talking excitedly about the great event. How splendid the king had looked in his uniform! Who would ever have thought that they, ordinary farmers from Kent, would ever be guests in the Palace! How proud they were of young Andy!

They paid little attention to Flo, slumped in a corner seat, ashen-faced and broken. She heard none of their chatter. Her mind was a blank, her body and soul engulfed in a deep, dark, terrible pain. She must have sat like that for a couple of hours, because slowly she became aware that they had arrived at Folkestone and that her companions had left the train. Shakily, she stumbled out on to the platform and headed towards The Leas.

As she reached the Appleby house, she paused, then wandered on aimlessly for some minutes, and sank on to park bench, looking across the sea. The sun was low now and fluffy clouds over the sea were tinged with pink and gold, but she saw nothing.

Part of her had died. The faint glimmer of hope she had always nurtured, the hope that she would one day regain her beloved son, had been snuffed out forever, in the most brutal way. All that remained was an unbearable pain.

"The humiliation! The cruelty of it! How he must hate me!" she agonised. *What poison had Josiah dropped into his heart?* she wondered, trying to blame his father. Josiah was basically a good man, she had to admit, but when it came to combatting what he held to be evil there was no reasoning with him, no compassion, no tolerance.

But the stern religious teaching she had received since birth took over and gradually, she began drowning in a sea of guilt.

"If only I had been a good, faithful wife, this would never have happened! All the heartbreak in my life—I've brought it on myself!" It was true that she had had some years of happiness with Darnley and their children—but there had been a cost: her immense suffering over his betrayal and later his death, their desperate poverty, Steinhauer, Hurst, being forced to send the children to the orphanage and betray her country … Would she ever finish paying for her sin?

Dusk was falling and, overhead, the seagulls were flying back from the shore to roost. There was almost no one around. The wind became colder, but she remained seated, oblivious. She was living again the moment when she saw Godfrey emerging from the Palace gate in his smart officer's uniform and his medals. How proud she had been of him! Her son had fought so bravely, had risked his life many times, had been wounded, had suffered appalling conditions which she could not even imagine, while she ... while she ...

She had betrayed him. All those thousands of young soldiers, marching so cheerfully along this very promenade day after day—she had betrayed them too. She strained to make out the coast of France across the darkening Channel, but in vain. How many of them had died in that hell over there, how many had been maimed and blinded because of her? And the sailors and airmen ... how many young lives had been cut short because of the messages she wrote on tissue paper and hid in hollow coins? She would never know, but that did not absolve her one iota.

Yes, she mused, she had had to support her children. She had had no alternative—or had she? If she had known then what she knew now ...? She had slid into it so naively, cushioned by her spymasters' assurances that it was all safe and harmless. Now, she was stuck, the prisoner of her crime. Whatever could she do?

She was stiff with cold. Her handkerchief was sodden with tears. She longed for the solace of her mother. "Oh, Mama!" she moaned quietly, "Mama, please help me!"

Thank God her mother never knew what had become of her, she thought. But in any case, her counsel would have been clear. Of course. She must stop spying immediately, cost what it may.

She stood up stiffly and walked slowly back towards the house. She was exhausted and drained, yet she felt strangely lightened. She did not know how she could extricate herself from her predicament, Hurst, of course would not hear of it. She would think about that in the morning.

Mrs. Appleby seemed weaker than ever. She only wanted to lie in bed, dozing or staring into space and mourning her beloved Richard. Flo felt more sympathy for the fragile older lady than ever. What was worse, she wondered, to watch one's son die or to have him reject one so brutally? Both were terrible. Trying to suppress her own pain and attend to her patient and her many daily tasks, she was unable to think about Hurst until after lunch when she had settled Mrs. Appleby down for a nap and retired to her own room.

Try as she might, she could not think of a painless solution. The truth was, she was frightened of Hurst. He had a cold, steely will, and she sensed that would stop at nothing to thwart her. She on the other hand, was totally defenceless.

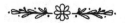

The next day, Mrs. Appleby developed a bad cough. Alarmed, Flo called the doctor who, fearing it could be the beginning of pneumonia, prescribed total bed rest, an array of medicines, and round-the-clock care. As she set up a camp bed for herself in Mrs. Appleby's bedroom, Flo realized that she would be effectively housebound for the foreseeable future. *Well, that solves the problem for the time being*, she thought to herself. She would let Hurst know she was out of action—at least it would put off the evil hour. Maybe she could put him off even further, and further.

That evening, she took out two postcards. On one she wrote the latest address Hurst had given her—he was always changing addresses—and, below the usual greetings, added in invisible ink: "My patient is very ill. No time, sorry." The other she addressed to Captain Miller telling him regretfully that owing to her patient's condition, she would not be able to see him for the time being. She gave them to James to post.

It was not pneumonia, however, and after a couple of weeks, Mrs. Appleby began to recover. As the spring came, she regained both her strength and her spirits. One day, to Flo's surprise and consternation she said, "It's such a lovely day, let's go for a little walk!"

Flo tried to discourage her, but the weather was indeed so sunny and mild that she had to give in and brought out the heavy old bath chair. The fine weather persisted, and it was during such a walk on The Leas a few days later that Flo thought she saw Hurst. She was standing by the bathchair while Mrs. Appleby greeted a neighbour when she became aware of a man looking at her from across the promenade. He was wearing workmen's overalls and cap, but she was sure she recognised him. Hurst! In an instant he had slipped behind a group of strollers and vanished from sight

"Now what do I do?" she worried. But the only possible answer, as she realized, once she was alone again in her room, was: nothing.

She was not surprised, however, when a few days later, a letter arrived for her from Hurst. Couched as usual in general terms so as not to arouse suspicion if it fell into the wrong hands, one phrase nevertheless made Flo very uneasy.

"I am glad to hear that all is well again, and I expect you will now return to your normal life, which will be so much better for your own health."

It sounded caring, but Flo, knowing Hurst, realised it was a threat. It plunged her once again into an agony of indecision. She could not continue spying, of that there was no question. Should she go to Captain Miller, confess all, and get Hurst arrested? Since Mrs. Appleby recovered, they had resumed their walks, and she had longed to tell him of her plight. But whatever he felt for her, he would be duty bound to arrest her, that she knew. There would be prison, a trial—she could even be hanged! She shuddered at the thought. Even if she were spared execution, the good captain would certainly not be able to save her from years in jail. And then what would become of the children?

She felt paralysed. "I've got to find a solution," she told herself again and again. But a solution would not come.

Chapter 36

DOVER, 1917

"Harris! Sergeant Harris!" A new recruit stumbled towards the tent where Cyril and three others were squatting on the ground, smoking and playing cards in front of their tent.

Cyril raised his head. "You looking for me?"

"Somebody wants to see you, sir," said the recruit, pointing towards the entrance to the camp.

"What does he want?"

"No idea, sir. He didn't say."

"Drat. Just a minute," he said to the others. "I'll see what he wants."

At the entrance stood a man astride a motorbike. He seemed to be a fisherman, with a navy pullover and trousers and a dark sailor's cap. He had a dark moustache and beard and from his mouth hung a briar pipe which, Cyril noticed, was not lit. He hesitated, puzzled.

"Cyril!" said the fisherman, moving towards him and holding out his hand. "Remember me—Uncle Peter? Peter Hurst?"

Cyril drew back. "You said we shouldn't have any contact. You know how dangerous it is for me."

Hurst drew closer. "Don't be afraid, it's perfectly safe," he said in a low voice. "As far as you are concerned, I'm your Uncle Peter. A distant uncle, if you like. But I need to talk to you. Not about business, it's about your mother."

"What's the matter with her?" Cyril was alarmed.

"She is not ill or anything, don't worry. But it is important. Let me buy you a pint or two, but not around here. Somewhere in town, perhaps."

"I can't. I'm on duty in half an hour."

"When will you be free?"

"Tomorrow is my free night but …"

"Fine. Meet me at the British Lion at seven. Just an hour or so with your old uncle, right? Important, purely non-business."

Reluctantly, Cyril agreed.

That night, as he and his mates swept the sky and the sea with their powerful beams, Cyril told himself he must not go. It was too risky. But by the following afternoon the prospect of beer and perhaps decent food outside the camp made him think again. Plus, he was curious to know what Hurst had to tell him about his mother.

It was a pretty good disguise, Cyril thought as he scrutinised Hurst across the wooden pub table. He would never have recognised him. Hurst, still in his fisherman's outfit, seemed to read his thoughts.

"It's real," he said, tugging at his dark beard. "It's just the colour that had to be changed a bit. Part of the job. Sometimes I don't even recognise myself. So, how's life treating you?" he went on, chewing on his pipe and leaning back in his chair relaxedly, the very picture of an uncle chatting to a favourite nephew.

"Oh fine," replied Cyril, still a little wary. "I'm quite enjoying it, as I have lots of pals from the tram company back in London. I'm learning a lot, and it's a good deal better than fighting on the front, I must say."

"Well, you are doing very well from our point of view. The powers that be are very pleased with your work." Cyril frowned. Hurst had said he would not talk "business."

Hurst ignored the frown. "And life must be good with all that extra pocket money your mother must be giving you. Fifteen pounds a go are not to be sniffed at."

Fifteen pounds? Cyril stiffened. His mother only passed him ten pounds for each piece of information. Was she cheating him? Hurst noted his discomfort with satisfaction and went on, "She is doing pretty well herself, I have to say. She will have a nice little nest egg put by when all this is over."

"She's had a difficult life; she needed it." Suspicious though he was, Cyril felt he had to defend her.

"The trouble is," Hurst went on, "I'm afraid that now she is reasonably well-off, she is not interested in working for us anymore."

Cyril was surprised. "What makes you think that?"

"She has stopped sending us information. She claims that she has no time because her employer is very ill, but even if she has been ill, she certainly seems better now. Has she said anything to you?"

"All I know is that she has been very busy because of Mrs. Appleby's condition. She told me to hold off for moment until she had time to, er, work."

"Well, she certainly seems to have time now. Could you be a good fellow, find out what's the problem and chivvy her on a bit? It's important, the war doesn't wait."

"Well, I'll do what I can," said Cyril, draining his glass. "But you know my mother, it's hard to get her to do anything if she doesn't want to."

Hurst looked at his glass. "Let me get you another pint," he said, rising. "Same again?"

Cyril looked at his watch. It was still early. "Thanks."

Could she be cheating him of his money? It wasn't in her nature, but the thought wormed inside him as he watched Hurst go to the bar.

"Don't get me wrong, I have great admiration for your mother," Hurst began again as he came back, deposited two frothing beers on the table and sat down. "Such an attractive woman. She could have remarried, found some wealthy man who would give her an easy life instead of pushing old ladies around in bath chairs and struggling to make ends meet."

Cyril's beer seemed unusually frothy, more so than Hurst's, but he took a deep draught, sat back, and said nothing.

"It's no business of mine," Hurst persisted, "but I've always been puzzled that she is alone. Did she have some great love who jilted her? Did she swear no man could match her late husband? Did she fall in love with a married man? Don't worry, I won't tell anyone."

A warm, mellow sensation was creeping over Cyril. He was feeling relaxed and at peace with the world. He did not usually feel like this after only a pint and a bit, maybe it was just the warmth in the pub. He took another long draught.

"She's not a widow. She's married."

Hurst looked at him intently. "You're pulling my leg!"

"No, I'm not." And slowly at first, then in a stream, as Hurst plied him with yet more beer, out came the whole story.

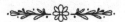

"I've never been as hung-over as this," thought Cyril as he threw up for the fifth time. It almost felt as if he had been poisoned. He could hardly lift himself out of his camp bed, his head was exploding, and his stomach seemed to want to leave his body. Miserably, he tried to piece together what had happened that evening. He had a foggy picture of Hurst riding beside him on his own motorbike and steadying him as he careened drunkenly back to camp. Hurst had put something in his coat pocket, what was it? Slowly it came back to him. A bag of fish and chips. Hurst had bought him some fish and chips to eat when he got back! The very thought of it made him want to throw up again. Why had he been drinking with Hurst anyway? Oh yes, something about his mother …

He must have fallen asleep again because the next thing he knew it was light and the men from the late shift were coming back to the tents, entirely unsympathetic about his plight. It was only as he was unsteadily washing that it finally came back to him. He had told Hurst everything about his mother. He had betrayed all her secrets.

He threw up again.

Chapter 38

FOLKESTONE, 1917

C aptain Miller was looking forward to the visit of his boss, William Melville. They had worked together in the Secret Service for many years and were good friends. Melville was quiet, unassuming, and workmanlike, but did not hesitate to put himself in danger's way if necessary—which it sometimes was, for their bureau was badly understaffed and underfinanced. Both Melville and Miller knew perfectly well that the public scare about thousands of German spies and saboteurs was nonsense and that their bureau, now called MI5, had been set up by the government, against the better judgement of certain ministers, largely to placate public opinion. At the same time, they knew that there was nevertheless a number of enemy spies in the country and their job was to make sure they were caught.

Miller met Melville at the station and took him to his office on the Marine Drive. It was important for both of them to meet from time to time because neither cared to entrust top-secret information to the post, much less discuss it on the telephone.

"I've got something that might interest you," said Melville, pulling a tiny cloth bag from his inside pocket as he sat down. He spilled the contents on the table. They were two copper pennies.

"Look," he said, and gently pulled at one with his fingers. It opened like a small tin. "My people found them on a young seaman on the ferry from Tilbury to Flushing. They asked him to empty his pockets and would not have noticed anything if one of the pennies had not dropped on the deck and opened. There was a small piece of tissue paper inside. The other one was the same. We are sure the paper contains messages written in some kind of invisible ink—we have a laboratory working on it now."

"Very clever," Miller said, inspecting one of the pennies admiringly. "Very clever, indeed. I wonder how long they have been using these. Did you find out how he got them?"

"The lad pretended to have no idea they were not normal pennies and made quite a good show of being surprised and intrigued by them. But we took him into custody and, by the time we had outlined all the consequences of working for the enemy in times of war, he caved in and told us everything."

"And …?" asked Miller expectantly.

"I say everything, actually it's by no means all, but it certainly gives you plenty to work on. He comes from Folkestone and joined the company when the ferries to Flushing used to run from here. He was given the pennies by his grandfather who is a verger at the church in Sandgate Road and was told to use them to pay for a newspaper at a kiosk at the port in Flushing that is known to take English money. He was paid a small sum for his services."

"Good work, William!" Miller exclaimed excitedly. "I'll get our people in Holland working on the kiosk in Flushing immediately, and I'll have a watch put on the church first before I go and have a cozy little chat with the verger."

"Good for you but be quick about it. It won't be long before the Germans realise what has happened and tip their people off." He gave Miller one of the pennies and kept one for himself, remarking, "We'll need these in court."

It was soon time for Melville to catch the 6:15 p.m. train back to London. Miller had been so focused on the pennies that he almost forgot to ask Melville who might have talked about the Russian anarchist plot to kill the Kaiser at Queen Victoria's funeral. Melville was just boarding the train when he remembered.

"Well, the Prince of Wales knew about it, the Prime Minister and the Home Secretary, of course" Melville replied, "but it was agreed nothing should be said about it in public. Just a couple of us in the Bureau, but of course we never reveal anything.

"Who else?" He paused for a moment. "Well, of course there was Steinhauer. He has been known to brag about things."

They said goodbye and Miller walked back along the platform with the things that Melville had told him passing haphazardly through his mind. The pennies and the verger … the Russian anarchists and Steinhauer … Steinhauer and the church in Sandgate Road … The church and …

As he walked out of the station it struck him like flash of lightning. That was it! No, it couldn't be! He stopped dead in the street, oblivious to the passersby and gasped out loud, "Florence!"

At that moment came a deafening roar overheard, and chaos. The horses of the waiting hansom cabs outside the station reared up in panic and several bolted. There was a huge explosion, then nothing.

At six p.m. that evening, Flo had been walking towards a stubby, round tower covered in dirty, white plaster perched on the cliff on a grassy promontory to the east of Folkestone. It was one of a long string of Martello towers that had been built along the south coast a century earlier to guard against a Napoleonic invasion. The invasion

never came and most had been allowed to decay. Some had been demolished, but several others were still standing in and around the town. She knew this was Martello Tower No. 3 because it formed the well-known starting point for a scenic walk along the top of the eastern cliffs, one which she had recently enjoyed with Captain Miller.

Flo was extremely nervous. She had ignored two more letters from Hurst instructing her to resume her task. Finally, she received quite a different one. Hurst had written in his usual enigmatic style.

I believe I understand completely the reasons for your reticence, so I will importune you no further. You may in any case be relieved to know that I am being sent away on a different mission. You should know that I am deeply aware of the debt that I owe to you and your admirable son and ask you humbly to meet me one last time so that I can express my gratitude and say farewell. I shall be at Martello Tower No. 3 at six p.m. on Friday, and I can assure you that if this meeting takes place no one will ever know.

Another threat. Flo did not believe that he had given her up or that he was being called elsewhere. The reminder that he still owed her money was bait—she had mentally written it off, but it would of course be useful. But the last line was unequivocal. If she did not obey, she would be exposed.

Friday was warm and breezy, as it was the end of May and already beginning to feel like summer. She had thrown on a light paisley shawl over her pink-flowered, cotton dress and walked towards the tower expecting to see the usual picnickers and strollers in the area. It somehow made her feel safer to think that there would be other people around.

But when she reached the tower, the place was deserted. Then she remembered: Sunday was Whit Sunday, and many people would no doubt be shopping, leaving, or preparing for the three-day holiday weekend.

There was a ladder up to the door halfway up the old tower. She knew from previous walks that these towers were being used by coastguards as lookout points, but there seemed to be no one there either. She began to feel a little scared.

Hurst was waiting a little way beyond the tower. He looked different. He was clean-shaven and dressed every inch a dandy, in a smart dove-grey suit with spats, a straw hat, and a polished Malacca cane. A pair of field glasses hung around his neck. He doffed his hat theatrically as he greeted her. She saw that his hair was now a caramel colour. Trying to hide her nerves, she dropped an equally theatrical curtsey and said, "My, sir, you are so elegant today!"

"Am I not always elegant?" he chaffed.

"But of course, sir, always! Even when you dress like a fisherman."

He mockingly offered her his arm and, mockingly, she took it, and they started walking eastwards, away from the town on a path along the cliff.

Their pantomime was so false, she thought, she could almost feel the tension crackling. She cast around for something to say.

"Such beautiful views!" she exclaimed, stopping and gazing around. Hurst took off his field glasses and offered them to her. Flo knotted her shawl under her bosom to free her hands and, trying to stop her hands trembling, raised the glasses to her eyes. Ahead she could see—so near!—miles of steep white cliffs scattered with scrub, and in the distance beyond, the sheerer, purer white cliffs around Dover. To her right, terrifyingly close, was the cliff edge and a vertiginous drop of some 300 feet. Below it, the sea, shimmering aquamarine, busy with naval vessels, cargo, and fishing boats. Turning to her right again, she could see the harbour and the town itself close-up, every house crystal clear.

"What marvelous things these are," she mused, handing the field glasses back. They walked on chatting about the scenery, and Flo began to feel less nervous.

But then, after a brief silence, Hurst began, again with untypical gentleness. "Tell me about your difficulties, Florence. Your old lady seems to have recovered now, so I assume they do not have to do with her."

"They do have to do with her," Flo retorted. "She is certainly looking a little brighter now, but the death of her son has ruined what was left of her health. She is very old and very frail and requires a great deal of care and attention. My free time is very limited; I can't leave her for long."

"Your free time is not so limited that you cannot go for long walks with your gentleman friend."

Flo stopped and stared at Hurst, outraged.

"You have been following me! How dare you! Do you have nothing better to do? You should mind your own business!"

"When an agent of ours allows herself to be courted by the very man most likely to unmask her and possibly destroy our whole network, it is very much my business," he replied. Flo could see he was making a visible effort to control himself. "You know he is the head of counterespionage in Folkestone, don't you?"

"I know that his job is in security, and he is looking out for spies, but I thought that that was the best possible protection. How could he possibly suspect a nurse like me, who is also a friend?"

"Florence, you are so naïve. In theory, you could be right, but you are so inexperienced, you could easily say or do something that would arouse his suspicion."

Flo thought of her gaffe about the Russian anarchist plot and said nothing.

"You should have told me immediately when you met him."

Flo became even angrier. "I'm not your slave! I can do what I want!"

Hursts voice became hard as steel. "Don't forget you swore an oath of allegiance to the Kaiser."

"Yes, I did, but you and Mr. Steinhauer made me think I would just be sending harmless information—not helping the Kaiser to mutilate and slaughter our young men, to rape young girls, to drive people from their homes—even to try and kill my own son. Have you seen what it looks like inside those hospitals?" She was shouting now.

"Florence, calm down," he snapped, looking around them anxiously. There was no one in sight. "This is war. It is not pretty.

Do you not think that the British and their allies are doing the same thing over there?" He gestured towards France.

"That does not make it any better! I don't want anything more to do with it. Who knows how many boys have been killed or injured because of what I have done! It's wrong! It's wicked! I wish I had never ever met you! or him!"

Hurst was silent for a while, then said slowly, "Florence, you are not personally responsible for what happens miles away from Folkestone. Now, you will go back home, and you will continue to send dispatches as instructed. Remember, you are paid well for them. If I can, I will try to get you paid a little more."

"You can keep your wretched money! I am not going to do it anymore!"

"In that case," he was speaking even more slowly, "we will have no option but to see that you are exposed as a spy. Would you want your family, your employers, your friends—in fact the whole country, to know that you have betrayed them to the enemy?"

Flo felt sick. It was the fate she always dreaded. But then, she thought in a flash, how dare he threaten her? He was a spy too!

"If you expose me, you expose yourself!" she retorted. "You are just as guilty than I am. No, even more!"

Hursts face had frozen into an icy sneer. "My dear," he said slowly and sarcastically, "do you think I would ever be so stupid as to let them catch me? You don't even know my name—my real name. You have no idea where I live. Those addresses I gave you give no clue whatever. If they ever started looking for me I would …" he made as if blowing away a leaf off the palm of his hand, "… vanish."

"You on the other hand, would be sitting in prison while all the newspapers would be reporting, as they surely will, that you are not a widow as you have always pretended, but that your husband, a clergyman, is alive and well and living in Canada. That you are an adulteress, that you have no less than five—five!—illegitimate children?"

"Who told you that?"

"Never mind who told me. In a way, you may be lucky, because it is likely that the

British, unlike the Germans and the French, would hesitate to execute a woman. But you must realise you will spend the rest of your life in prison."

Flo went cold. The black terror that had gripped her at critical moments in her life now engulfed her completely. This time there was no way out. Except one. In a flash she turned and ran toward the cliff edge.

Hurst shot after her and seized her shawl. The knot held. He pulled her back towards him and grabbed her tightly. She screamed and fought, tearing viciously at his hands and face, but he gripped her even harder. She burst into wild sobs, shaking and choking. He was saying things to her, but she did not hear. Slowly, her sobbing subsided. His grip seemed to become more of an embrace, the sound of his voice gentler. Exhausted and helpless, she laid her head on his chest. He was saying something that sounded tender and, astonished, she raised her head to look at him. As she did so, something caught her eye, and she stared over his shoulder in horror.

Flames and smoke were shooting into the air above the town. An instant later there came a loud explosion, then another. A host of what looked like huge birds were flying low over Folkestone, their two tiers of silvery wings swaying and glinting in the sunshine. Hurst abruptly released her and turned, raising his field glasses.

"Gothas," he said. "Bombers. It looks like they've got Shorncliffe, good lads ..."

"But that's where the Canadians are!" gasped Flo, horrified.

More explosions. "That is probably Central Station. Why are they not bombing the harbour, the fools?" Hurst seemed to be talking to himself. "Now they are going for the town centre ... Good work!"

"But they are killing people! Ordinary people, not soldiers—children, women! How can you?" Folkestone was being bombed, people must be dying, and he was exulting!

The planes were coming nearer, flying parallel to the shore, one was roaring directly towards them. They could see its vast wings and boxy fuselage, the black crosses painted on its side, pilot and the two gunners in their helmets and goggles. Flo threw herself down onto the grass, but Hurst remained standing, shielding his eyes against the sun. She saw him give a wave to the men in the plane.

Flo went wild with rage. "You monster!" she shouted.

His cane was lying just beside her, dropped in the struggle to pull her back from the edge. She grabbed it in fury and, as he turned slowly away from her, following the planes with his field glasses as they flew eastwards, she rammed it into the small of his back and ran, pushing him ahead of her to the cliff edge. He cried out, tried to turn but lost his footing, and catapulted over the edge, his body bouncing down the rough cliff face, down and down, to the huge boulders below. Flo teetered for a couple of seconds, then straightened up and stepped back away from the edge. She threw his cane after him.

Then, she gathered up her skirts and ran hell for leather towards the smoking town.

Part 5

Chapter 39

Queensland, Australia, 1920

A small cloud of dust followed the horse-drawn buggy as it jolted along the dirt road through the lush, green Queensland countryside. The lady in a wide-brimmed hat sat silent and preoccupied in the passenger seat, fanning herself and oblivious to the rolling hills, the woods, and the mountains in the distance.

"Been out here long?" the driver asked. He could tell from her pale complexion, chic haircut, and fashionably short, loose dress that she was new to these parts.

"I came out to Brisbane last year," was the reply.

"Like it there?"

"Hmm," was all the answer he got.

Flo did not feel like chatting. The news she had received that morning was much too alarming. *So much for the wonderful new life I was to have here*, she thought.

Instead, her old life seemed to have come with her, and the good Lord had found new ways of punishing her.

She still had nightmares about that moment on Copt Point. She could still see the explosions, the columns of smoke rising from the town, the bombers coming towards them, Hurst's body crashing down the cliff. She had run frantically, like a woman possessed, all the way back to the Appleby house and collapsed on the doorstep in a state of shock. James had carried her in and laid her on the sofa, assuming that, like everyone else, she was devastated by the bombing.

Her only thought as she ran back to the house had been to leave immediately—leave the Applebys, leave Folkestone, and escape to somewhere where no one would find her. But by the time she arrived, she was so confused, stunned, and terrified that she could do nothing but lie and sob for hours on end.

As she gradually came to, she was surprised to hear that Mrs. Appleby had slept through it all, but the older lady had been badly shaken when Dora, who had been out shopping, returned, supported by a young Canadian soldier, both covered in blood and dust. She had been heading for the town centre when she was thrown to the ground by a violent explosion. Bleeding from being struck by shattered glass, she struggled to her feet and tried to help people who were badly injured to reach ambulances that were arriving. Moving closer to the street where the bomb had hit, she saw the carnage, blood, severed limbs and heads, baskets, shopping, wreckage everywhere. She fainted and was rescued by one of the many soldiers who had rushed to the scene to help. In the following hours, news flooded in of people who had been killed and maimed in the attack, friends, acquaintances, tradesmen—also two of the young Canadians from Shorncliffe who were billeted on them, including Antje's admirer.

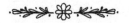

Flo soon realised it would be much safer to stay where she was. Her sudden departure would immediately raise questions whereas her frenzy and the drama that had led up to it was likely to escape notice in the general aftermath of the bombing. Nevertheless, each day she anxiously scoured the local papers for any mention of Hurst's demise. Several days passed in suspense before she finally spotted a report that the body of a "mystery man" had been discovered at the bottom of a cliff near Copt Point. Police said they had found no clue as to his identity and had been unable to determine whether the cause of death was an accident or suicide. A little later, she found another report: after an inquest the coroner had returned an open verdict. She felt immense relief. She was safe, at least for the present.

Flo had heard nothing from Captain Miller but assumed that he would have been busy, possibly investigating what everyone now wanted to know—why no one, least of all the RAF, had had any warning of the impending attack. After a few days, however, she grew a little anxious and sent him a brief note asking how he was. Rationally, she knew he posed her greatest danger and—Hurst was right—she had not been as careful as she should be. She hoped against hope that he had forgotten her remark about the Russian anarchists for, paradoxically, after her years of lonely struggle, she felt safe with the captain, almost protected. She needed his quiet strength, his warmth, and his affection. She realised she had become deeply attached to him. Was it love? It was not the romantic passion she had shared with Darnley, but she found herself often wishing that they might have some kind of future together. If only!

More days passed, and she heard nothing. Could he have been involved in the investigations into Hurst's death? It suddenly occurred to her, and she grew alarmed. One evening, she asked Gerrit if he had seen him.

Gerrit stared at her in consternation. "Have you not heard, Nurse? He was killed by a bomb that day. Just by the station."

Flo felt that she was falling to pieces. Hurst, the bombs, and now Miller's death—her

life had been blown apart. It was all she could do to pull herself together enough each day to go on tending to Mrs. Appleby and to behave as if nothing had happened. She was mourning Miller deeply, and even more so when the news reached her that Josiah had died in Canada—she could have married him! It was weeks before she recovered sufficiently to be able to think clearly about her own life and about the future.

Mrs. Appleby was in visible decline. Matilda had begged Flo to stay with them until she died, and Flo, who had become very fond of the older lady, and indeed everyone in the house, had willingly agreed. But afterwards? She longed for a new beginning, to go far away from the country and society where she had had such a bitter struggle for survival and respectability. Somewhere where she could leave her past behind and feel safe—for she was constantly dogged by the fear that one day someone might find out the truth about Hurst and her spying.

A letter from Lizzie, expressing excited at the prospect of emigrating to Australia when the war was over, that gave Flo an idea. Australia! Why should she not go too? Godfrey, of course, would be there, and she had little hope he would ever agree to see her again, but she would be near Lizzie and—why not?—she would bring the children with her, she would recreate her family and they would all become enthusiastic new Australians. Young Frank, currently apprenticed to an engineering firm, was already planning to go out there with Lizzie. Cyril, to her great relief, had left immediately after the war for Martinique, in the French Antilles, where, she hoped, he would be safe in case of possible investigations, but the others, she thought, could be easily persuaded to come. She began putting out feelers about selling the house in Littlehampton and gathering information about assisted passages to Brisbane, where they would all be near Lizzie and Fred.

Two years passed, however, before she finally stood on the deck of the *RMS Ormuz* listening to the long, mournful boom of the ship's horn announcing its departure from Tilbury docks. It should, she thought, have sounded like a trumpet heralding the start of her new life, but it was more of a heartrending farewell to all those who had become dear to her. Fragile Mrs. Appleby, whom she had cared for as if she were her mother, was dead, and she was sad to leave Matilda, who had become a firm friend. James and the two Mrs. Janssens had died of the Spanish flu, as had Mrs. Snodgrass's husband and several other friends. She would never see Klaus and June Frantzen again. The flu had raged in the orphanage, but mercifully, all the children had survived. After working round the clock helping to nurse the family's and Folkestone's sick, she had contracted it herself, but recovered.

When Flo spotted Lizzie among the jubilant crowds on the quay as the ship docked in Brisbane, her sister looked as if she was dabbing her eyes with a handkerchief. *Tears of joy, no doubt,* thought Flo fondly, *Lizzie is so emotional.* But when the two sisters finally embraced, Lizzie could only blurt out, "Poor Flo! My poor, dear Flo!" And, finally, "Frank is dead!"

Frank—the first of her love-children with Darnley. Darnley's favourite, her favourite, everyone's favourite—Frank was dead? Flo almost fainted. He was so young! It couldn't be!

Flo sat on her luggage on the quay, tears running down her face, while Lizzie told her the tragic story. She had brought Frank out on the same ship as her and without telling Godfrey in advance, taken him to the farm, both hoping that Godfrey, who had never met his young half-brother, would give him a job. At first, Godfrey, whose rejection of his mother extended to her younger family, had been furious and refused to have anything to do with him, but Frank, with his boyish charm, managed to talk him round and, egged on by Lizzie, Godfrey finally agreed—on condition no one should ever know they were related. Frank had to drop the name Harris and have himself called by his first names: Frank Hunter. Even Lizzie was not allowed to tell anyone she was Godfrey's aunt.

Just a week ago, while Flo was still on her way, Frank and another farm hand had gone swimming in the river close by the farm. Frank dived in, hit his head on a rock and, probably knocked unconscious, drowned. It was the day before his twenty-first birthday.

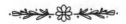

And now Godfrey. Still mourning Frank, Flo had managed to buy a little house in Brisbane with the proceeds from the sale of the one in Littlehampton and found a job nursing. She was hoping that at last her life would run in calmer, happier channels. Then that morning she received an urgent telegram from Lizzie at the farm, "Godfrey critically ill. Come quickly."

Flo feared that that could only mean the worst. Godfrey had always flatly rejected Lizzie's efforts for a reconciliation and her message implied that Godfrey was no position to object. Who knew what was awaiting her at the farm.

"Here we are, ma'am," said the driver as he turned the horse off the dirt road and into a long drive through fields dotted with black-and-white cows. Ahead of her, she could see a cluster of farm buildings and, in the middle, a charming, low, white-painted wooden house. A veranda with graceful balustrade was wrapped round the sides with slim posts and elegant latticed arches supporting a large, pitched roof. As they drew nearer, she was puzzled to see that, although low, the house stood on stilts which raised it a couple of feet from the ground.

The buggy stopped by the front steps, Flo paid the driver, and turned to see Lizzie come out onto the veranda holding her apron to her eyes.

"Lizzie, dearest! Oh, no!" exclaimed Flo in consternation, running up the steps. Lizzie threw herself into her sister's arms, crying uncontrolledly.

"He's dead."

There was little time to talk. The doctor was just leaving and expressing his condolences, the undertakers had to be telephoned, and the farm workers informed. The sun had almost set, and a welcome cool breeze had got up before the sisters were able to sit down at the white wicker table on the veranda for a cold meal that neither felt like eating. Lizzie turned to make sure that the maid who had brought it was out of earshot then leaned over to Flo and said in a low voice, "It was suicide."

"Suicide!" Flo gasped. "No! Why? How?"

"Two nights ago," began Lizzie, "before going to bed, he said he was very tired and would sleep in the next day. On no account was anyone to wake him, he was very insistent about that.

"The next day there was no sign of him, and by late afternoon I was beginning to get uneasy. He had not called for any food, and he did not seem to have gone to the bathroom. The old gardener, Joe, and I tried the door gently, but it was locked. The curtains were drawn so we could not see in through the windows. We thought of forcing the door, but Godfrey could get so angry when anyone disobeyed his orders, so we decided not to."

"And?"

"The next day it was the same again. Nothing. But he was needed on the farm; there were telephone calls, people delivering things. I banged on the door and shouted but still no reply. So, I plucked up courage and told Joe to force the door.

"He was lying in bed and seemed to be asleep. I went over to him calling, 'Godfrey, Godfrey,' but he didn't move. I gave him a shake, still nothing. Yet he was breathing, just. He was warm. So, I called the doctor. It seemed like hours before he came."

Lizzie began crying again and hid her face in her hands. Flo reached out and stroked her knee.

"The doctor said he was in a coma. He gave him an injection but warned that there was little hope he would recover. That is when I sent you the telegram.

"There was an empty bottle on his bedside table with some scientific name on it. The doctor said it was some kind of opium compound and was more than enough to kill a person. I had never seen it before, heaven knows where he got it. He had obviously drunk it. Oh, if only I had tried to wake him up sooner. It's all my fault!"

"Of course it isn't, dearest. But why on earth would he want to do it? He had this lovely farm; he seemed to be doing well."

"Well, in a way he was. He worked hard, invested a lot in it. But all the time, something seemed to be eating him. He had always been a difficult boy after you left Josiah and even more so after Martha died. But when he came out of the army, he was even worse. The young lady he courted in England did not want to come out with him, another one he took a liking to here went and married someone else, and I think each time it broke his heart. He avoided company, he would even shut himself up in his room for hours on end, leaving the farm to run itself. He was nice and polite enough to neighbours when he met them, but he would fly into rages with his workers if things did not go as he wanted. I can't tell you the number of times he would storm at me and tell me I was sacked. I learned to shut myself in my room and wait until he simmered down and pretended nothing had happened. He never told anyone about his war record and would not let me tell them either."

"Why not?" asked Flo

"Who knows. The doctor said he was suffering from shell-shock, whatever that means. I think he did not want to be reminded of the war. He must have had a terrible time; his lungs were in a dreadful state—you know he had been gassed more than once … He was a sick man, and I begged the doctor to put something else, not suicide, on his death certificate. He put 'acute respiratory illness.'"

"Did Godfrey leave a note?" Flo asked.

"Just this." Lizzie pulled a piece of paper out of her apron pocket, put it on the table, and smoothed it open.

Thank you for everything, Auntie, and sorry. Godfrey.

"That's all."

The two sisters sat in silence for a while. Then, Flo said, "May I see him?"

Lizzie led her to Godfrey's spacious bedroom and pulled down the sheet which had been laid over his body.

Flo stood at the end of the bed, looking down at him. Her son. And yet a complete stranger. Could that be the eight-year-old boy she had left crying in the house in Pillowell? A man whose whole life had been lived in rejection of her. A hero who had risked his life a million times and been wounded in body and soul, while she … while she …

Nothing would ever free her from his eternal reproach.

She broke down, and the two sisters clung together, weeping.

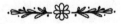

Few people attended the funeral, just Flo, Lizzie, the farm staff, and a couple of neighbours.

On their way back in the farm buggy, Lizzie told Flo that Godfrey's lawyer had informed her that he had left her the farm and all his belongings.

"Will you stay here then?" asked Flo. She could not imagine Lizzie as a farmer.

"No!" replied Lizzie emphatically. "I mean … I have been very happy here. I made the house and the garden nice for Godfrey but … first Frank, now Godfrey … I feel there is a curse on the place. And the lawyer warned me that Godfrey was deep in debt. I am going to sell it."

"Well," said Flo thoughtfully, "then maybe you could come and stay with me in Brisbane while you decide what to do. We might be able to find you a job somewhere as a housekeeper."

Lizzie liked the idea. "It would be nice to live near each other now, at our age."

They both fell silent, contemplating the future.

After a while, Lizzie put her hand on her sister's knee and said, "Flo, after all these years perhaps you can tell me why you *really* left Josiah."

Epilogue

And thus, the two sisters returned to Brisbane where they lived quietly and uneventfully for the remainder of their days. "Lizzie" died there in 1937. "Flo" lived on for many more years, during which she took to frequenting spiritist seances, presumably in the hopes of contacting lost loved ones. A faded photograph taken, judging from the twenties-style dress she was wearing, soon after she emigrated, shows her walking down the street with a handsome, white-haired man. Both are smiling and looking happy together. Had she found a new lover? No one knows.

She was never able to gather all of her remaining children around her. "Mollie" joined her for some years, having escaped to Australia during the Japanese invasion of the Philippines where she had been working as a nurse. But "Prue" went to Nyasaland (now Malawi) as a missionary nurse, then resolutely settled in Devon. The two sisters later retired together to a cottage in the picturesque seaside village of Clovelly.

"Joanna" rejected her mother as bitterly as "Godfrey" had. She flatly refused to go back to her but stayed on at the orphanage, first to study on a scholarship at Blackburn Grammar School,

then as a member of staff until she won another scholarship
to a teacher-training college in London. Bright, vivacious, but
scarred for life by her childhood traumas, she became a teacher,
married, and had two children.

Then there was "Cyril." After the war, he left for the French
Antilles—was he afraid he might be found out?—but later returned to Britain and had a successful career as an electrical
engineer. He travelled widely, working on British government
projects to install electricity in developing countries. He was a
moody, difficult, and domineering man with few friends except
a mysterious German called Eikermann or perhaps Eichermann,
who in the years after the war would turn up periodically on a
motorbike and be closeted with Cyril in their front room. No
one ever knew who he was or why he came. On retirement,
Percy lived for a time in Australia and it was he—the son who had
been closest to Flo in the dramatic moments of her life and the
sole custodian of all her secrets—who arranged the funeral when
she died in Brisbane in 1955 at the venerable age of eight-seven.
Then in 1968, aged seventy-seven, he sat down and, to his
family's astonishment, began writing a book. Of this, more later.

I can reveal all this because, as the reader may already have
guessed, it is part of my family history. "Flo" is modelled closely
on my maternal grandmother—Sarah Ida Harry, nee Bleath-
man—and this book on what I know of her scandalous life. Her
children are based on my aunts and half-uncles: "Joanna"—in real
life Joan—was my mother.

Yet, no one in our family ever spoke of Ida, as I believe she
was called. I grew up without knowing she existed. It was only
when I was in my mid-teens and it finally dawned on me that
my mother must have had parents, that I began to ask—and was

astonished to hear that Ida was still alive, albeit far away in Australia. Then for the first time, my mother, through gritted teeth, spat out a few bitter words about her. She had been beautiful, flighty—and deplorable. She had dumped her and her siblings in an orphanage—a terrible place, she said. She hated her for it and would never forgive her.

I do not think there was a deliberate conspiracy to keep silent about Ida. I believe that she and those around her who knew or had suspicions about her disreputable sex life simply kept quiet for fear of scandal which could also bring shame on the rest of the family. It seems likely that my mother and her siblings—apart from "Cyril", in real life Percy—knew very little about her past but did not care to confront their own illegitimacy or revisit the traumas of the orphanage. I am convinced that no one other than Percy ever knew about the spying.

All these skeletons would probably have remained locked in their cupboard forever if it had not been for a strange incident one afternoon in 2014. I had got stuck with a tricky passage in a book I was writing and, seeking distraction, began idly surfing the Internet. I started looking for traces of my late brother and to my astonishment came upon a message for the two of us on a find-your-relatives website called Curious Fox. A woman wanted to contact us: "I am a niece of her mother," she declared.

I was baffled. My mother's sisters and brother Fred ("Frank") had, of course, all died childless. But I answered the message and met, via email, a woman living in Australia who turned out to be, indeed, a half-cousin. She was called Anne Delisle and she revealed to me that Ida had had two older sons, half-brothers to my mother. Anne was the daughter of the older one, Percy, the other was Gilbert ("Godfrey").

We Skyped and emailed. I sent her copies of old family photos, she sent me copies of birth, marriage and death certificates, and census extracts. And she sent me something else: page after photocopied page of four school-type exercise books, handwritten and sometimes hard to decipher. It was Percy's "book."

It was ostensibly a novel, but it was patently the story of his outrageous mother and, to a lesser extent, of himself. There were scenes which he had obviously witnessed himself as a boy and young man and which had burned into his memory. He described little-known events and historical details which on investigation turned out to be astonishingly accurate. But they were strung together by rambling, often irrelevant passages which seemed pure invention. And the story stopped just after Ida had been recruited by Herz/Hurst. He had died before he could finish it.

I was as amazed as Anne had been when she first read it. It seemed clear to both of us that Percy had wanted to get it all off his chest before he died, at an age when he need no longer fear retribution. "It was so unlike him to do something like that. He had no imagination whatsoever," she told me. "I don't remember him ever reading a book in his life. And then he suddenly started to write this."

And so, I began to search for more about Ida. I hunted in archives and museums in Britain and Germany, scoured the Internet, contacted distant relatives and organisations that might have some record of her, engaged a professional researcher when I got stuck, and visited the orphanage and places where Ida and her children had lived until the COVID-19 pandemic put a stop to my travels. And I found much to support Percy's account. There was indeed a top German spy called Peter Herz. There are indeed dispatches in the German archives about troop shipments from the south coast and a message about British searchlight units being ordered to sweep the skies for Zeppelins. There were indeed, as Percy described, early flying experiments on Little-hampton beach, a man with a German name did live next door to Ida and the father of her children (my grandfather!) did die of pneumonia in 1914. And I found much, much more, particularly about Gilbert's war record, about "Darnley" (real name: Alfred Walker Dolby) and about Fred and Ida's other children. But I still was not able to dig up enough for a proper biography. How, for instance, do you find out about the activities of a spy who was never caught?

So once again, Ida is the subject of a novel, based on all I have learned and filling in the remaining gaps in an endeavour to reconstruct not just what happened, but also—why.

About the Author

Patricia Clough, a journalist with a degree in German and French from Bristol University, has had an extensive career, including training at the Bolton Evening News, and working for Reuters, the Times, and the Independent. Her postings took her from Geneva, Bonn, and Rome to covering significant events such as the collapse of Communism, the fall of the Berlin Wall, and the "Tangentopoli" scandals. She transitioned to Warsaw in 1990 to report on Eastern Europe's move to democracy, which earned her the Anglo-German Foundation's journalism prize. Clough, who also had stints at the Baltimore Sun, the Sunday Times, and the UN World Food Programme, has one daughter and resides in Italy. She is a well known author in Germany and Britain.